# BENEATH THE CYPRUS SKY
## A STORY OF LOVE, LOSS AND HOPE

### SARAH CATHERINE KNIGHTS

SARAH CATHERINE KNIGHTS

Copyright © 2025 by Sarah Catherine Knights

All rights reserved.

No portion of this book may be reproduced in any form without written permission from the publisher or author, except as permitted by U.S. copyright law.

# DEDICATION

I'd like to dedicate this novel to Peter, my husband, who is always there with ideas when writer's block kicks in.

# CONTENTS

Part 1
1999

    1. Chapter 1      3
    2. Chapter 2      23
    3. Chapter 3      39
    4. Chapter 4      65
    5. Chapter 5      81
    6. Chapter 6      93

Part 2
2012

    7. Chapter 7      109
    8. Chapter 8      119

Part 3
2018

    9. Chapter 9      129
    10. Chapter 10      147
    11. Chapter 11      159

| | | |
|---|---|---|
| 12. | Chapter 12 | 171 |
| 13. | Chapter 13 | 183 |
| 14. | Chapter 14 | 189 |
| 15. | Chapter 15 | 201 |
| 16. | Chapter 16 | 217 |
| 17. | Chapter 17 | 235 |
| 18. | Chapter 18 | 245 |

Part 4
2024

| | | |
|---|---|---|
| 19. | Chapter 19 | 253 |
| 20. | Chapter 20 | 265 |
| 21. | Chapter 21 | 281 |
| 22. | Chapter 22 | 299 |
| 23. | Chapter 23 | 315 |

| | |
|---|---|
| Also By Sarah Catherine Knights | 325 |
| About the Author | 331 |

Sarah Catherine Knights

# PART I
1999

Sarah Catherine Knights

# CHAPTER 1

Charlie Greene's first morning as a sports teacher at a comprehensive in Swindon had been a disaster. She'd felt out of her depth and exhausted, having been up since five am with Lou, her five-year-old, who'd chosen that day, of all days, to wake up earlier than usual. By the time Charlie had attempted to make herself look respectable and had dropped Lou off with the child-minder, she'd been ready to crawl back to bed, but she'd had to face her new reality of dealing with other people's children. Why had she ever thought *that* was a good idea? She'd done a degree in sports science because she loved sport, but then couldn't work out what to do with it. Teaching was a career that was touted to women in the nineties, so she'd stayed on for another year to get a post-grad certificate of education. She'd enjoyed being a student, so why not delay real life for a year?

But life'd had other plans for her. Charlie had ended up delaying her career as she'd met David, married him a year later and then had got pregnant virtually straightaway. She'd had a few years as a stay-at-home mum, which she'd loved, but it was now time to start her career.

That first morning had gone by in a blur. She'd just about survived, but had felt overwhelmed with the sheer number of children she had to deal with, finding her way around the new environment and all the demands on her. Charlie had muddled her way through a gym session with Year 7, netball with year 9 and hockey with year 10. She'd felt very much 'the new girl' and had met no one at break-time she could chat to. Everyone else appeared to know what they were doing and were busy getting on with it. Now, it was lunchtime, and she flung herself onto a chair in a corner of the staffroom, hoping to merge into the background. How was Lou getting on with Barbara, the childminder, she wondered? She'd seemed nice, but lots of nightmare scenarios were whirring around her head. Should she ring, just to find out if Lou was ok?

"Hi there! How's it going?"

Charlie looked up from the book she was pretending to read and found an absolutely stunning young woman sitting next to her, who was staring straight at her with huge, almond-shaped green eyes. She had short, jet black hair and her smile lit up her high-cheek-boned face and drew Charlie in, instantly making her feel better about life.

"I thought I'd come over and introduce myself: I'm Beth Harris: history, married to Alex, as yet no sprogs. How about you?"

Charlie was relieved to see someone about her age. She said, "Oh ... Hi, I'm Charlotte Greene, PE, married to David, one child. Call me Charlie. Probably pretty obvious I'm a sports teacher, in this get-up," she laughed, looking down at her tracksuit and trainers.

"Are you new, too, like me? You don't look worn down like the rest of them," said Beth quietly in Charlie's ear. "In fact, you look positively enthusiastic," she whispered, pulling a face. Everyone in the room had their noses in books or were marking exercise books; nobody else was chatting. They lowered their voices so that people wouldn't hear their conversation.

"Yes. First teaching job since uni, having had a long gap to give birth ... and totally losing touch with anything to do with education."

"So, you're really on top of your game, then?" said Beth, laughing.

"Yes, totally," Charlie said with a grimace. "I've actually been up since five, dealing with a three-year-old and have spent most of the morning worrying about her. Not sure how I got through the actual teaching," she said, trying to be light-hearted about it, but not succeeding.

"She'll be fine. You know what kids are like, she'll be having a whale of a time with new children to play with and new toys. I'm assuming you haven't left her to fend for herself?"

"Er, no. You're right. She's probably fine, but I could do without the stress. How do people do it? Being a mum and having a career? It must be nice being David. He just goes to work, and that's it."

"That's men for you. What does he do?"

"Well, to be fair, he can't really combine his work and being a dad. He's in the Air Force. A Hercules pilot. He's either away for days or at home, really. There's no in-between. But he's not a particularly hands-on dad when he's home. Too many sports to play," she laughed.

"Couldn't you have stayed being a housewife and done the whole 'Air Force wife' bit? It might have been easier than this."

"I could, I suppose, but I didn't want to. Flower arranging in the Mess isn't for me. I wanted to get off the camp as soon as possible. We moved into our own place last year." Charlie took a sip from her coffee and had a bite from a rather dry sandwich she'd made that morning. "You sound as if you know about military life?"

"Well ... my father was an Army colonel. Say no more. My childhood was all boarding schools and army camps. I couldn't wait to get away. He's retired now, and he's become a different person. He's very chilled, unshaven and possesses no smart clothes. It's almost as if he's rebelling against years of military discipline."

"Ha ha, that's funny. I can't imagine David being like that in the future. So, you know what it's like, then? Teaching seemed like a good option and to be honest; as much as I love Lou, I thought it would be a bit of a break from her. Being one-to-one with a three-year-old tyrant can be overwhelming! She's a gorgeous child but ... enough about me ... how about you? How long have you been teaching?"

"Well, I did some supply teaching, and I covered a maternity leave, but this is my first 'proper' job since leaving uni. Alex is still studying ... he's training to be a vet. He's in his last year, so we're still leading a studenty life. He's starting work next summer. It's so tough becoming a vet, but one advantage is that your clients can't answer back."

"I love animals ... but I'd find it too hard dealing with injured and dying ones; he must be a very special person."

"He is ... it's what he's always wanted to do since he was a kid. His mum says he was always bandaging their old labrador's paws. I wish I'd had that kind of ambition. I drifted into teaching, really."

"Me too," said Charlie, smiling.

And that was it ... Beth and Charlie formed a bond over lunch in the staffroom, each recognising in the other someone they could talk to.

From that moment on, every lunch break, they sat next to each other, chatted about how horrendous the children in their classes had been that morning; found out about each other's pasts and laughed at each other's jokes. Beth made coming to school fun and Charlie positively looked forward to seeing her.

They became best friends and soul mates.

---

They soon started socialising and there were several girls' nights out, Charlie leaving David to babysit, much to his dismay. She always got Lou into bed before she left, so it wasn't as if he had to do anything. On a couple of occasions, she got home worse for wear after drinking copious amounts of sparkling wine. David wasn't best pleased at her drunken attempts to stumble into bed quietly, but she didn't feel too guilty. She always spent hours on her own with Lou, waiting for him to come back from various air crew nights in the mess. It was almost compulsory, it seemed, to have drinks after a flight, so he couldn't complain if she had a couple of drinks with Beth, could he?

Charlie settled into the routine of teaching; she couldn't say she enjoyed it, but she kept her head above water and there was a part of her that enjoyed the feeling of having something for herself, something that placed her outside the realms of 'David's wife' and 'Lou's mum'. Some kids in her classes drove her mad: the ones that were always talking; the ones with all the backchat; the ones that were always late and the ones that were always trying to wind her up, but she was learning how to deal with them. There really wasn't anything she'd learned during her PGCE which could have prepared her for the practicalities of dealing with actual children; it was only something you could learn on the job. She could see now that if Lou was older, she'd have had personal experience of teenagers, but she had all that to come ... oh the joys. She thought that if she was in Beth's position, it would seriously put her off having any children at all.

On their nights out, they got to know more about the other's partner. They both thought it would be good if they actually met up as a foursome, so Beth invited Charlie and David round to their cottage, "to give you a break from Lou". This was a marvellous idea in theory, but finding a babysitter wasn't so easy. She asked around and eventually found Saskia, a sixteen-year-old 'A' level student who lived down the road. She arranged for her to come at seven; David was due back from flying at four; she hoped he didn't spend too long in the bar before he got home.

By six, she was getting anxious; David still wasn't home. If he'd got back at four, that was quite enough time for a quick drink, surely? She was keen for this evening to go well; she loved Beth's company and couldn't wait to meet Alex. She'd seen a picture of him a while ago; Beth had proudly shown her a black-and-white photo of him she kept in her wallet. Her husband was extremely handsome from what Charlie could see (the picture was quite creased and 'well-used', so wasn't that clear). He had dark hair that flopped over his face, angular features and gorgeous, kind eyes. He had a wide, friendly smile that shone out of the photograph. What a great couple they made. She said, "Wow, very handsome ... " as she handed the picture back to Beth. She didn't have a photo of David to show Beth there and then, so she'd tried to describe him. "Well ... David is six feet tall, has light auburn hair, greeny/grey eyes and quite a few freckles. He goes a lovely golden brown in the sun and his freckles come out. Tennis is his favourite sport, so he's very athletic; he's great at cricket too. He looks hot in his flying suit, with all those zips. Ha ha."

She was just beginning to get seriously pissed off with him, when he wandered in at 6.30 pm, unaware that they were in a rush to get ready.

"Don't worry, you know what I'm like. I can get ready in two minutes. We were late back, and we just had a couple of beers in the bar. Honest."

"Not sure I believe you, but ..." she grinned.

"I'll nip upstairs and change. Won't be a sec."

He still wasn't down by the time Saskia arrived. Charlie quickly showed the sitter around and told her to help herself to food and drink. Lou was sparkers; they both gazed at her in the darkness of her room, listening to her quiet breaths, before they tiptoed out. Saskia seemed to be a mature girl and quietly capable; Charlie gave her Beth's number, just in case she needed it.

"We won't be later than 11.30. Is that okay?"

"Yes, fine. You go and enjoy yourselves. I've got loads of homework to do. Don't worry about a thing. If she wakes, I'll sort her out and attempt to get her to sleep again. I've got two younger sisters, so I know what to do."

"She's dry most nights these days ..."

David appeared, looking clean and tidy, smart/casual, being the way to describe his clothes. He was a typical Air Force type, somehow managing to look smart in jeans. He had a green top on which suited his colouring, and brown brogues. Charlie was also wearing jeans, and she'd put on a v-necked striped jumper, which she thought was flattering. She'd added a matching gold pendant and earrings and tied her blond hair back in a loose ponytail.

"Okay, Saskia, we're off now," said Charlie. "Ring if you need us and help yourself to anything. See you later."

Charlie was surprised when they drew up outside the address Beth had given her. She was expecting something more basic, but this was a quaint old cottage, all hollyhocks round the door, leaded windows and old stone. It was gorgeous and was just the sort of thing she'd wanted to buy when they moved off the camp, but David had wanted a new-build, as it wouldn't involve him in any maintenance. As it turned out, there had been quite a few 'snags', ranging from leaks round the shower to cracked plaster and a roof that needed repairing twice. Fortunately, it all fell under the guarantee, but it hadn't been the stress-free move he'd hoped for.

They parked on the road and walked up the garden path. Charlie saw Beth through a small window; she'd obviously been looking out for them and rushed to open the door.

"Hi you two ... Welcome."

She ushered them through, hugged Charlie, pulling her in and kissing her on both cheeks and then turned to David and did the same. "It's so nice to meet you at last; I've heard so much about you," she said, grinning.

"Nice to meet you too," said David, returning the smile.

"Alex, they're here," Beth shouted.

They heard a distant, "Coming!"

"Come into the kitchen," said Beth. "We don't stand on ceremony here. Beer, wine, gin? Any preference?"

"You know me, I'd love a white wine. Oh, I forgot — here's a bottle," said Charlie, handing over a bottle of Sauvignon.

"Thanks ... David?"

"Beer for me, please."

At that moment, Alex walked in.

"Hey, sorry — I was a bit late home and had to have a shower to wash the animal smell off," he laughed. He was wearing black jeans, brown leather boots and a dark blue top with a short zip, which was undone, revealing a white t-shirt underneath. He went straight over to Charlie, giving her a bear hug and kissing her on both cheeks. She could smell his lemony shower gel; his arms felt remarkably strong.

"So, you're Beth's partner in crime. It's so nice that you've got each other to confide in."

"Yes ... Beth's been my saviour, to be honest. Everyone else is rather ancient. A bit of an exaggeration, but we hit it off from the start."

"So ... David, nice to meet you," said Alex, shaking his hand and clasping his other arm with his free hand.

"Yes, nice to meet you, too. I was late home too. It's compulsory in the Air Force to have a drink afterwards, you know how it is. I've probably got a head start on you; downed a couple of quick pints in the bar." He looked at Charlie and raised his eyebrows.

She said, "Normally, I don't mind, but I didn't want to be late ... life in the Air Force revolves around the bar. Your house is gorgeous, by the way."

"Oh, thanks," said Beth. "We're so lucky; both sets of parents helped us buy it. We couldn't have done it otherwise."

By now, they all had their drinks. Gorgeous smells wafted from the oven; Beth had already laid the table.

"Come through to the sitting room," said Alex. "How long till we eat, Beth?"

"About fifteen minutes. It's simple, just lasagne and salad; I hope that's okay?"

"Perfect," said Charlie. "You could have given us beans on toast, to be honest, and I'd have been happy. It's just great not to have to cook!"

The sitting room was small, cosy and warmed by a blazing log burner. There were candles flickering on the coffee table, giving off a wonderful spicy scent. Beth put some nibbles and dips on a low, square coffee table, and sat down with a sigh in the nearest armchair. Charlie took a crisp and wandered over to the bookcase, always drawn to other people's book choices. To the left of the bookcase there was a collection of photos, some old and faded, some more recent. She couldn't help peering at them.

"Sorry to be nosy, but can you tell me who they are?" she said. Alex came and stood next to her, his presence feeling comfortable, even though they'd only just met.

"Well, that one there is me and my brother and my parents, taken years ago. I was about fourteen, I think. It's special to me because Jake and I had just won a junior sailing race. You can just see our boat in the background. We lived in Chichester and spent our entire childhood there, messing about in boats. My parents still live there and I'm the joint owner of a yacht with my friend Benji, but I have to say, he gets far more use out of it than me," he laughed.

"I've always wanted to sail, but never got round to it," said Charlie. "I've done just about every sport you can think of and I *love* swimming, but the problem was we never lived near enough to the sea. We lived in Surrey when I was a child. That's my excuse, anyway." She turned towards him. He was staring at the photo and even in profile, his face looked sad.

"I go as often as I can, but my work's so full-on, I don't have the time ... and it lost its appeal a few years ago," he said.

"Jake died of cancer when he was only twenty," said Beth, coming to stand next to Alex. She took his hand. "I never met him, but Jake was the life and soul of everything, apparently,"

"I'm so sorry, Alex. How awful for you. Do you have any other brothers or sisters?" asked Charlie.

"No, it was just Jake and me. It was devastating for Mum and Dad."

They continued to stand in front of the pictures and, in order to divert the conversation away from the sad family history, Charlie pointed to another one on the next shelf down. "So, where was this one taken? Is that you, Beth? You haven't changed much at all!"

"Yup, that's me. I'm about fourteen too. I always think how weird it is, that we were living just a few miles apart and didn't know we would live together forever. I didn't sail, so it wasn't until we went to uni in London that we met. Those are my parents, my sisters, Jo and Alice, and our beautiful Lab, Daisy. It was taken at our family home. We lived in Arundel."

David, all this time, was not really partaking in the conversation. To him, people's pasts, dead siblings and long gone pets weren't of much interest. He liked the here and now and, sensing that he was appearing rude, Charlie attempted to engage with him.

"David, you and I could have 'missed' each other if you hadn't come to that party in Birmingham. Fate's odd, isn't it?" she said, going to sit on the arm of his chair and putting her arm round his shoulders.

"I don't really believe in fate. There are thousands of people you could potentially meet, but you don't."

"Very romantic," said Charlie, nudging his arm and laughing.

"But probably true," said Beth. "Life's pretty random. My sisters live in the States now, both married Americans. How weird's that? Anyway ... let's eat; don't want the lasagne to burn."

They went through and Beth rushed to the oven. "God, just in time," she said, grabbing some oven gloves and opening the door. There was indeed a faint smell of burnt cheese, but when she put the dish down on the table, it was just nicely brown, with lots of dripping cheese round the edges. "I think it was the cheese on the bottom burning," said Beth, peering into the oven. "I know if I was well-organised, I'd clean it off right now, but I can't be bothered," and she slammed the door shut.

They sat down, Alex next to Charlie, Beth next to David. There were a couple of bottles of wine on the table and before starting to eat, Alex poured the wine and they all chinked glasses.

"Here's to many more suppers like this," said Alex.

"Yes, cheers," said Charlie. "You'll have to come to ours next, but the food might not be as good as this."

"Wait till you've tasted it," said Beth, inserting a large serving spoon into the cheesy dish. They helped themselves to salad and large chunks of soft, white bread. Beth got up and dimmed the lights a little and, with yet more candles burning in the centre of the table, the atmosphere became intimate and friendly.

"So, David, tell us about your job. My Dad was in the Army, so I know a bit about military life, but nothing about flying," said Beth. "When did you know you wanted to be a pilot?"

David took a large swig of wine, finishing the glass. Beth re-filled it quickly and David said, "My parents made me join the Air Cadets. To be honest, I didn't want to join at all, but it got me out the house and I found I preferred it to school. They took us gliding when I was about seventeen. I got a taste for it and I seemed to have some aptitude. I applied when I was nineteen, as I realised I didn't want to go to university; seemed like a waste of time to me. It was a toss up between commercial airlines or the Air Force and the RAF offered me an interview first."

"Wow, amazing. How do they know you're going to be any good?" said Alex, before taking another sip of wine.

"Well, it's a physical skill, really. You can either do it or you can't. Loads of people fail the training, but they found out I was pretty exceptional," said David with a grin.

"And modest," laughed Charlie, looking a bit embarrassed.

"You have to be confident when you're in charge of a machine worth millions of pounds," said David. "No point pretending you're not."

Charlie was well aware of this. She often wished she had half his confidence. That was the problem with her and teaching. She didn't believe enough in herself and always thought she'd picked the wrong career.

"So, what happened after you got accepted?" asked Alex.

"Well, basic flying training, then I specialised on the Hercules. That's how we've ended up here." David reached for another chunk of bread and started wiping up the cheesy sauce with it.

"It must be a very satisfying job," said Beth. "Have you had any hairy moments?"

"Loads, but you kind of have to get on with it. I'd hate a boring job, stuck inside all day. I like the unpredictability, the weird hours, the foreign trips, the danger. It's also great in the military because you can play all sorts of sport."

"Yea, that's great," said Alex. "What's your main sport?"

"Tennis, I suppose. I'm in the RAF team, which involves loads of matches all over the place."

"Do you play?" asked Alex, turning towards Charlie, smiling at her. She was always prone to self-deprecation, didn't enjoy blowing her own trumpet, so said,

"Yup, but I wouldn't say I'm up to David's standard. We play social tennis together, but he poaches my shots."

"Only because you're not always quick enough ..." said David, laughing.

"We'll have to have a four; Alex is pretty handy with a tennis racquet and I can just about hold my own," said Beth.

"Yea, let's," said David. "We can always play at the camp."

They all had seconds, more wine and then Beth bought out a spectacular Pavlova, covered in fresh strawberries.

"Wow, you never told me you had Delia Smith tendencies, Beth," said Charlie.

"I don't, really. This is my only claim to fame in the pudding department. It's the one thing I can do that impresses people and I think I've succeeded?" she grinned, as she cut large slices, placing them carefully on small, flat plates. It was perfect: fluffy and chewy in the middle with a golden sheen on whirls of meringue on the top.

"You're a lucky man, Alex. This is delicious," said David. "If you come to ours, a bowl of ice cream is about the limit." He laughed at his own joke, but nobody else laughed. Charlie felt mortified and glanced at her watch, thinking maybe it would soon be time to go, before David drank any more.

"Well, it's scrumptious," said Charlie. "I think I could rise to something more than ice-cream. You'll have to tell me how to make a Pavlova, so I can have a go myself."

"Who've you got sitting for you tonight?" said Beth, deliberately changing the subject.

"A nice young girl, Saskia. She's never been before, but she seems competent. I gave her your number, but everything's obviously okay as she hasn't rung. I hope you don't mind. Just in case ..."

"No problem at all," said Alex, smiling at her. "I'm sure she'll be fine. Your daughter's called Lou, isn't she? Short for Louise or Louisa?"

"Louise," said Charlie. "She's a handful, but we wouldn't be without her. I can't remember life before ..."

"I can," chipped in David, laughing. "Peace, long lie-ins, adult conversation ..."

Ignoring him, Beth said, "Do you think you'll have any more?"

"Maybe one," said Charlie. They'd always talked of a pigeon pair, one girl, one boy.

"Not for a while," said David, polishing off another glass of red. "What about you two? Are you going to add your 2.4 children to the planet?"

Charlie was always wary of asking people questions like that; for all they knew, Beth and Alex might be desperately trying or indeed, found out they can't have any children. Never a good idea to ask, but to be fair, Beth had asked if they were going to have more.

"We'd love to, but no luck yet," said Alex, reaching across the table and taking Beth's hand. "I'd love three, and Beth would love at least six."

"Don't do it," said David, grinning. "Think of the expense."

No one said anything. They'd all finished their puddings, and every plate was left spotless.

"I've left what I didn't want," laughed Charlie, wiping her mouth with a paper serviette. "Wow, that was amazing."

"Shall we go through to the sitting room and have some coffee?" said Beth, standing up. "Alex, you take them through."

"I'll help clear the table," said Charlie. The men disappeared, and the girls took the dirty dishes into the kitchen. Beth switched on the kettle.

"Sorry about that," said Charlie, grimacing.

"What do you mean?"

"Oh, you know ... David asking about children."

"Oh, that's okay. I'm sure it'll happen one day. I just hope it doesn't take too long. Ticking clock and all that! David likes his wine, doesn't he?"

"Yes, he had a bit of a head-start on us."

"Will you be ok?"

"Yea, I'm used to it. We'll go when we've had some coffee. He'll fall asleep in the car and wake up as right as rain tomorrow. I don't know how he does it. Air Force training!"

They sat chatting, with the flames in the log-burner giving a warm glow to the room. Even Charlie felt a little woozy, with the heat and alcohol. The coffee woke her up a little and, looking at her watch, she said, "I think it's time we were getting back, to be honest. I said to the sitter we'd be home soon," said Charlie, standing up.

"Are you sure?" said Beth, reaching for a box on the coffee table. "I've got some mints ..."

"No thanks. It's been absolutely lovely but ... come on, David. Time we were going," and she went towards him, grabbed his hand and pulled him up.

"Oh, shame. I was just getting started." He stood up reluctantly with Charlie's helping hand.

"Thank you so much, you two, for a really lovely evening. I'll see you on Monday, Beth," said Charlie, hugging her friend maybe a little too tightly. Alex hugged her too; she could feel tears spring to her eyes. She wasn't sure why she was upset, but she'd really wanted the evening to go well.

"Thanks, mate," said David, slapping Alex on the back. "And Beth, you did yourself proud. Lucky man, Alex. Your wife is beautiful ..."

"Yes, come on, David, enough flattery for one evening."

They walked down the garden path, the automatic light coming on, showing them the way. The stars were glowing in the coal-black sky, the near full moon hanging behind some trees.

"Bye ... see you soon," called Charlie, waving as they reached the car.

"I'll drive," she said to David.

He slumped into the passenger seat and was asleep in seconds, before she'd even turned right onto the main road.

# CHAPTER 2

It was at the start of the following academic year. Beth told Charlie she was pregnant during their lunch break, as they were sitting side by side in the staffroom.

"I'm up the duff," she said, in her ear, her smile lighting up her face.

"I knew it. I KNEW there must be something up. When I saw you earlier, there was just *something* about you, a radiance ... like a halo."

"Don't be ridiculous."

"No, seriously. Talk about blooming! How far along are you?"

"Three months. Alex didn't want me to tell you until now. He said it would be pushing our luck. So, you see, if your theory was right, you would have known before; I would have been radiating ..."

"Well, whatever ... I knew today, anyway," Charlie laughed. "So exciting. If only I could get on and get pregnant again, they could be birth buddies. I really want another one and unless I get pregnant soon, the gap between them will be crazy. Lou's already four, for goodness' sake."

"Alex is going to be such a wonderful dad. I don't know whether it's because he loves baby animals or something, but he's just a natural. We went to see my cousin a couple of weeks ago. She's had twins. Well ... Alex was just amazing with them. There was no awkwardness or nerves; he was just straight in there, getting them out of the cot, cuddling, rocking, and he even changed a nappy. I had to fight with him to get a look in."

Charlie couldn't help feeling a bit jealous. David was a good father, but it didn't exactly come naturally to him. The day Lou was born, you could see he was overwhelmed, joyful even, but he was reticent to pick her up and when he *did* eventually, he looked almost frightened of her. It got better as time went on, but as she became a toddler with tantrums and opinions of her own, he found it difficult to cope, often resorting to shouting and anger instead of adult reasoning. Lately, Lou seemed to have the capacity to wind him up, and he couldn't see how ridiculous he was. These situations often ended up with *them* having a row, which Charlie tried very hard to hide from Lou, who was getting very observant and picked up on vibes between them.

"That's so nice. I can just imagine Alex with babies. He's such a softie," said Charlie, picturing his kind face in her mind's eye. She'd grown more and more fond of him. She noticed the way he looked at Beth with such love; it wasn't put on or exaggerated, he'd simply follow her with his eyes and smile. They were so perfectly at ease together, laughing at each other's jokes and respecting each other's opinions. This made them sound dull to be around, but the opposite was true; there was always so much fun and laughter in their company.

"Yes, he's going to be a pushover; when the kid's a teenager, they'll be able to wrap him around their little finger; they'll convince him they *must* go to whatever party they're talking about and that everyone else in the entire form is going. It'll be a nightmare," Beth laughed.

"I think David will leave that stuff to me. He finds it difficult enough dealing with Lou now, never mind as a teenager."

Beth looked at her with a 'knowing' expression. She didn't have to say anything, having already witnessed several of David's rather unreasonable outbursts. It was understood between them that they didn't talk about it, but Beth knew what Charlie had to put up with.

Beth had a difficult birth. She went into labour at seven in the morning when her waters broke as she waddled downstairs to get a cup of tea. Fortunately, Alex was at home when it happened. They'd practised what they'd do and were very well rehearsed, but the reality of it made them both panic. The contractions started soon after the waters broke and on the way to the hospital, which was only twenty minutes away, they both thought it might all happen in the car. Alex drove as fast as he could under the circumstances, while Beth tried to concentrate on her breathing.

Once in a room, they were told they had a way to go yet, by the very young-looking midwife who was in charge. She was bright, cheerful and oozed confidence, which helped, but they both felt as if they'd lost control of the situation. A 'way to go' turned out to be eight hours of intense pain for Beth. She'd opted not to have an epidural and when she'd realised that was a stupid decision, she was told it was too late to have one. The baby wasn't in the right position and had to be manipulated; Beth had so many monitors on, it was impossible to get off the bed, so all the pain was in her back.

Alex had, of course, attended many animal births, so he knew what was going on. He gave Beth instructions and got told off by the nice midwife.

"Mr Harris, it's very confusing for your wife, with the two of us giving her advice. Could you please just leave it to me, please? Could you comfort her? Hold her hand?" Duly put in his place, he moved up to the 'head' end and tried stroking Beth's head and whispering encouragement, only to be sworn at. He felt utterly helpless and hated seeing his beloved wife going through such pain. After what seemed like hours of pushing, a mass of dark hair appeared and he was allowed down the other end to watch the miraculous arrival of his daughter.

Alex was so overwhelmed with love for them both that he collapsed on a chair and sobbed with joy. While Beth was being sewn up, he held his daughter in his arms, gazing into her eyes, as if it was the only place to look in the world. In that moment, he loved Beth and Darcy (as she immediately became) more than any man had ever loved anyone, or that's how it felt.

He vowed he would protect them against everything the world could throw at them. He would love them both forever. Nothing bad would ever happen to either of them.

Charlie was so excited when she heard the news. It was as if a member of her own family had been born.

"She's here ... she arrived at ten past six this evening," said Alex. "She's absolutely beautiful, Charlie." She was one of the first people he'd rung, after family. He caught her just before she went to bed.

"Oh, my goodness ... it's a girl. I *knew* it. That's brilliant news. How's Beth? How did it go?"

"It was awful, to be honest. I'm sorry I didn't ring you to let you know while it was happening, but it all started so quickly and then we just went into panic mode and it went on forever. All our preparations went out the window."

"Don't be daft. I'm sure you had too much to deal with, to think about ringing me. I'm just so happy for you both. How's Beth? You didn't say."

"Beth's okay now, but exhausted. She was amazing, Charlie. I don't know how you women cope with it. I really don't. She had to have a few stitches; she was sleeping when I left. I've just staggered home in a state of ... I don't know what you'd call it ... euphoria, I think. My head's spinning with it all."

"Have you chosen a name yet?"

"As we didn't want to know what sex the baby was, we had a few boys' and girls' names we liked, but the moment we saw her, we both thought she was definitely ... Darcy. So ... she's Darcy Elizabeth Harris."

"That's gorgeous. What a lovely name. I can't wait to meet her. When can I come? What's the plan?" Charlie was in the kitchen and turned the kettle on for a celebratory cup of cocoa.

"I think if all goes well, we should be able to get her home the day after tomorrow. Why don't you come to the hospital tomorrow? I'll ring you before school and let you know a good time."

"Okay. Just let me know when, and I'll be there."

They said their goodbyes and Charlie piled her cup with lots of cocoa powder, and pouring the steaming water, she could see the three of them in her mind's eye. Those two would make such great parents, she knew they would. It was a precious moment in a marriage, straight after the birth of the first child. She couldn't wait to meet Darcy.

Alex rang in the morning; mother and baby had had a good night and Darcy was feeding well.

"Are you okay? You sound knackered," laughed Charlie.

"Yea, I feel as if I've been hit by a truck. I couldn't sleep at all last night. I was on such a high! Couldn't stop thinking about it all. I think I must have only got about two hours. Sorry to ring you so early, by the way."

"I've been up since six. You've got all these delights to come," she added. "Could you try to go back to bed for a bit? I'm presuming you're not going to work today?"

"No, I've got a few days off, thank God. I'm just so wired, I don't think I'd sleep."

"Maybe your body's getting you used to all those sleepless nights you've got coming."

"Thanks, Charlie; you know how to cheer a chap up."

They arranged for her to come into the hospital at five. Charlie put down the phone as David came into the kitchen. "Who rang so early?"

"It was just Alex ..."

"How's the baby? Is it okay?"

"Yes, fine ... we were just arranging a time for me to go in and see them all. She's not an 'it', by the way."

"Oh ... why don't you wait and see them when they're home? The baby's not going to change in a couple of days."

"The baby's name is Darcy ... and I know she won't change. I just want to see her and Beth as soon as I can."

"Oh well, your choice. I won't be back tonight, by the way. I'm flying to Cyprus. Will be back, hopefully, late tomorrow evening."

Charlie was so used to their weird life, when things changed constantly, that she didn't react. This was just another time, like all the others, when she'd be on her own for the evening, dealing with their daughter alone, preparing for tomorrow's classes and feeling like a single mum.

David kissed his daughter's head in passing; she lifted her arms to him for a cuddle, but with a backward wave, was through the door and gone. It was as if he didn't make a fuss of leaving, for fear of upsetting everyone but leaving was part of their life together.

In her lunch hour, Charlie rushed out and bought a card and a cute teddy. She spent ages choosing both and was nearly late for her afternoon class, running into the staffroom just in time, flustered. She told as many people as she could about the good news and started a whip-round for a present for Beth and Darcy. It seemed to cheer them all up: the grey clouds and the tedious relentlessness of teaching groups of surly teenagers had taken its toll on everyone and the good news of a new life lifted them all.

When she arrived at the hospital, she remembered that special time with Lou: the look of her, the smell of her, the feel of her. All her own hopes and dreams lay with that little person ... all the future.

She asked where Beth's room was. She didn't want to barge in, so knocked quietly. A voice murmured something from inside, so she pushed the door open slowly. Peeking in, she saw Beth sitting up in bed with a sleeping Darcy in her arms.

Beth looked pale and tired, but her smile on seeing Charlie burst forth like the morning sun through clouds. Alex was sitting next to her on the bed, his face weary, but beaming.

"Is it okay to come in?" Charlie whispered as she glanced round the door. "If it's not a good time ..."

"Come in ... she's fast asleep," said Beth, looking down at her. "Sleeping like the proverbial baby."

Charlie felt she should tiptoe; the scene was so peaceful, and she didn't want to wreck it. She came and stood near Alex and gazed down at Darcy's black hair.

"Oh my goodness, guys, she's absolutely beautiful. She's got masses of hair, Beth ... she looks as if she's going to take after you."

"I know, it's incredible, isn't it? Do you want to hold her?"

"Can I? Are you sure? I don't want to wake her."

"She'll be fine ..." she said, expertly shifting the baby into her hands and passing her over.

Charlie had forgotten how light babies were; she was like a doll, so fragile. Even though it wasn't that long ago that Lou had been so small, she felt awkward and worried with the responsibility of simply holding her. There was a chair by Beth's bedside and she sat down with her precious bundle, Darcy snuffling a little, but sleeping soundly throughout the manoeuvre. Charlie gazed down at her with wonder: her little button nose, her rosy cheeks, her almond-shaped eyes. Perfect.

"She's tiny ... how heavy is she?" she whispered.

"Seven pounds three ounces, so a good size ... just right, in fact. Although she felt a lot bigger than that when she was coming out. Why didn't you warn me, Charlie? You made it sound easy."

"I didn't want to frighten you, but ... it's a strange pain; the moment it's over, it's totally forgotten. All you can remember is the relief ... and the sheer gratitude. You men just don't know what actual pain is all about," she whispered, grinning at Alex.

"No, you're right. We can't remotely compare the pain of childbirth to anything ... mind you, I lived through every contraction," he laughed, "and my hand will never be the same again after Beth squeezed it for hours on end. So we do suffer, you know."

He took Beth's hand and kissed it.

"I actually wouldn't want to watch someone go through that," said Charlie. "I'm sure you feel totally useless. All you can do is give encouragement. Hey, I've forgotten something. Alex, can you look in that bag? I've bought a little something for you all."

Alex bent down and found the card, the squashy, pink-wrapped parcel, a bottle of champagne, and some strawberries.

"Wow, Charlie, what's all this?"

He opened the card and read out loud. "To Darcy, Beth and Alex. This is the first day of your future together. I'm so happy to share it with you. Love Charlie."

"Oh, that's so lovely ... now let's see what's in here ..." and he tore the paper off the cuddly teddy. "Her first toy ..." he said, as he put it in her cot. "Thank you so much, Charlie ... and for the champagne."

"You won't be allowed to have it here, but I thought you could celebrate when you get home. Hopefully, you can eat some of the strawberries, Beth."

They chatted for a few more minutes. Both sets of grandparents had been in touch and had arranged to come to meet Darcy when they were at home. Alex had spoken to his parents soon after the birth. Having lost Jake, Darcy was extra special to them, he said. They were so excited. Beth said she was going to call her sisters in America later.

Darcy woke and started rooting around. "I think you might need to take over from here, Beth," she said, standing up slowly and handing her back so gently it was as if she might break.

"What are you doing for supper tonight, Alex?" asked Charlie. "Why don't you pop round to ours on your way home and I'll cook you something? I'll leave you two lovebirds alone now, but you're very welcome later."

"Are you sure? That would be amazing. I've done no shopping and haven't given eating any thought."

Charlie went to kiss Beth goodbye. "Well done. She's an absolute stunner. Life really is miraculous." She bent down and hugged her, breathing in the newborn smell again. Darcy was beginning to cry, straining to find the source of her food.

"Hurry up and have another one yourself ... what are you waiting for?" Beth laughed.

"Well, I'll give it a go ... I'll see you soon when you get home and ... I'll see *you* in a couple of hours, Alex," said Charlie. "Enjoy your night in hospital with her, Beth. It's such a special time."

---

Charlie collected Lou and raced home, wondering what on earth she was going to cook. She'd blithely invited Alex, but had no idea what she had in the cupboard or freezer.

The doorbell rang just as she'd got Lou out of the bath a bit earlier than she'd expected. She opened the door to him, with Lou wrapped in a towel.

"Come in, come in. I've just got to get this one into bed and then we'll eat something. Not sure what, yet. David's not here. Gone to Cyprus."

Alex looked worn out. "Oh, right. All the more for us. I'll eat anything you give me. Honestly, I don't mind what."

"Why don't you come upstairs and we'll read Lou a story," said Charlie, as she closed the front door. "She loves it if someone reads to her, even though she loves looking at books herself, too. Or would you rather collapse in a heap?"

"No, I'd love to."

They all went upstairs and Lou ran down the corridor to her room, giggling and excited to have someone different in the house. She jumped on her bed and started singing a loud song. After a struggle, Charlie managed to get her dressed, blowing on her belly and making raspberries. Charlie loved this time of day, when Lou smelt clean and her body was warm from the bath. Alex perked up and joined in the games. Charlie was secretly thinking they'd never get Lou to go to sleep after all the fun.

She tried to calm things down by taking her to the pile of books in the corner. They chose one and Charlie sat on the bed too and listened as Alex read the story, using lots of different voices and accents for each character. Lou insisted on another book, so Charlie left them to it and went downstairs to start the supper; she had spaghetti and veg and a tin of tomatoes, so threw together a spag bol with plenty of cheddar to spread on top. She had to rescue Alex; he was on his fourth book by the time she went back upstairs again.

"Beth said you'd be a pushover and I can see you already are," she laughed. "Lou, it's time for bed now. Uncle Alex is exhausted. Come on, lie down." She beckoned to Alex to make a hasty retreat, which he did, blowing a kiss to Lou at the door. She turned on the night light and Lou lay down.

"Night night, poppet. Sleep well," she said, hoping she'd go down without a fight.

Lou said, "Can Uncle Alex come back and say night, night?"

"No, it's time for sleep now. Close your eyes, sweetheart." Charlie bent down and kissed her sweet cheek. How she loved her. She'd die for her.

She went out, turned off the main light, and waited a few seconds outside. When all was quiet, she went downstairs, where Alex was sitting at the kitchen table.

"That was such fun," he said. "I love the thought of reading Darcy stories …"

"It's a wonderful stage. They're so innocent, so cute, so …"

"So gorgeous," he added.

"She *can* be a little monster sometimes," Charlie laughed.

"No, surely not? I don't believe it; you're making it up. She's like a cherub."

"Believe me … anyway, I hope you like a very basic spag bol, as that's all I had. It's not even a meat one."

"Honestly, Charlie, that sounds amazing."

They sat down and polished off an enormous pile of food, Alex eating ravenously. There was no need to fill any silences; they were perfectly comfortable just eating. Charlie could tell that all the excitement of the past days and then the frivolity of Lou's bedtime, had completely sapped him dry of energy.

When they'd finished, she said, "Why don't you go to the sitting room and I'll bring you through a coffee …"

and with no further need of encouragement, he got up and disappeared.

Charlie quickly threw the plates and cutlery into the dishwasher, made some coffee and went through. "Let's just watch the telly," she said. "You look past it."

"Thanks ... I don't think I could have a conversation," he grinned.

She turned on the TV; he sipped his coffee, and they settled down to watch a drama that neither of them had watched before. It didn't matter that they hadn't got a clue what was going on; they were both exhausted and before long, Alex's eyes were tight shut and he was snoring. She continued watching, hoping that it would all come clear, but it didn't, so she turned it off and looked over at him again. He really was out for the count.

Standing up and going over to him, she lifted his legs onto the settee and slid his shoes off. He didn't even stir, so she went upstairs, grabbed a blanket, and covered him gently. She felt somehow protective of him.

She found herself staring at him, sleeping. He was utterly still; she could hear his soft breaths. There was a small part of her that was jealous of what Beth and Alex had. She loved them both so much, and now there was Darcy. They really were the perfect family.

What an absolutely lovely person he is, she thought, as she turned off the light. She knew he'd probably be embarrassed in the morning about falling so heavily asleep.

She went round the house, turning everything off and then made her way upstairs to bed. Charlie tiptoed into Lou's bedroom; she was snuggled under her duvet, cuddling her favourite bunny. Charlie gently kissed her forehead, went to her room, and quickly undressed. She too fell immediately asleep.

In the morning, she found a note on the kitchen table:

> Sorry about my complete lack of social skills … I don't know what happened. I must have just passed out. I woke at 5.30, so I'm going to go home and prepare for the big homecoming. Thanks so much for being such a good friend … to both of us. See you soon. Alex xxx

# CHAPTER 3

Alex and Beth settled into parenthood as if they were born to it. Darcy was what people call a 'good' baby; not only did she sleep through after five weeks, but she hardly ever cried. Was this because they were such good, calm parents, or was it that she'd inherited their laid-back characters? Whichever was the reason, she was a delight; they could go out to the pub for lunch and she was quite happy to be passed around and admired by complete strangers. When it was time for her to smile, her entire face lit up like her mum's and when she discovered her laugh, she sounded just like her dad. She was the happiest soul.

When Darcy was a one-year-old, Charlie gave birth to William, or, as he became almost immediately, Will. It was a hard labour which went on for hours. Charlie also left it too late to have an epidural and only had some gas and air. David was with her and helped her through it, but it was Charlie who had to suffer the agony, fear and intense relief when he finally made an appearance.

Will came out the way he meant to go on ... absolutely yelling his head off; there was no lull when everyone waited for that sound of the baby taking his first breath. Will cried the moment he was in the world.

With tears streaming down his face, David, who had watched him come out, said to Charlie, "It's a boy ... it's a boy." They'd decided not to find out beforehand, but David had confidently predicted the outcome. He'd felt throughout the pregnancy that it was his son kicking and turning in Charlie's belly, keeping her awake at night. He'd say things like "That's my boy" when he saw or touched Charlie's bulging bump, or "I can't wait for that time when we can watch rugby together and go down the pub". A boy would complete him.

Beth's serene mothering of Darcy made Charlie feel like an awful mum; nothing she did seemed to placate Will: he cried, he struggled, he screamed and ... never slept. If two babies were polar opposites, it was them. Poor Charlie had thought that she'd got the whole motherhood thing hacked as Lou had been relatively easy, but Will taught her a valuable lesson: that children will be who they are, with no input from their parents.

Will continued to be 'difficult' as a toddler and, however hard Charlie tried, he was determined to have his own way. They had terrible 'set-to's' when Charlie felt she was continually losing the battle. She tried to see the funny side of it. How could a child be such a powerful adversary? But she found him exhausting. Beth would support her and tell her it was nothing she was doing wrong. If it was *her*, then Lou would have been the same, wouldn't she, she said.

Despite everything, Charlie absolutely adored Will. He was funny, feisty, and she actually admired his powerful will. She was sure he would be an incredible adult.

Darcy and he were the best of friends from the start. Being a year older, she tried to mother him; he was like her living, crying, baby doll. When they were four- and five-year-olds, they were always up to mischief together; they were almost closer than Will and Lou. They all went to the same school and the three of them were like family: always in each other's houses, with sleepovers, parties and shopping trips.

Beth and Alex tried to have a brother or sister for Darcy, but after four years of trying unsuccessfully, they were told it was unlikely ever to happen. It turned out they'd been lucky to have one child; Alex had a low sperm count, which made Darcy a miracle. They accepted it, but were heartbroken that Darcy would never have a real sibling. Alex knew what it was like to have your parents' undivided attention, and it put a lot of pressure on you.

Beth had handed in her notice soon after Darcy was born; she said she knew she wouldn't want to go back after maternity leave. Charlie fell out with her new Head of Department when she returned after her maternity leave and decided she couldn't hack it at that school any more. He always seemed to pick on her; she wanted to call him out as a bully, but decided she couldn't be bothered. Trying to prove it would be too stressful, so she threw the towel in.

That situation had actually put Charlie off teaching altogether for a while; she wondered if she was cut out for it, but a job in a posh, private girls' school came up, and to her surprise she got offered it. It was a part-time role and fitted around the children perfectly. She rather liked the longer holidays; she had a few days when she was off, but her children were still at school. A real bonus. As in any school, there were still problems, but they were easier to handle.

Having a young child completely changed Beth's attitude to teaching secondary school kids. She started going into Darcy's school to help with reading and assisted on outings; young, primary-aged children were much more 'her thing', she thought, so when she got a job offer as a teaching assistant at Darcy's school, she never looked back.

---

When Will was about four, Charlie and David decided that they'd like to go to the RAF Officers' Mess Summer Ball. Charlie hadn't wanted to go in recent years, having two young children to contend with; she hadn't got the energy or inclination. David was always keen to go out anywhere, but Charlie had won the argument in this case, and they hadn't gone to many Air Force social do's since Will's birth. David had plenty of opportunities to socialise with his colleagues anyway, so didn't make too much of a fuss, but he was thrilled when Charlie decided she'd like to go again.

"Can we ask Beth and Alex to come too? I reckon they'd love it," she said.

"Yea, why not? The more the merrier. Find out, and I'll get the tickets. We'll pay for theirs; I'm sure we owe them. I feel as if we've been to their place more than they've been to ours. What do you think?"

"Yes, I agree. That would be a friendly gesture, David. I'll ask Beth tonight."

Of course she agreed; she couldn't wait. "How often do we get to dress up these days? I'm in jeans and food-covered t-shirts most of the time. Why wouldn't I want to go to a glamorous ball? Mind you, it might take me a while to get presentable."

"Don't do yourself down, Beth. You're gorgeous. If fact, you're annoyingly slim and beautiful," said Charlie.

Beth looked down; she found compliments difficult, and she didn't know how attractive she was. "Are you sure we can't pay for our tickets? It's so kind of you both ..."

"Don't be daft, of course you can't. We're just pleased you're coming. I never feel I have any friends amongst the RAF wives. I've got a few acquaintances, but no one I can have a laugh with. It will be a really fun night."

On the evening of the ball, Alex and Beth drove round to their house; they were going to get a taxi to the Mess so they could all have a drink. They'd arranged for the same taxi firm to pick them up at half past midnight to take them home; Alex would leave his car at theirs and collect it in the morning. The ball would, of course, go on much later than that, but they knew the kids would be awake early the next day, and that was late enough.

"Oh my god, Beth, you look stunning. I love your dress. Emerald green really suits you," said Charlie when she opened the door. "And you've scrubbed up well, too, Alex."

She kissed them both warmly. Alex was so handsome in his dress suit; she was used to seeing him in jeans and had never seen him look so smart.

"I feel very odd in this," he laughed. "I had to hire one. I possess nothing quite this sophisticated. You, Charlie, look amazing."

"Thank you, kind sir," she said, doing a twirl. She was pleased with how she looked. After three months of dieting, she felt less bulky around her tummy. She was wearing high heels which were, in fact, already killing her, but they made her feel powerful, as if she could conquer anything. Her dress she'd found in John Lewis and it fitted her well, emphasising the good bits and hiding the not-so-good. The colour suited her colouring, she thought; it was burnt orange.

David, as usual, had gone up late to change; he'd been watching some rugby match that was vital, apparently. He always thought he was a quick dresser, but getting into the Air Force dress uniform was far trickier than he'd remembered. The major problem was the bow tie, which always proved tricky to get right and tonight was doubly so. He now emerged into the sitting room, looking flustered.

"Wow, look at you," said Beth, kissing him on the cheek. "I've never seen that uniform before. Very posh. Is it comfortable, though? I hope you don't mind me saying it, but you look rather 'stiff'!"

David was, in fact, standing ramrod straight and trying to pull his collar away from his neck. "Yeah, so would you be in this wing collar, cummerbund and ridiculous pointed shoes. Thank god I don't have to wear it very often."

"Well, I think you look very smart," said Alex, coming over and shaking his hand. "Thanks so much for inviting us, mate. I can't remember the last time I went to anything like this."

Thankfully, the children were already asleep, so they could enjoy a glass of bubbly before they left. "I haven't provided any nibbles as we're going to eat so much tonight, I think we can do without them," said Charlie. "You'll be amazed, there's so much food. The main meal and then there'll be other things like a barbeque, Chinese food, a salad bar, pancakes; it's crazy."

"Sounds incredible. The army used to do things like this, but I, of course, didn't go as I was only a child. I remember Mum and Dad coming back really late and not wanting to get up," said Beth. "My sisters and I took advantage and ran riot in the morning without their supervision."

David went to the window and looked through curtains. "The taxi's here. Come on troops. It's time."

With instructions to the babysitter to call if there were any problems, Charlie put her light coat round her shoulders and David held the door open for her and Alex and Beth. He also held open the back door of the large car he'd ordered and the three of them got in, the girls trying not to stand on their long dresses. Alex sat with the two girls and made a joke about being the thorn between two roses. David climbed in next to the driver and they drove the twenty minutes to the camp. The atmosphere in the cab was warm and fun, the girls' perfume permeating the air.

As they pulled up outside the officers' mess, there were many other people arriving and decanting from vehicles. All the men looked extremely smart and the women, so colourful. They entered the main hall and joined a hubbub of people, all talking loudly, surrounded by paintings in gold frames of aeroplanes and past commanders. A huge glass chandelier hung above, lighting the scene with its brilliance. Waiters in uniform were standing with trays of champagne glasses and they were handed one almost immediately they got inside. They stood together in a group, chinked glasses and tasted the sharp bubbles. The girls were standing next to each other and Beth leant into Charlie and whispered, "This is the life. I feel I'm in a parallel universe. Our lives aren't usually this glamorous, are they?"

"Not exactly, no," Charlie laughed. "But you really look the part; I keep seeing men taking sly looks at you."

"Well, I only have eyes for Alex," she laughed, "so they can sod off."

At that moment, an insanely good looking man in an army dress uniform walked by. He looked spectacular, and both girls gawped intensely. Not noticing them, he marched past, through the melee, with purpose. They looked at each other and giggled.

"I might make the odd exception," said Beth. "Men really improve with a uniform, don't they?"

"Yes, you're right. The most ordinary-looking bloke can be elevated to idol-level with the help of a few gold buttons and spurs."

"That sounded very sexist, ladies," said David, as he caught the end of their conversation. "They are objectifying us, Alex. Are we going to stand for it?"

"They can objectify me as much as they want," he laughed, grabbing Beth's hand and kissing it ceremoniously.

After a few more minutes of idle chatter, they wandered through to the rest of the mess, David showing them around proudly. There was already a band playing in one room, but no dancing as yet. They sat and listened for a while as the band played classic songs from the past. David said they were RAF musicians, and they were undoubtedly talented. When one particular song came on, *Luck be a Lady Tonight,* Alex jumped up and insisted on dragging Beth onto the empty dance floor. She looked back at Charlie with a look of *Oh god, here we go,* on her face. He whisked her around like a professional, and all David and Charlie could do was watch with total admiration.

"Wow," said Charlie, "I had no idea you had that in you," as they came back to them, beaming and excited. "Where did you learn to dance so well? Not being mean, Beth, but I could see it was Alex who knew what he was doing."

"Charming!" exclaimed Beth, sitting down with a bump.

"Well, I've always loved dancing and when I was at school, they made us have lessons. I went to a posh, private school, you can tell."

"Yea, you wouldn't get ballroom dancing lessons in most schools," said David, who'd shown no interest in dancing in his life.

"And I love that song ... mainly because I had to sing it in the school production of 'Guys and Dolls'. It was my big moment; I can still feel the spotlight on me and hear the standing ovation at the end. I really miss singing and dancing."

"Very modest," said Beth, as she looked at him with love.

"You've got lots of hidden talents," said Charlie. "And there were we, thinking your whole life was animals."

"And sailing, don't forget," said Beth. "He's a man of many parts. Trouble is, when you grow up and get a job, there's not much time for anything else, is there? You're so exhausted just trying to make it through another day. And then children ..."

"Maybe when I retire, I'll take up amateur dramatics and sailing again," said Alex. "I love the life I have now, but wow, I enjoyed that." He appeared to be on a high and at that moment, the band started playing *Why Do Fools Fall In Love.* He jumped up again, saying, "Come on, you two lovebirds, let's shake our stuff," and he pulled both the girls up by the hand and forced David to stand up too.

Charlie felt a little shy, dancing on an empty floor; she wasn't the best dancer, but she loved it; she just needed more champagne inside her to lose her inhibitions. David wasn't bad at dancing, but you always got the feeling he was going through the motions and doing what was expected of him. As it was a fast song, the two of them just twisted and twirled about to the music, laughing and falling over each other's feet.

Charlie looked over David's shoulder, fascinated by how good Alex and Beth were. They made it look effortless and timeless and made her and David's efforts look amateurish. But she shouldn't worry about what other people were doing; they were there to enjoy themselves.

Sitting back down again, quite breathless from all the effort, Charlie said, "Hey, I wouldn't mind a cold drink ... where's the bar?"

"It's all right; I'll go and get you something. Orange juice?" asked David.

"Yes, with lots of ice and fizzy water, please. Can you get Beth one too? I'm sure she'll want a drink when she's allowed to sit down."

"Okay," he said, and David wandered off.

Charlie sat and watched as her two best friends danced on and on. There seemed to be no song they couldn't look good to. Her feet were already aching and while she waited for David, she took off her shoes and rubbed her toes; she was already regretting her decision to wear those heels. By now, there were a few more couples dancing and she happily 'people watched' until David came back, brandishing a tray with long orange drinks and beers.

Alex and Beth eventually came over, both panting and sweating, and downed the cold drinks with gusto. "I'm exhausted already," said Beth. "I'm not used to all this exercise. It's going to be a long night if you insist on dancing this much, Alex."

"I'll give you a rest, don't worry. Maybe I can persuade Charlie to join me later?"

"I'd love to, but I'm not as good as Beth," she said, feeling embarrassed.

"Let's have a meal now and we can all chill for a while," said David. "Follow me," and he marched purposefully towards the exit.

They walked down the corridor to the dining room; they could choose from a vast variety of food, but they all went for the roast beef and vegetables option. David grabbed two bottles of red wine and they sat in the candlelit serenity, away from the frenetic music. David poured the wine, and they did cheers again, revelling in the atmosphere of friendship and glamour. Charlie looked at Alex and Beth, who were sitting opposite and thought how lucky she was to have met them. This wouldn't have been half as fun without them.

The wine flowed; the girls had wonderful puddings of meringue, fresh fruit and copious cream and the boys went for sticky toffee pudding and treacle tart, covered in custard; such a typical gender divide making them laugh.

"Why do men love those old-fashioned English puddings so much?" said Beth. "It's as if they think they need building up, or maybe it's memories of their mother's cooking?"

"Actually, I love them too," said Charlie, "but even here, at something like this, I'm worrying about my weight."

"Why do you worry about your figure?" said Alex. "You always look slim and gorgeous to me."

"Thank you," said Charlie, feeling stupidly pleased. "But it all goes back to uni when someone, probably not maliciously, said I had 'child-bearing hips'. It was a joke in their head, but unfortunately, it's stayed with me ever since."

"That's such a shame," said Beth, "but it's true ... it's so important to think about the effect of your words on people."

"I don't let people's opinions affect me; they go right over my head. You should try to be less sensitive, Charlie," said David, his words sliding into each other.

"We can't all have your confidence, though."

"Well, I stand by what I said," said Alex. "You're slim and you look absolutely amazing tonight. Just enjoy it and eat what you want."

Charlie wished it was that easy, but the mind was annoying; there was always that nagging voice in her head telling her she was fat. But Alex was right, she really ought to enjoy herself for one night. All the alcohol was so calorific, anyway. Who was she kidding? On which note, David grabbed another bottle of red and a bottle of white for Beth and he took them to a quiet sitting area where they could get coffees. As they walked there, Charlie felt decidedly wobbly and realised she'd drunk too much. David was slurring his words; he must have had some sneaky glasses at the bar, as it took a lot to get him drunk these days.

"I'm going to the Ladies, Beth. Do you want to come?" she asked. "Can you order me a coffee and some fizzy water, David?"

"Yeah, I think I ought to," said Beth. "See you in a bit, guys. Same for me, David. Thanks."

As they walked into the brightly lit bathroom, they saw themselves reflected in several mirrors.

"Oh my god, I look horrendous," said Beth. "My face is crimson and look at my hair!"

"Blimey, I think we ought to slow down. We both look as if we've had a shitload of booze. Despite the dresses, we look as if we've been out on the razzle all night, in some dodgy nightclub," Charlie giggled.

They tried to repair the damage with some powder and lippy, and a quick brush of the hair. Staggering into the cubicles, they relieved themselves and then, when they emerged, they linked arms and barged back through the door, hooting and laughing as they went. On entering the quiet room, they saw the two men downing brandies. This evening was turning into a booze fest. Things usually went pear-shaped, when spirits were imbibed.

They both sank into squashy sofas, flopped backwards, took off their shoes and relaxed. There were loads of people milling around and the noise level was high; Charlie felt herself drifting off.

"Wake up, sleepyhead," she heard someone say after a while. She wasn't sure how long she'd dropped off for; she'd had to force her eyes open. Alex was standing next to her, holding her coffee. "Drink this; it'll wake you up. There's a lot of dancing to do." She tried to focus and eventually took the coffee, nearly spilling it. It was cold, so she'd obviously been asleep longer than she'd realised.

"Where are the others?" she said sleepily.

"David wandered off and Beth's gone ahead to listen to the band. There's another lot who've just started up and they sound incredible. They're playing modern stuff. I said I'd wait for you."

"Thanks ... you didn't need to," she said, smiling up at him. She slurped her coffee and, with a lot of effort, put her shoes on again and gave her hand to Alex.

"Pull me up!" she said, and he took her hand and pulled backwards. She staggered upright. "Right ... let's go. Did David say where he was going?"

"No, not sure."

"The bar, probably. I'll leave him to it."

When they arrived, they spotted Beth; she was sitting to the left of them at a little table at the edge of the dancefloor; she was chatting to a guy in a naval uniform. They were laughing and Alex said, "I'd better see who's chatting who up." He wasn't the jealous type; Charlie knew he was perfectly at ease with Beth speaking to other men.

"There you are," laughed Beth. "Finally woken up, then? This is Geoff; I was just telling him about you and what a lightweight you are."

"Hi there, Geoff," Charlie said. "I'm not used to all this booze. I feel more awake though now. Alex, are you going to put me through my paces, then? I love this one."

The band had a girl singer, who'd started singing, *I just can't get you out of my head,* by Kylie. Alex grabbed her hands, and they joined the throng of people who had now filled the dancefloor. There were several sparkly disco balls showering them with pink and green lights. The music was deafening and Alex started throwing her around in a mixture of styles; one minute they were dancing a kind of waltz and the next, they were disco-dancing round each other. He could somehow force her to go where he wanted her to go and, at the same time, make her feel as if she was flying. The song merged into the next, an S-Club Seven one, and by this time, Charlie felt totally uninhibited; she was, in her own head anyway, dancing like a diva, not caring what she looked like.

"Oh Alex, that was great," she shouted in his ear as they walked back, hand in hand, towards Beth and Geoff. "I can't remember the last time I had so much fun."

"You're good ... much better than you implied," he said, undoing his bow tie and the top button of his shirt. He then took off his jacket and hung it on the back of a chair. "I'm far too hot now," he shouted. "I'll go to the bar and get some cold drinks and try to track down David."

"Poor Geoff's girlfriend's ill, so he's had to come on his own," shouted Beth into Charlie's ear.

"Oh, bummer," said Charlie, looking at Geoff with a regretful smile. "Not the same on your own ..."

"I know a few people here, so it's okay, I suppose. Are you on your own?"

"No, I've got a husband somewhere ..."

Alex came back with the drinks and a worried look on his face. "He wasn't in the bar. I had a look around, but I can't see him anywhere. I'll drink this and then go for another wander. Maybe he's gone outside to cool down or something."

"He often does this at do's," said Charlie. "He gets talking bollocks to his flying mates; they drink far too much and then he disappears. It's happened before. He kind of forgets me. Don't worry, I'm used to it."

They all looked at each other; no one was sure what to say. Both Alex and Charlie drank their icy water as if they'd just emerged from a desert crossing and then slumped onto some chairs and were happy to sit and watch the dancing. Then the two girls took Geoff onto the dancefloor, feeling rather sorry for him. He wasn't a superb dancer like Alex, but they all sang to the music, twirled round each other and enjoyed themselves. Alex took the opportunity to go off in search of David again.

"Hey Charlie, I think you'd better come with me. I've found him," he said, quite a long time later.

Charlie and Beth looked at each other, and leaving a bewildered Geoff to fend for himself, they followed Alex down the corridor. When they got to the entrance hall, Alex went out through the main door, turned right, and went through a side gate into the garden. It was a warm evening, and the moon was almost full, casting a ghostlike silver light over the trees and shrubs.

"He's over here. I don't know why I came out; I think it was instinct, but I found him."

In the middle of the lawn, under a large tree, there was bench and David was lying down on it, completely wasted. His bow tie was missing, as was his jacket, and there seemed to be what looked like blood on his face.

"Oh god, here we go," said Charlie.

"What do you mean?"

Charlie walked over to David and gently shook his shoulder, but there was no response at all; it was as if he was dead. She looked round at the other two and said, "He's done this at various things before. He can hold his booze well so you won't have seen him like this before in normal, everyday socialising, but when we go to Air Force things with alcohol everywhere, he can't resist and then he just passes out."

Alex and Beth were holding hands in the moonlight and Charlie could see the concern on their faces.

"I didn't see him drinking more than the rest of us, though," said Alex.

"No, that's what's so clever. When he went to the bar for our cold drinks earlier, though, he will have had a couple of whiskies. I know what he's like." She pushed his shoulder harder this time. No response. "And he will have polished off the third bottle of red."

"What shall we do? We can't leave him here," said Alex. His face was full of worry. Charlie didn't want to ruin their night.

"It's not cold out here. He can stay out here till we want to go home and then we'll have to get him into the taxi somehow." Charlie knew it sounded hardhearted to leave him but, what else could they do? Why should he ruin everyone's night?

Alex and Beth looked at each other. "Seems a bit off, leaving him out here. We can't just carry on, as if nothing's happened," said Beth.

"Why not? He did this to himself; we're not to blame," said Charlie. She felt so fed up; she didn't care how she came across.

"What's the time?" said Alex, jerking back his sleeve to look at his watch. "Quarter past eleven. Mmm ... quite a long time till the taxi comes."

"By the time we've had a few more dances ... he'll be fine for an hour. We'll have to come and drag him to the taxi at twelve fifteen; it will take ages. He'll be a dead weight."

Beth and Alex, she could tell, didn't like this idea at all, but Charlie marched off, back through the garden, on a mission to get away from him. They followed reluctantly, looking back at David. Beth squeezed Alex's hand and whispered, "It's not exactly love's young dream, is it? I've never seen Charlie like this before. She's so angry with him."

Alex drew her hand up to kiss it. "We'll just have to support her."

Charlie was far ahead and was striding down the corridor towards the dancing, despite her high heels. She went and lent against the wall with a furious look on her face.

"Come on, let's all dance and enjoy the last hour," said Alex, catching her hand, "otherwise we might as well go home."

"I'm so sorry that he's ruined it for you," said Charlie.

He pulled her away from the wall and drew her into a hug. Beth put her hand on her friend's back and rubbed up and down.

"He's not ruined it for *us*," said Beth. "I'm just sorry for *you*. It's such a shame for him, too."

"Oh, he won't care. He'll be all bright and breezy tomorrow, and won't remember anything about it. I've seen it too many times before."

"Why have you never mentioned it, Charlie? I knew he enjoyed his booze, but I didn't know it was this bad."

"It's embarrassing, and every time he does it, I naively think he won't do it again, but, of course, he does."

"Do you ever discuss it with him?"

"No, not really. We kind of ignore it, well, I do. He just forgets about it."

"Well, we should forget about it for now and have a boogie," said Alex, taking both their hands, walking backwards towards the dancefloor, smiling. The band was playing some eighties hits: Madonna, The Police, Blondie and everyone was going wild. They joined in and for a while, the sight of David, so comatose, faded from their minds, as the lights sprinkled them with colour and the beat of the music entered their bodies. Alex had endless energy and enthusiasm and encouraged the girls to keep dancing until it was time to go.

They left the room in search of the bar to get some more cold drinks before facing the task of getting David to move. The girls went to get their coats from the cloakroom, and then they stepped out into the night air. It was cooler than earlier and they went round into the garden, wondering if he'd still be there.

But yes, there he was, in exactly the same position. Charlie bent down and said loudly right by his ear, "David, wake up!" and shook his shoulder. There was a groan and a slight movement.

"DAVID! For God's sake. We're going home." She shook him roughly.

At this, he mumbled and stirred, trying to sit up. His feet fell to the ground as he pushed himself into a sitting position. His eyes opened, he looked around in a daze and said, "Wha ...ar ...ye ... doing?"

"You need to stand up. The taxi's here."

Alex and Beth were looking on, helplessly, wondering what to do. Alex stepped forward and said, "Okay, old chap, let's get you up and in the taxi." He put his arm under David's and hauled him upright, Beth quickly stepping forward to take the other arm.

"Where ...am ...I?"

"You're at the mess, mate," said Alex. "Come on, one step forward."

Between them, they managed to get him staggering towards the gate. His legs gave way a couple of times, and it took all their strength to keep him standing. Manoeuvering him through the narrow gate was tricky and when they got to the front of the building, they scanned the cars to see if they could see the taxi. With relief, they saw it parked up, and it took a tremendous effort to get him there and in the backseat. The driver didn't look pleased and said, "I don't want him throwing up," in a very disgruntled voice.

Charlie sympathised with him, but politely said it would be fine. She wasn't lying when she told him that David had never been sick in these circumstances before. David immediately fell heavily asleep with his head against the window, and they drove back home in silence. They all heaved him out at the other end and deposited him on the sofa. The babysitter looked askance and left immediately, saying that she hadn't had a peep out of the children, which was at least good news.

They couldn't keep the taxi waiting for long, so Beth and Alex kissed Charlie goodnight. Beth took both her hands and looked her squarely in the face. "Will you be okay? Promise me you'll call if you ..."

"I'll be fine, honestly. Thank you for helping ... and I'm sorry for spoiling tonight."

"You didn't spoil it. We had a wonderful time, Charlie. See you tomorrow; we'll be back for our car," and she gave her another kiss. They both looked back and waved from the taxi.

Charlie just stood there, feeling drained and depressed. Why did the night have to end like this?

She had no desire to make David more comfortable or take off his clothes and shoes. He could sort himself out when he woke up. She went upstairs, took off her clothes and, without taking her makeup off, she climbed into bed and fell into a deep sleep.

Beth came round the following morning to collect the car. When she arrived, she knocked tentatively on their door, not knowing what to expect. Charlie came to let her in and ushered her into the kitchen for coffee. The kids were quietly watching some cartoons in the sitting room; there was no sign of David.

"How are things?" Beth said, looking around.

"Coffee?" said Charlie, filling the kettle.

"Yes, please, lovely."

Charlie switched on the kettle, got a couple of mugs out and came and leant on the kitchen unit next to Beth.

"When I woke up, David wasn't on the sofa where I'd left him. He must have woken and gone and slept in the spare room. He hasn't emerged yet," she said with her voice lowered.

"How are you feeling?"

"Oh, you know ... pissed off with him. I think that's why I don't enjoy going to social do's in the mess. I should have remembered ... anyway, enough of that ... how are you two? I hope you enjoyed it? It was so lovely to see that other side of Alex. I had no idea he loved dancing ... and how he used to sing and act."

"Yes, when we met, we were always out partying. I used to get exhausted from all the dancing. I'd never danced before I met him. He's so much better than me, but he somehow pushes and pulls me in the right direction," she laughed.

"Yea, I know what you mean. I'm hopeless, but he made me feel as if I could dance! Such a skill."

They both sat down at the kitchen table and sipped their coffee. The TV was muttering in the next room and the children occasionally giggled. They heard footsteps upstairs thumping along the corridor.

"He's up," said Charlie.

"What's your plan for the day? I can't stay long, as we're off to see Alex's parents for the day. We want to leave by ten thirty."

"Oh, that's nice. Not sure what we're doing ..."

At that moment, David appeared at the kitchen door, dressed and looking awake and ready for action. He was wearing a tracksuit.

"Hi Beth. You're here bright and early! Did you enjoy it last night? It was great, wasn't it?" He went over to the kettle and put a tea-bag in a mug and two slices of bread in the toaster.

"Yea, it was amazing. A great night," said Beth, looking at Charlie with a raised eyebrow, as David had his back to them. "We both felt worse for wear this morning, though."

David turned round, holding the mug of tea in his hands. "Well, I feel fine ... hey Charlie, did I tell you I have a tennis match this morning? I'll have to get a move-on. I'm just going to have a couple of pieces of toast and then I'll be off. Back around two, or maybe three. Is that okay?"

"Yea, fine. I wasn't planning on doing much," said Charlie, her voice flat. The toast popped up and David quickly buttered it, took a large bite out of one of them, and headed to the door.

"Thanks for coming, Beth. Send my regards to Alex," and with that, he left the room.

"See?" said Charlie. "Literally, no recollection of anything."

"Do you think it's genuine, or is he covering it up with jolliness?"

"I'm pretty sure he doesn't remember. Either way, it's as annoying as hell." Beth came and stood next to her and put her arm around her.

"It must be."

They stood like that for a short while and then Charlie said, "We get on really well most of the time. It's such a shame he has to spoil it, but he doesn't even realise it. Anyway, you must head off if you're going to Sussex."

They kissed each other on the cheek and Beth left, leaving Charlie feeling lonely and sad. She went to join the children in the sitting room, hoping that the cartoons would cheer her up.

# CHAPTER 4

The two men continued along their career paths as planned. Alex became a partner in his practice; he dealt mainly with people's pets, one of the other partners specialised in farm animals and another in horses. They made a good team and Alex became well known in their local town: he was kind and caring and as good with the owners as he was with the animals. He once said to Charlie and David that being a vet was rather like being a psychologist, counsellor and social worker, all rolled into one. When a pet died, you had the humans to deal with, and Alex got a reputation for someone you could trust in horrible circumstances to be empathetic, practical and caring.

David was so involved with the Air Force that it was like he had a separate existence from the rest of the family. He was often away on detachments abroad: The Falklands, Cyprus, Malta, The States ... and Charlie had to get on with it. He was never happier than when he was with his colleagues, talking planes or sport, and propping up endless bars. She got used to the total unpredictability of their life; he could be called in unexpectedly to fly off to some far-off country, just when they thought they knew what was happening, so the upshot was she grew used to making her own plans and leading her own life.

When the kids were older, Beth and Charlie decided they were all going to go on holiday together. They'd talked about it for years and never got around to arranging it, but it was *definitely* going to happen this year, they said. David promised he could take leave in July and Alex had organised time off with his colleagues.

"But where shall we go?" said Beth. "Home or abroad?"

"I definitely want the sun, so that means abroad. I know the UK can be okay in July, but imagine if we trekked all the way to Cornwall, and we got two weeks of rain? That happened to us last year, and I said, *never again*."

"Where are you absolutely guaranteed wonderful weather that's not too far away?"

"Well ... the south of France? We could all drive down there; we wouldn't have to have all the hanging around in airports ..."

"But *imagine* being stuck in the car with the kids for that long? Sounds a bit of a nightmare to me. Or we could go really mad and fly to Florida ... do Disney? The kids are just at the right age ..."

"That would be cool ... but expensive, surely? What about Portugal? It's only a two-hour flight and they're in the same time zone. I've always wanted to go there ..."

The conversation went back and forth; they couldn't make up their minds, but were determined to do something together. They could only do two weeks, no longer.

It was David who suggested Cyprus; it hadn't crossed the women's minds but when he started describing it, they listened. He'd been out there so many times now and had got to know it well. He said they were absolutely guaranteed wonderful weather in July; in fact, he said they'd probably find it too hot, which Charlie and Beth laughed at, as they thought heat was just what they needed. The kids would love it too; they could spend their entire time in the sea. He hadn't ventured too far from the camp, but knew that the area around Akrotiri was great, so they started looking at places near Paphos and Limassol. They'd decided on a 'package'. They were good value, and the women liked the idea of not having to do any catering; two weeks without lifting a finger is how Beth put it. They all liked the look of a hotel on the seafront in Paphos: breakfast provided, close to the airport, lots of tavernas nearby. It was a simple decision.

The holiday was booked.

"Oh my god, it's so hot," said Beth, as she stepped out of the plane, surveying the dry, brown landscape around Paphos airport. Charlie, who staggered out, pulling her small carry-on behind her, followed her.

"Wow, it's heaven! Come on, you lot," she said, as she started walking down the steps. The kids were trailing behind, followed by David and Alex. They all had to walk across the tarmac towards an arrivals building, with the sun beating down on them. They were all sweating by the time they joined the queue inside, in a snaking line, to show their passports. At least the building was air-conditioned.

When they'd got their luggage, which came off virtually straightaway, they made their way over to the car rental place, David taking charge, while everyone else hung around. After what felt like an age, they had to find their car, hoping they could get the enormous suitcases in the back. They'd hired a big people carrier, so they could travel together.

"What the hell have you bought with you?" said David, as he heaved one case into the car. "You're hardly going to need any clothes here."

"You never know what you're going to need," said Charlie, "and the kids wanted to bring a lot too. It's not just me."

"You'll end up not wearing half of it," said David, looking hot and bothered. "You'll probably be in your swimming costume all day and then just a light dress at night."

"I'm not a very seasoned traveller," said Charlie, trying to hide her annoyance. "I didn't really know what to expect."

Eventually, they all got in and David shut the back, after a lot of swearing and organisation of cases. The small bags had to be on people's laps.

"Do you know where we're going, David?" said Beth, "or do you want me to look at a map?"

"I'm fine. I've been to Paphos before, so I know roughly where I'm going; I think I know where the hotel is. So, we're off," he said and started the car. The drive was simple and soon they were entering the front entrance to a modern, grand hotel. It was a four-star and first impressions were promising. Palm trees on either side of the entrance and they could pull up directly outside the doors. A porter stepped forward, helped them extricate the cases, and he put them on a large trolley. Six of them went to the check-in desk and David went off to park the car in the car park. An efficient, friendly woman did all the admin they needed to do at the desk, gave them their keys, and the porter went off with their luggage to the lift. After David had reappeared, they made their way up to their rooms; each couple having a double with a connecting room for the children. They disappeared into each of their rooms, arranging to meet downstairs in half an hour.

"This is so cool," said Lou, as she ran into the room. "It's huge. Where are we sleeping?"

"Through here," said David, opening the adjoining room.

"Wow, we've even got our own bathroom, Will," said Lou, opening yet another door.

Each room had a balcony with a sea view, but by now, it was pitch black, so they couldn't see the ocean. They could, however, see the most beautiful pool lit up below, again surrounded by palm trees. There were walkways meandering around the grounds, highlighted by foot-level lights. They all stood and gazed at the sight, not quite believing they were there for a whole fortnight. The kids had never been abroad before, so it was overwhelming.

"Let's unpack and get sorted," said David, walking towards the suitcases.

"Do we have to?" shouted Lou from her room.

Charlie agreed with her, but said nothing, as she knew how David would react.

"Yes, we do. Once we've unpacked, it will feel more like home and we'll know where everything is. When I go away with the Air Force, it's the first thing I do."

The kids reluctantly started unpacking, but soon forgot that they hadn't wanted to do it, and started arguing about who was going to have which drawers.

In their own room, Charlie looked around at what the hotel provided: tea and coffee making facilities; fluffy towels; loads of free bottles of shampoo and shower gel, and a fridge full of bottled water and other drinks.

"This'll do, I think," she smiled.

"Yes, good choice," said David. "I hate it when you can't make your own coffee in the room. I wonder if there's an iron?"

"Why on earth do you want an iron?"

"Well, when we go out in the evening, I like to have ironed trousers. Actually, there is one here and a board. Sign of an excellent hotel."

Charlie was glad that the crisis had been averted, but had no intention of using it herself; ironing was the last thing she wanted to do.

They went down to the ground floor to meet the others; they were going to eat in the hotel tonight, as it was the easiest option. While they waited for them, Charlie looked around the entrance hall. It really was quite grand: marble floor, large chandeliers and everything shiny and pristine. On a glass table in the middle was a huge vase full of large, heavily scented irises; there seemed to be many doors leading off to unknown parts of the hotel. They'd have to explore tomorrow and find out where everything was. The decor pleased her sense of well-being; it was the first time since they'd had the children that they'd gone anywhere like this. She was determined to enjoy every minute.

The food turned out to be good and catered to the kids' fussy tastes. While they ate, a slightly dodgy pianist entertained them with 'unusual' versions of popular songs. They all got the giggles trying to work out which song he was playing, but it all added up to a jolly evening, despite the tiredness that descended on them all.

After a quick discussion about what they planned to do the next day, they said their goodnights and went to bed.

---

They met in the restaurant at 9.30 am; everyone was dressed in summer holiday clothes. David still looked 'military' in a beautifully ironed, casual shirt and khaki shorts. (Charlie couldn't believe it when she woke up to find him at the ironing board). She'd thrown on a crumpled sundress over her swimsuit and shoved her feet into flip flops.

They had to queue for a while as a waitress checked people's names to ensure their hotel registration, then a waitress seated them at a large, round table. Having made their order for tea all round for the adults, they went in search of food. There was the most magnificent array of every type of breakfast you could wish for. Both men went straight to the English-type cooked breakfast. The kids went immediately to the pastries, coming back to the table with plates laden with croissants, Pain Au Chocolat and whatever they could get their hands on. Beth and Charlie went to the muesli, fresh fruit, seeds and nuts and yoghurt area.

"This is amazing," said Darcy. "Can we really eat whatever we want?" Her face was a picture: a broad smile, her eyes dancing with anticipation of all the treats in store.

"Of course, Darce," said Beth, "but don't take more than you can eat. It's always tempting at this sort of buffet breakfast to have eyes bigger than your stomach." She grinned at Alex, who had so much food on his plate it was toppling off.

"Don't you worry about me. I'll eat all this. Might even go back for more," he laughed. "I might be a little more selective tomorrow."

David had two fried eggs, fried bread, mushrooms, bacon, fried tomatoes and beans. "I'll definitely go back for toast after this," he said, tucking in.

"I just couldn't eat all that; I'm definitely not an egg person in the mornings," said Charlie.

"Me, neither," said Beth. "This is my idea of a feast," she said, as she picked up a piece of over-ripe melon that dripped juice everywhere.

The kids were soon up and roaming for more food, and came back with a mixture of cheese, fruit, and toast. "If this is what it's like to go to hotels, I love it," said Will, layering loads of butter and strawberry jam onto thick bread.

"Well, you'll have to get a good job like mine, to afford it when you're older," said David. "Money doesn't grow on trees." Will ignored this comment and tucked in.

"David, let him enjoy the delights of breakfast, without a lecture," said Charlie, smiling encouragingly towards her son.

"Well, it's true. The sooner he understands it, the better. You've got to choose a job that will earn you money."

"I'm not sure I entirely agree," said Alex, wiping up the yolk of his egg with a piece of bread. "I think you should find something you really enjoy doing *first* and if it pays well, that's a bonus. You've got to work for at least forty years, so you might as well do something you like. I was lucky ... I'd always wanted to work with animals and so I didn't have that awful dilemma when I was eighteen, wondering what I wanted to study at uni. My life was mapped out and fortunately, I got in. The money never entered my head, though."

He sat back in his chair, wiped his mouth with the linen serviette, and smiled. "Right, I'm off to find some toast," he said and wandered off.

"Don't listen to him, Will," said David. "Lifestyle's everything. The Air Force has given us an amazing life. You can't choose some arty-farty subjects at school and expect to live like us. You've got to study maths and the sciences, so that you can get a decent job."

Beth looked at Charlie out of the side of her eye, knowing that if anyone questioned him, David would argue. She'd found over the years it was best not to contradict some things her friend's husband said. He had no qualms about telling her to mind her own business or butt out. She was willing Charlie not to react.

"Oh well," said Charlie, "he's got ages before he has to decide."

She stood up, putting an end to the discussion. "I'm dying to explore this gorgeous place. Did you see the colour of the sea? It's so beautiful ... I can't wait to get in it."

Alex came back with enough toast to feed ten people, and the two men began wading through it. Beth, Charlie and the kids started walking towards the exit and Charlie called back, "See you two at the pool!"

As they walked along the corridor, Beth whispered, "Well diverted," and squeezed her arm.

The three kids were way ahead, walking towards the door that took them out onto the patio and the pool beyond.

Charlie replied, "Why talk about Will's future career when we're trying to enjoy a holiday? It just doesn't make any sense. I don't think Will has a clue what he wants to do yet and why should he? He's still a child. He never seems to say things like that to Lou, and she's older."

"Come on, forget about David. Let's lounge by the pool. I've already got my costume on, have you?"

"Yup! The kids have too. Has Darcy?"

"Of course. We can all go straight in, although my mum would say we should wait at least an hour after all that food," she laughed.

"Yea, that's just a myth, I think. I just need to get in that water."

There were plenty of sunbeds ranged along the side of the pool with neatly folded hotel towels on each one.

They found seven together, stripped off, and were in the pool in minutes.

---

The men joined them about half an hour later; they'd gone up to their rooms and changed into their trunks. Alex looked good in his. He was wearing board shorts and his toned physique already was dark before it had even seen the sun. David insisted on wearing proper trunks; he said shorts interfered with his legs when he was swimming. He looked good (all the sport he played had kept him slim) but he looked like a Brit on holiday: pasty and sun-deprived. *Mind you, so do I,* thought Charlie with a giggle.

David dived straight in and started pounding up and down the length of the pool with an impressive crawl. Alex, however, lay down on one of the sunbeds.

"I need to let my breakfast go down first, I think. It's so nice to feel the sun on your skin, isn't it? As much as I love the UK, the weather really is a bit shit, isn't it?"

The two women had been lying down, while the kids mucked about in the pool. They'd both been in to cool down, but were keen to relax. "Can you imagine living in such a hot climate?" he said, to no one in particular.

"I think I can," said Charlie. "I'm such a sun worshipper."

"I can imagine living somewhere like this for a while, but I don't think I'd want to live abroad forever. I'd miss the UK too much," said Beth, sitting up to put sun cream on her legs. "Alex, can you put some on my back?" She got up and went and squatted by his bed. He sat up and she handed the bottle to him. He leant forward, kissed her back and then gently rubbed in some cream in round movements.

"There you are, Darling. Yea, I love the sun too; it makes you feel more relaxed, I think. But I agree, I'd miss the UK."

"I'm not sure," said Charlie. "What would you miss?"

"Oh, I don't know ... the landscape, the pubs, the culture, the people ... everything. It's home, isn't it?" he answered.

"Yes, I suppose it is."

Charlie closed her eyes and at that precise moment couldn't think of one thing she'd miss. The feel of the sun was so heavenly. She could hear the children's voices coming from the pool; there was some gentle Greek music emanating from the poolside bar and a few sparrows were chattering nearby. It was peaceful, and she drifted off.

David woke her up by shaking some water over her. "Thought you might enjoy a few cool drips," he laughed.

"Thanks," she said, sarcastically ... but actually it was quite pleasant. "We were just talking about living in a hot climate," she said to David. "I said I could imagine it, but those two said they'd miss the UK too much."

"I can definitely imagine it," said David. "In fact, every time I come out here, I think I'd like to retire here."

"Really?" said Beth.

"Yes ... it's full of ex-Air Force people who've retired."

"Well, that's news to me," said Charlie. "I've never heard you say it before."

"It's something I've been thinking about. Last time we came here on detachment, I met a couple in a taverna who'd actually done it, and they said they'd had no regrets. They were living the dream and ... it got me thinking."

"Were you going to share this dream with me?" said Charlie, grinning.

"It's only a vague thought, but what do you think?"

"I'd like to see the island, outside the environs of a four-star hotel first," she said. "Then I'll be able to answer. It's certainly worth thinking about."

"Thinking about what?" said Lou, who'd appeared by her side and was looking for a towel to dry herself.

"Oh, Daddy was just talking about us coming to live here when he retires."

"Wow, that would be amazing ... I could swim all the time."

"By then, you'll be off doing your own thing, Lou. It's not for ages yet."

"So you two would come out and leave us kids in the UK? Charming," she laughed. "Wouldn't you miss us?"

"Yes, of course we would," said Charlie, stroking Lou's back.

"I can't imagine ever leaving Darcy and going to live abroad," said Beth.

"No, neither can I," said Alex. "I never want to retire, anyway. I love my job."

Lou went running back to the pool and the three of them lay back and zoned out. Charlie's mind went to the future ... would she want to leave the kids and run away to a sun-drenched island? There were so many pros and cons, her brain couldn't cope.

It was all a bit pie in the sky at the moment.

# CHAPTER 5

They'd all eaten sandwiches from the pool bar for lunch; the kids persuaded their parents to let them have cans of Coke; the men had pints of Keo and the women, brandy sours. It was unusual for Charlie and Beth to have alcohol at lunch time these days, but the barman said it was a local drink and they went for it; first day of the holiday and all that. It turned out to be delicious: sweet and sour at the same time ... and strong, with a crunchy layer of sugar round the rim of the glass.

"Oh my god, I think this could be my new favourite drink," said Beth, licking the sugar off her lips and swirling the ice cubes round her glass.

"Mmm, gorgeous. I feel squiffy, though. Better just stick to the one, or I'll forget how to swim," Charlie laughed, taking another large slurp.

Afterwards, they walked the short distance from the pool to the sea. There were hotel beds on the grass overlooking the ocean and they plonked everything down on them and made their way down to the water, the children running ahead. There was a lovely little sandy cove off to their right and they went down some steps to get there.

The sea was calm, with just a faint ripple at the edge. There were strands of odd-looking seaweed about, but it fazed none of them and they ran into the sea together. The children immediately dived under the water, but the adults floated, or stood admiring the view of azure, sparkling water stretching to the horizon.

"It's even warmer than the pool," said Beth, kicking her legs, floating on her back. "I prefer swimming in the sea. It's so invigorating. Wow, it's very salty, this water." She scraped her wet hair back and squeezed the water out, which dripped down her back and she licked her lips.

"Do you fancy swimming out a bit? The men can oversee the kids," she said to Charlie.

"Yes, definitely. It's heavenly."

They started doing gentle breaststroke, closing their eyes to the brightness of the sun. They could hear the children's voices recede behind them and soon it was just them in the deep, aquamarine sea, the sun's diaphanous rays surrounding them with light. It was as if they were in a world of their own, far away from the stresses and strains of their lives.

"I feel so lucky to be here with you, Beth," said Charlie, treading water. "Just imagine, if you hadn't come and talked to me that day in the staff room ... I'm useless at just going up to someone I don't know and introducing myself. Thank you for being better at it than me. And to be here with you and your family, it really is a gift." She swam a little closer and lowered her voice. "Do you think Alex and David get on okay?" She shaded her eyes and looked towards the shore. Alex was in the water, playing ball with the children and she could just make out David, wading slowly back towards the sand. "Is it difficult for Alex? I know it must be hard for him; I realise we're the friends and we've slightly forced the men on each other."

Beth's eyes followed Charlie's, and she gazed at her husband in the distance. "Alex is such a laid-back kind of guy. He's fine. If I'm honest ... they probably wouldn't be friends if it wasn't for us, but it's good to get to know people you don't meet in the normal run of things, isn't it? He's learned a lot about planes and flying ..."

"Oh god, does he go on about it all the time? I wonder if he ever asks Alex about *his* job?"

"Yea, I think he does. Don't worry, they're fine."

"They *are* very different. I wish David had more of Alex in him ... Alex is so good with the kids and I love his chilled personality. Sometimes David's too intense ... too opinionated. He can be very self-absorbed."

"But his heart's in the right place," said Beth. She was good at putting Charlie's mind at rest, although she wasn't sure she agreed with herself about David, often having had to bite her lip and keep her mouth shut where he was concerned. She loved Charlie though, and she was prepared to do anything to make her happy.

"Let's swim over to that buoy," said Beth, pointing. "I'll see if I can beat you. One, two, three, go!" and she set off at a good pace. As Charlie followed and tried to catch up, she realised Beth was right. David's heart *was* in the right place; he wanted the best for Will's future, but she wished he'd approach it differently. Will's so sensitive. If David had a go at Lou, she'd stick up for herself, but Will ...

"Beat you," shouted Beth, as she flung her arms around the buoy.

"Ha, Ha, you're fast when you set your mind to it," said Charlie, panting and grabbing the buoy too. "This is going to be such a fun holiday ... thank you for being my friend."

"You soppy twit," laughed Beth. "We'll be best friends forever. Soul sisters. Now come on, stop being an emotional wreck. Beat you back to the kids," and she set off in the same determined way. This time, Charlie was convinced she would beat Beth to the shore. She put her face down and did her best crawl; she wasn't looking where she was going though and eventually bumped into Alex, who grabbed her round the waist and threw her back into the water. The kids took it as an opportunity for him to do the same to them. With shouts and splashes, Alex threw them all in quick succession, while Charlie and Beth left them to it.

They decided they'd walk into the town around six to find a good taverna. David explained they could either go along the road and pass loads of potential eating places along the way or walk along the shoreline. They opted for the second choice.

"Do you see that large building at the end of the peninsula? We're heading there. It's the old fort and there are loads of places to eat around there. The sun will set around 8 pm too; it's one of the best places to see the sunset in Cyprus."

The kids still had masses of energy; they ran ahead of their parents, shouting and having fun, trying to trip each other up. Lou had reverted to behaving like a twelve-year-old again. The adults wandered more sedately, Beth and Alex walking hand in hand. Charlie and David weren't a 'hand in hand' type of couple, but Charlie put her arm through David's and drew him closer.

"Thank you for suggesting Cyprus, David. What a beautiful place."

The women were in sleeveless dresses; a warm breeze blew gently around them, but it was still about 27 degrees and they all were sweating, despite the lateness of the day.

"Thank goodness we bought some water with us," said Beth, unscrewing the top of a bottle and taking a long drink. "I love warm evenings like this. Anyone else need a swig?" and she handed it to Charlie, who was looking hot and red-cheeked.

They passed a watersports business offering sailing, windsurfing and banana rides. Stopping to read the price list, Alex said, "I think I'll come down here tomorrow. I really fancy a sail; I haven't got to my boat for ages. I'm even thinking of selling my half, as I get so little time to go these days."

"Oh, that would be a shame," said Beth. "Don't. It's your favourite thing to do."

"No, I don't think you should, either," said Charlie. "Not that it's anything to do with me, but ... I was rather hoping you'd teach me to sail, some day."

"Why don't you come and have a go tomorrow? I'll take you out and see if you like it. What about you, David?"

"No, I'm fine. Never been one for water, me. I like a gentle cool off in the sea, but I'm more of a ball sports guy. You two go."

"How about you, Beth?" said Charlie.

"No, I'm fine. I'll stay and look after the kids and chill."

They were relieved when they reached the main drag. There were so many tavernas to choose from, they didn't know where to start. Waiters were trying to entice them into every one and they were eventually persuaded by one particularly charming chap, to take a table right next to the sea.

The menu was extensive, and they all spent a while reading their way through it. Darcy didn't want traditional Cypriot food and opted for pasta. Lou and Will liked the sound of chicken and chips. The adults, at David's insistence, all went with fresh fish: sea bream or bass. They ordered a huge village salad to share.

Baskets of local bread came out first, accompanied by hummus, tahini and taramasalata. They also added small olives with an intense taste, along with lemon slices. The women had ordered a small jug of brandy sour and the men had large Keos. When the main courses came out, they wondered if they could ever eat it all. The fish had been filleted and was spread out flat on the plate, covered with parsley and lemon juice. They hadn't realised the fish came with chips.

"I'm never going to walk back to the hotel, after this lot," laughed Beth, eating a delicious, salty chip.

"Fish doesn't fill you up, though," said David. "You'll be fine."

"You have more faith in me than I do," she laughed. The kids were extremely happy with their meals, and silence descended on the table as they all tucked in.

The light was fading as they ate. Pink streaks appeared across the sky, mixed with apricot and purple, and the sun was hovering above the horizon line, a burning orange ball. The blueness was fading fast. The lights along the promenade were now on, the palm tree emerging as majestic silhouettes.

Somehow they all finished what they'd been given, the village salad being particularly enjoyed by Charlie and Beth. They'd drenched it in olive oil and squeezed lemon juice all over it; the crumbled feta was so good. Despite their former desires not to eat many chips, they'd both eaten loads of them. They were too delicious to resist.

Everybody somehow found room for ice cream and as they spooned the creamy gelato into their mouths, the sun made its last drop and was gone. "Wow, what a place to eat a meal! It's like your own personal light show, given by nature itself," said Alex.

The kids were seemingly unimpressed and asked if they could go for a walk down towards the fort. "Yes, but stick together and come back in ten minutes," said Charlie. They pushed back their chairs as if they wanted to be anywhere but there and before any more could be said, they were off at a run.

"What energy," said Beth, wistfully. "Shall we have a coffee?"

"Yes, definitely," said David, and he called over the waiter. They ordered Cypriot coffee and loved the small cups, the strength and the taste. The waiter also brought over some Cypriot Delights on a small plate, small squares of jelly sweetness covered in icing sugar.

"We better save some for the kids or they'll be furious," laughed Charlie.

They soon reappeared as if they could smell a treat from a mile away, grabbing their share without too much politeness.

The walk back was long, warm, and beautiful. The stars were coming out, and the moon was nearly full. Its light shone on the water like a silver runway.

"This has been magical, David," said Charlie, this time taking his hand. "What an amazing start to the holiday. Maybe I can imagine living here. Just think, we could eat like this all the time and watch sunsets like the one tonight, on our future unknown patio," she laughed. The romance of it all had affected her, and she could seriously see herself living this life.

"Didn't I tell you?" said David.

Next morning, they walked along to the water sports place. It was already thirty degrees, so there was a clamouring by the children to get into the sea as quickly as possible.

"Let's just see what the situation is first and then you can do whatever ..." said Alex. He walked down the jetty and was greeted by a guy who looked as if he'd spent his entire life in the sun: white-grey hair and the most incredible mahogany tan. He must have been in his mid-sixties, but his body was muscular and on display. He was bare-chested and was wearing only a pair of faded blue board shorts. He was even barefoot.

He held out his hand to Alex, beaming. "Hey, my man, what can I do for you? The name's Nick Brown."

Alex was surprised to find himself talking to a fellow Brit; he'd expected this place to be run by a local. He explained his love of sailing and how he was a part-owner of a boat in the UK and his wish to go out on the water.

The kids were getting restless and so Alex suggested they went off and swum; they were all excellent swimmers and didn't need babysitting, but David and Beth went with them. "We'll be by the pool when you're ready," said Beth as she left.

Alex introduced Charlie to Nick, and he showed them what boats were available. "If we take that one out," he said, pointing, "I'll come with you as it's actually my boat. I'll show you around it, then later, you can go out on your own. I've got a guy who works for me who can take over here. When would you like to go?"

"Maybe around one? That would be great."

"Suits me," said Nick. "I don't get many people like you here. Not knocking the tourists or anything, but they mostly want to have a banana ride. I'd love to go out with a fellow sailor."

"Do you live in Paphos?"

"Yeah, been here for fifteen years now. My wife and I came out for a different life and we loved it ... but she died three years ago. It's not the same without her ... but I decided to stay. I couldn't imagine going back to the grey skies of England. This weather suits me." A sadness came over his face, dimming the gorgeous, friendly smile that was on his face like a mask. "How lucky am I ... to hang out by the sea all day?"

"What do you do in the winter when all the tourists have gone?"

"I can still go out, but you have to be more careful; the sea can be very changeable. I do all the maintenance during the winter months too. After that, it's walking in the Troodos, skiing if the snow comes, and reading any book I can get my hands on."

"Sounds like a lovely life," said Charlie, "but I'm sorry your wife isn't here to enjoy it with you." She wondered if he was indeed rather lonely in a foreign land, on his own. "Do you speak Greek?"

Nick laughed. "A little. Sara made me take lessons when she was alive, but I confess they've rather lapsed. I can get by, but I can't have a good conversation like this. The Cypriots make us Brits lazy; so many of them can speak such good English. No excuse, I know, but ..."

"Well, it's a pretty good excuse, to be honest," laughed Alex. "So, look ... we'll go and do some swimming with the kids and we'll be back later. Thanks so much for the opportunity."

"Look forward to it, my friend," said Nick.

The sail out on the bluest of blue seas was a great success. Charlie loved it, although she didn't know what she was doing. Nick and Alex gave her minor tasks, and she fulfilled them to the best of her ability, but mostly, she simply sat back and enjoyed the ride. It was burning hot, and she had to keep sloshing water on her face; *thank God I put on a lot of sun cream*, she thought. She pulled her cap right down to cover her face, but when she got back to the hotel later and looked at herself in the mirror, her face was bright red.

Alex and Nick got on like a house on fire; it was if they'd known each other for years. There was much laughter, and each of them had stories to tell of past sailing exploits. They were out for an hour and a half, and by the time they got back, they were firm friends. The age gap didn't seem to matter at all; they were kindred spirits.

They planned to come back the next day and as they walked back to the hotel, Alex said to Charlie, "Shall we invite him to come out with us one evening? I really like him and I think he'd enjoy the company."

"Yea, that's a great idea. Why not?"

# CHAPTER 6

The holiday continued like that first night and day: walks along the seafront to different tavernas; so much swimming that they all laughed that they were turning into mermaids and mermen and Alex and Nick going out most days for a sail. Charlie went three more times, but Alex was so in his element, she felt he ought to go out without her. He protested, of course, but the two men were so enjoying each other's company, she rather felt in the way.

Alex, as planned, asked Nick to come with them one night towards the end of the holiday, and he was thrilled. Alex asked if he had any recommendations.

"I'm sure you'll know somewhere that's not on the main street in Paphos," he said. "Something a bit more authentic?"

"Mmm ... I know just the place, but we'll have to drive. It's not far, but it's too far to walk."

That night, he led the way in his beat-up, old truck down the coast towards the airport. He pulled up outside a taverna that was right on a beach. Parking outside on the road, they made their way inside, past some luscious plants in beds on either side of a walkway: huge flowering cactuses, postbox red hibiscus, white cyclamen and pink bougainvillea.

The path led them to the busy outdoor restaurant. It was very 'unreformed', basic even, with plastic tablecloths and old metal chairs; everything higgledy-piggledy and spread over a large area. There were small candles on each table and lights hanging from trees. Tree canopies spread everywhere, creating a 'covered' effect.

"Wow, what an amazing place," said Charlie. "I feel I'm in genuine 'old' Cyprus at last. What are those trees everywhere with the white-painted trunks?"

"They're mulberries; they're coming into fruit now. Maybe you can even pick some," said Nick, looking up.

They chose a table next to the beach, and a waiter handed them the menu. There was all the usual fare. They were beginning to know what their favourite things to eat were. The kids were happy to have endless chips with something, but the adults had discovered the joys of calamari, halloumi, and a vast variety of fish. The piquant olives were so different in Cyprus to any back home; they were full of flavour; hard little green or black nuggets of sharpness.

There was a low wall, painted bright blue, running around the restaurant to stop the beach encroaching, and suddenly, a friendly cat appeared, sauntering along it, picking its way between the fallen mulberry fruits. It sat, as if invited, next to their table.

"I hope you don't mind cats," said Nick. "This place is famous for them ... and lots of other animals, too."

"I love them," said Darcy. "My dad's a vet, so we love animals in our house."

"I hate the things," said David, pulling a face. Fortunately, he was sitting at the far end of the table.

"You really can't hate cats in Cyprus," said Nick. "They're absolutely everywhere. They do a good job of keeping down the snake population. Maybe this place was a mistake?"

At that moment, three more arrived around the base of the table; they all sat patiently waiting for scraps. David looked at them, and Charlie could tell he was having to control his instinct to push them away. Some of them looked dirty, but the one on the wall was pristine and had a funny little Hitler moustache effect on his face, which made him very endearing (to her, anyway).

"So, Nick, do you think you'll live here in Cyprus forever?" asked Beth, trying to divert attention away from cats. She dipped some bread in hummus and poured olive oil over her salad. "It seems like a wonderful life, but do you get lonely without your wife?"

"I love it but, of course, it's not the same as it was ... we had imagined getting old together here, watching sunsets and slowly fading away ... But it wasn't to be. I try to make the best of it."

"Did your wife go sailing with you?" asked Charlie.

"Yes, she was as keen as me. It was great to have a hobby we both enjoyed. I think couples need something like that to help bind them together. We might have a row or something ... but all would be forgotten as we bobbed around on the sea."

Charlie nodded her head in agreement, realising at the same time that she and David did very little together. They sometimes played doubles in tennis, but she always got the impression that he'd much rather play men's singles. Other than that, they existed together in the same house and brought up the children.

"Yes, I wish I'd learned ..." said Beth, "but now Alex is so busy with his work, he hardly has time to go sailing. That's why it's been so great for him here. I think he would have been bored stiff, lazing in the sun all day, wouldn't you, Alex? So, thanks for all the entertainment, Nick," and she raised her glass and said, "To Nick" and they all chinked their glasses together. The children enjoyed doing 'cheers' with their Cokes and Charlie was left wondering whether life out here with David would be a good idea after all. She loved him ... but would they be flung together too much here? Maybe this entire retirement plan would go away. It was a long time in the future.

Nick said with a grin, "It's been really great to meet you all. I *do* get lonely, even though I've got quite a few friends here. They're a mix of ex-pats and Cypriots, but it's been so nice to meet someone who shares my passion. And thank you all for inviting me out tonight; I've loved it. My wife and I didn't have any children, unfortunately, so it's nice to spend time with some."

The children were being well-behaved tonight; there'd been no arguments or shouting, so he'd seen them on their best behaviour, but Charlie felt sad for him; she couldn't imagine a life without them. They were what kept her and David together; they were the 'hobby' he talked about.

The children had finished their food and, surprisingly, *asked* to leave the table. They got up and wandered off to the far end of the restaurant. They didn't come back for a while, but when they did, they were full of stories about various animals wandering around: piglets, two goats, a cockerel and some chicks. Health and Safety would have had a field day in the UK; here it seemed perfectly natural. Beth, Alex and Charlie got up to have a look, too.

"What a place," said Charlie when they came back to the table. "It's like a farmyard up there."

"They love animals here, but generally, the Cypriots have a very different attitude to them from the Brits," said Nick. "I've had to accept it, but I find it very hard."

"What do you mean?" said Alex.

"Well, you see a lot of abandoned dogs; hunters just dump them, if they're no good at hunting. Unwanted puppies are left to die; cats are starving; horses are left tied up in the sun with no water. It's pitiful to see. A lot of Brits complain about it and try to rescue dogs and feed cats, but unfortunately you're fighting a different culture and it's their country, after all."

"God, that's awful. I'd find that too hard. What are the vets like out here?" asked Alex.

"You have some very caring ones, but it's rather a losing battle."

"Surely their attitude could slowly change, though?" said Alex.

"Yes, maybe, but I wouldn't hold your breath. It's sad. I just have to look away. I've got two cats that I rescued back home, but you can't rescue them all."

"I wouldn't have any problem *not* rescuing cats," laughed David.

Charlie gave him a look across the table, and silence fell. She'd always wanted to have pets for the children, but David hadn't wanted any. She wished she'd stood up for herself, but she hadn't.

"We'd be hopeless if we lived here, wouldn't we, Alex? We'd end up with hundreds of rescued dogs and cats."

"I'd love that, Mum," said Darcy. "Can we come and live here?"

"No, darling, I'm afraid not; Dad's got all those animals to look after, back home."

"And I'm not sure I could cope with it," said Alex, ruffling his daughter's hair. "I love animals too much. It's the other extreme in England; we treat animals as part of the family."

"I'd rather it was that way," said Charlie. "Shall we get the bill?"

They insisted on 'treating' Nick and wouldn't let him contribute. When they got back to the cars, they promised to visit him the next day, and he drove off.

Charlie couldn't help feeling sorry for him. He cut a lonely figure, going back to his solitary flat and his two cats.

---

The end of the island holiday was looming; they had two more days.

They hadn't ventured far from Paphos; they all decided it was far too hot to explore the island extensively, but on their second to last day, they visited Limassol seafront and had a meal in the old part of town at lunchtime. Afterwards, they drove down to the port and along the track that ran alongside the coast, known as Lady's Mile beach. They'd gone right to the end and David had shown them a distant view of RAF Akrotiri, seen through rolls of barbed wire fencing.

They stood and stared, trying to make out the beach that David had visited so many times. A propeller-driven plane took off and rose slowly before disappearing.

"There goes a Herc right now, probably off back to the UK," said David. "It's a shame we didn't visit the camp while we were here, but it would have been a hassle to get you all in there."

"Is the beach like this one, Dad?" asked Lou.

"Yes, it's just a continuation. You would have loved it, Alex. There's a sailing club next to Arabs beach, where I go, and loads of windsurfing goes on there too."

"Wow, what a life. Are there any jobs for vets there?" he laughed.

"Why can't you get posted out here, Dad? Why are we in boring old Wiltshire?" said Lou, splashing her feet along the water's edge.

"Yea, it would have been nice ... but you have to be offered a posting and it's never materialized. Not sure your mother would have been very keen."

"Why on earth wouldn't you want to come here for Dad's job, Mum?"

"Oh, I have mixed feelings about it. A three-year posting would be okay, I suppose, but I'm not sure that I'd really want to live in Cyprus full time. It's gorgeous for a holiday, but I realise I would definitely miss England and it's so bloody hot. Lou, you'd have to go to boarding school; not sure you'd like that, would you?"

"I'd hate it," said Will, pretending to be sick.

"There are schools out here for military kids, you know," said David. "But I'm never going to be sent here now anyway, so it's immaterial, kids. I've told Mum I'd like to retire out here one day, though."

Lou and Will both looked at Charlie, waiting for her to respond.

"Let's wait and see ... I don't feel old enough to even *think* about retirement plans. You two would have to be well and truly established in your own careers and lives, before I went abroad to live, anyway."

"I think it's a great idea, Mum," said Lou. "You'd see us all the time; I'd be out here for holidays every five minutes, like a shot."

"And me," laughed Will.

"You see, *they* think it's a good idea, Charlotte, even if you don't," said David. "We've only got one life; we may as well try to live our best lives."

"Well, that depends on what you think *is* your best life," said Charlie. "I like Wiltshire!"

"It sounds pretty idyllic; you might as well consider it," said Alex. "I think I agree with David ... shall we come too, Beth?"

"Okay, that's settled," laughed Beth. "Meet you out here is ten years."

"Charming, Mum. You're going to leave me on my own?" said Darcy.

Beth scooped her up and wrapped her in her arms and said, "Only joking, Darce. I'll never leave you, you know that. Let's have a swim, everyone. Last one in's a sissy," and she ran full tilt into the sea, followed by Darcy and Alex. Once again, Beth had diverted attention away from something David had said. *What would I do without her?* thought Charlie.

"Come on, David, catch me if you can," Charlie shouted and ran after them. The kids followed, but David sat on the edge, his bottom on the sand, his feet in the water.

She dived into the warm waters, loving the cooling effect on her scalp and her hot, dry skin. Little brown fish darted around her. Standing up again, waist-deep and facing out to sea, she could make out the outlines of buildings in Limassol off to her left, with the heat-hazy mountains ranging off into the far distance behind. Beth, Alex and the kids were all playing a game of chase in the water, but she was content to look at the surrounding landscape. It tugged at something inside her.

Could she be happy here one day?

They lay on sandy towels and dried off in the baking sun and then set off across the vast expanse of the salt lake towards Akrotiri village. David had been this way before and wanted to take them home a different way. It was a surreal landscape: acres of salty, sandy nothingness. They followed a well-trodden road across the basin of the lake, but could see that others had been more adventurous; wheel tread marks were going in large circles off to the side. It felt like a forbidden place, a dangerous place, somewhere your car could sink, if you weren't careful.

Soon, they were on safer ground; the track was more like a road and they travelled between trees, past a mysterious sign that said 'Monastery of the Cats'. To their right was more salt lake, and they could make out a few flamingos standing long-legged in a pink mirage. David pointed out the entrance of the camp at the end of the road, but they were forbidden to enter, so they turned right and travelled through a sea of pylons and aerials guarding the camp, into a long, dark road, lined by tall pines, behind which were lines of orange trees.

"Who fancies supper at another beach?" said David, his arm leaning casually on the open window ledge, letting the dry, scorching breeze into the car.

After a chorus of "Me, me," he said he knew *just the place*. They'd spent all day wandering and driving and they looked forward to food, drinks and relaxation.

He took them down to Curium beach; a long expanse with spectacular cliffs behind it. Small waves were rolling in and having parked up, the children wanted to frolic in them before supper. Three of the adults went into the taverna, but Charlie volunteered to go in the waves with the children, to make sure they were safe. The waves weren't like huge Cornish ones, but she wanted to be sure there wasn't an undertow and secretly looked forward to jumping around in them herself.

Everyone was in shorts and t-shirts and they forgot they had nothing dry to change into. They dived over and under the waves, marvelling at their warmth; Charlie remembered the last time they played in waves in Polzeath: stronger but much colder waves had engulfed them. These were gentler, massaging their bodies with their soft, salty caress and there were no dangerous currents. It was still so hot that many people stood thigh deep in the water simply to keep cool, hats on, admiring the cloudless, darkening sky.

After twenty minutes, she herded the children together and persuaded them to get out of the water. With all the energy of youth, they ran along the beach to dry off; she watched them, envious of their endless vitality. She tried to shake herself like a dog, squeezing water from her hair and running her hands down her arms and legs. They walked into the taverna, saw the others, and waved. There were already pints of Keo on the table. It really didn't matter that they were wet; the floor was bare wood and the furniture, basic. The table was against a railing; it was as if they were on the deck of a boat they were that near to the sea.

As the late arrivals sat down and ordered more drinks, Charlie realised how bizarre this was: she was as warm as newly baked bread, despite sitting in wet clothes at seven at night. It was almost a relief to have the layer of dampness keeping her cool.

At the end of the meal, they were given the most spectacular natural performance. The sky was awash with oranges and soft blush pinks. Shadowy grey-black clouds hung above the horizon. The sun sank slowly, setting the sea on fire. Even when it was gone from sight, its peach glow lit up the sky. Charlie felt full from the food, exhausted from all the playing in the sea, and optimistic. Life was good, life was peaceful; her children were the loves of her life and if David thought coming here was his dream future, maybe it could be hers too. If only she could 'see' herself as an older empty-nester, but she couldn't.

On the last day, they all went down to Nick's spot to say goodbye. Alex went out for one last sail. The two men swapped emails and vowed to keep in touch. They had bonded, like a father and son, and Charlie could feel the sadness oozing out of Nick as they walked away, his arm raised in a wave of farewell.

The holidaymakers had to catch a late flight, leaving at ten pm. As the plane sped up down the runway, the children were already looking sleepy; David, the relaxed professional flier, was snoring and Charlie, in her window seat, was peering out of the round window into the darkness. The others were in the row across and silence reigned; she could see Beth and Alex holding hands (poor Beth was a nervous flier) and Darcy was looking at her book.

As the plane rose, she could see amber lights spread out, shadowy hills emerging, car lights making their way along distant, unknown roads.

Cyprus was receding, leaving part of her still there.

# PART 2
2012

Sarah Catherine Knights

# CHAPTER 7

How could Charlie, or any of them, for that matter, have known that the two-week holiday in Cyprus, would be the last time ever, that they'd all spend time together?

It was as if the holiday was a dividing line between 'life before' and 'life after'. A catastrophe of the worst kind was going to rip them apart and nothing would ever be the same again.

The day was just another normal day ... as they always are.

The kids had gone back to school; Charlie and Beth were also back in their respective schools; David was away, as usual, and was due back at the end of the week. Alex had a full day dealing with people and ill pets. The day was straightforward and at four o'clock they were all back home, bar Alex and David.

Alex was due home at six when Beth was going to leave him in charge while she went to the theatre in Bristol with a group of friends from work. She had decided to meet them at the theatre; she lived in the opposite direction to the other four and they were sharing a car. It would be just over a forty-minute drive, but that didn't worry her; she was actually looking forward to some solitary time in the car, when she could listen to her music (Alex didn't particularly like her choices).

"I should be back around 11.15," she shouted to Alex from the sitting room. "It finishes at 10.30, so, all being well, I won't be too late. Make sure Darcy finishes her homework and please get her to go to bed by 9.30; she keeps going to bed far too late. Are you listening?"

She joined Alex, who was in the kitchen, stirring the pan of mince that Beth had prepared earlier. "Yes, I'm listening," he said and came through the kitchen door, wiping his hands on a t-towel. "Don't worry, Darling, we'll be fine. You have a lovely time; enjoy yourself," and he kissed her on the cheek. "Love you," he said.

"Love you, too."

And the door closed.

Alex went back to the cooker, checked on Darcy (who was, in fact, watching telly, but who convinced Alex that she was definitely going to start her homework in fifteen minutes). Alex went back into the kitchen, turned on Radio Four and listened to "I'm Sorry I haven't a Clue" while cooking spaghetti and preparing a simple salad.

They ate their meal together at the table, Darcy telling her dad about how annoying various teachers were. He chuckled to himself, secretly wondering whether they found their daughter equally annoying; he was sure she probably never stopped talking in class. After some ice cream for pudding, he persuaded her to go upstairs to work. She'd got a desk in her bedroom; given the chance, however, she'd prefer to sit on the sofa with the TV on, and do her work on her lap. But he was determined she was going to work upstairs tonight.

"You'll finish it much quicker if you focus, Darce. You can't possibly concentrate, with the TV blaring."

"I *can*, Dad."

"Well, not tonight, you aren't," he laughed. "Go on, up you go. You know it makes sense."

"All right ... but can I come down again and watch something?"

"Yes, of course. We'll watch something together, but your mum wants you in bed by 9.30."

"Okay, okay," and she disappeared. Alex cleared the table, filled the dishwasher and then did some of his own work that he needed to do on the practice's accounts. Darcy later proudly showed him what she'd achieved, and then they settled down to watch TV. On the dot of nine, he sent her up, so that she could read for a while before going to sleep. He popped up to give her a kiss goodnight and then settled down to read the paper and watch the ten o'clock news. It was just a pleasant, ordinary evening.

But how quickly the ordinariness of life can change. He fell heavily asleep on the sofa and must have been there for at least two and a half hours.

A knock on the door woke him up.

"Good evening, sir. Are you Mr Alex Harris?"

There were two uniformed police officers standing there, in the light of the front porch light.

"Yes, I am."

"May we come in, sir?"

"Why, what's happened?" said Alex, sounding defensive.

"Can we come inside, sir, and we'll explain."

Alex ushered them into the sitting room, where the TV was still murmuring in the corner of the room.

"Would you like to sit down, sir?" asked the lady officer.

"No, I'm fine," said Alex, "I'll stand. What's all this about?" *Had he been done for speeding or something* he thought?

"I'm afraid I've got some very bad news, sir."

The blood drained from Alex's face; his legs began to shake.

He knew, he *knew* ... what they were about to say.

"Your wife, sir, Beth Harris ... has been involved in a car accident on the M4."

"Oh my god, how is she? Is she all right?" Alex whispered, sitting down in a heap on the nearest armchair.

Even though he'd asked those questions, he *knew* the answer.

This was the end of his life.

"I'm very sorry to inform you, sir, that she died at the scene. She suffered catastrophic injuries ..." Both police officers were standing near him, towering above him like malevolent birds.

Alex heard them, but it was as if he wasn't in his own body. He was floating ... floating around the room, disengaged, dismembered, disassociated ... in fact, he'd disappeared from reality.

"Mr Harris, Mr Harris, did you hear me? Is there anyone who could be with you, Mr Harris? Are you okay?"

Of course he wasn't okay ... his darling Beth, his soulmate, his daughter's mother, his one love, was *dead*.

He would never be *okay* again.

He tried to speak, but no words came. He looked up at the officers, trying to understand. His mouth was dry. His lips were dry, his eyes were wet. He opened his mouth and stuttering said, "What ... happ ... ened? What do you ... mean?"

"Your wife ... Beth ... was driving on the northbound carriageway. As far as we know, at this stage, a car travelling in the same direction hit her."

So, she was dead. Did it matter how it happened? Beth was gone.

Forever.

He did not know how to continue ... with anything.

Charlie got a text from Alex at school the following day that simply read:

> Charlie, please come. Alex

She made it a rule not to look at her phone at school, but for some reason, this time she did. She was waiting for the under 14's netball team to arrive for a practice, and when she felt her phone vibrate, she took it out of the pocket of her tracksuit bottoms.

She thought it odd; the tone of it worried her and the complete lack of any context was strange. She couldn't leave school until 2.30 pm, so she texted him back and said she'd be there as soon as she could. The children were both going to after-school activities until 5 pm, so she didn't have to worry about them. Why was Alex at home, anyway? Why hadn't Beth contacted her, as usual?

There was something definitely wrong. She felt her stomach churning.

She left the school car park far too fast and made the brief journey at a speed she never usually drove at. There was no sign of anyone when she drew up outside the cottage, so she knocked loudly on the front door. She heard someone come to the door.

When Alex opened the door, the look of utter desolation on his face scared her. He almost fell onto her, his arms round her for support. He started sobbing; she could feel him shaking.

"She's dead, Charlie ... Beth's dead."

The words that came out of her mouth made no sense. She could hear herself saying, "Oh my god ... Beth? ... what are you talking about? ... you can't be right." She gripped him for what felt like an hour; they were holding each other up, as if they could crumple together to the floor. Her mind and body were in total turmoil; she couldn't take it in. It was as if she'd taken a large quantity of drugs. Her brain flew to another level but couldn't function. In the end, she had to pull away from him or they were going to dissolve into each other's tears. Alex turned abruptly and staggered to the kitchen. He fell into a chair, his head in his hands.

After a while, Charlie said, "Where's Darcy, Alex? Where is she?" She leant against the wall for support. Her legs had turned to jelly. All she could hear were the birds outside the door, chirping.

"She's gone with Beth's parents." He kept his head down, his speech was muffled. "They came last night. We all had to tell her, our beautiful daughter, that her mother was dead. They took her back to their house."

"So, you're here all alone, Alex?"

"Yes."

Her mind was racing. What had happened? She wasn't dead, she just *couldn't* be. She was too full of life. Her own grief was all-encompassing, but she knew Alex couldn't stay here on his own.

He said, "I told them to take her ... I couldn't cope ... I begged them to take her."

"Where are your parents, Alex? Could they come?"

"I've rung them. They're coming later. How will they ever cope with another death?" He sobbed into his hands. Charlie drew up a chair next to him. She rubbed her hand up and down his back as he cried. How would he carry on? How would any of them carry on?

Alex suddenly got up, paced around, and then left the room. Charlie knew she had to act, to do something to help him. She couldn't think of anything she could do that would help ... so she boiled a kettle. As it came to the boil, he came back in with a photo from the sitting room, clutching it to his chest. His dear face was contorted and tear stained.

"Show me," she said.

He held it out to her, and she took it. And there she was ... her wonderful smile, her beautiful face. It was a black-and-white photo; its timelessness, making it even more poignant.

That was all they had left of her.

"Oh, Alex ... she's so beautiful," she whispered. Her heart lurched in her chest, realising she'd used the present tense. All she could say was, "Tell me about it."

He stared at the photo, as Charlie held it for him to see. "I took it in Cyprus," he murmured. "I loved it the moment I saw it. She's so ... so ..." but he left the sentence unfinished.

Seeing her best friend's face made everything real ... she'd never see her again.

What an impossible thing to contemplate.

The following hours, days, weeks ... went by in a blur of confusion, grief, sadness and despair for Charlie. She missed Beth so badly, it hurt ... but she knew what she was feeling was nothing compared to Alex.

His parents came and stayed with him. They tried to be strong for him, but their grief for Jake came back with a vengeance. It had, of course, never gone away, but the arrangements for the funeral, the burial, everything in fact, compounded their own grief. Darcy came home to be with her father; she needed to be back in the family home. She, too, tried to be strong for her father. Alex knew he was the one who had to protect Darcy, but he struggled. Darcy was in her own world of grief and he couldn't reach her. She changed for a while from a gregarious, cheerful person into one that was withdrawn, silent and angry.

They were *both* angry. How could the world have taken such a beautiful soul away from them? There was no rhyme or reason to it. There was a gaping hole in both their lives.

But life had to carry on; Darcy had to go to school when she felt able to, and Alex had to earn a living.

# CHAPTER 8

The police report told them later that Beth had been driving in the middle lane; the driver of the other car had recklessly gone from the middle lane to the slow lane to undertake her, but had then swerved into the middle lane in front of her, clipping her car, which made his car overturn directly in front of her. Beth could do nothing ... she drove straight into the upside down car, at approximately fifty miles an hour. It was all caught on camera.

As with accidents worldwide, there was no explanation as to how the other driver survived. He was found hanging upside down by his seatbelt with a few injuries, but nothing life-threatening. Beth took the full force of the impact.

He was prosecuted for dangerous driving and for being under the influence of alcohol and was sent to jail. He seemed genuinely remorseful, especially when Alex's impact statement was read out in court; it was indeed heart-rending to hear. The driver, who was only twenty-two, had his whole family there, and they were crying, but all the tears in the world could not bring Beth back. She was innocently going about her day, driving safely, and coming home to be an amazing mother to Darcy and a wonderful wife to Alex, and her life was ripped from her in a second.

Alex wasn't a religious person before but, now, he was adamant that there was no God. How could a loving God end the life of such a wonderful person so mercilessly? Nothing made sense anymore.

He got comfort from his work; animals were innocent creatures who only ended the lives of other animals in order to eat them. That was the true order of things.

It was as if his life stood still. The silence in the house was invasive; Beth's absence was like a palpable thing you could feel the moment you entered.

Charlie found herself putting on this false, bright voice whenever she spoke to Alex.

"How are you feeling today?" she'd say, as if she was a care-worker in an old person's home, trying to jolly the troops. "Have you seen your therapist this week?" "How's Darcy being?" Constant questions to fill the silence. There was very little in response. Alex had lost the ability to have a conversation.

She asked David to take him out for a drink, thinking another man might get through to him, but after one outing, when Alex got blind drunk, he wouldn't go again and David gave up asking.

A few months down the road, when nothing much had changed, Charlie contacted Nick. Maybe sailing was a way to get through, she thought? In the upheaval of everything, so soon after the holiday, no one had thought to contact him and tell him the awful news, so Charlie had to tell him and ask for his help in one email.

The message she got back from him was truly heartfelt; perhaps because he'd lost his own wife, he could understand what Alex was going through. He gave such good, kind advice and wrote wonderful words. It was as if he was there in the room.

Charlie read his email out to Alex and he listened distractedly. It ended:

*I've been wanting to come to the UK for a few months now and have not found the motivation to do it. But now I will come and if Alex agrees, I could stay with him and Darcy for a few days? Maybe we could even go sailing together in his boat?*

*What do you think, Charlie? Let me know. I will come whenever it suits you all.*

*I am thinking of you. Beth was a truly remarkable person.*
*With love, Nick.*

"Wow, that's so nice of him, Alex. What do you think?" said Charlie, in her usual sing-songy voice, hoping that maybe she'd get a reaction. She was sitting next to him on the sofa and she linked her arm through his. "I think it would be so lovely to see him," she continued, "and what a good idea of his to go sailing together." Charlie looked at him, but he just stared ahead, not a flicker of anything on his face. Blank.

"Alex ... I think it would be good for you to have some male company here. Don't you?"

Nothing.

"You could show him around, go for drinks together ... I'd look after Darcy ... she could come and stay with us. She loves being with my two."

There was a long silence and then he muttered, "Yeah, maybe."

That was all he said ... but it was a start. She replied to Nick's email saying they were just trying to work out dates, glossing over Alex's reaction. She said she'd write again the following week.

She persuaded Alex to let her arrange it, telling him that if it was all too much for him when Nick came, he could stay at her place.

The visit was arranged for the following month. Nick was going to visit some other friends first and then come to them. Alex didn't complain, but he didn't exactly seem to be pleased, either.

Nothing pleased him any more.

---

Charlie met Nick at the local station and as his train pulled in, she could feel her heart thumping. She wasn't sure if this was a good idea or not. Had she made a stupid decision to invite Nick, who, let's face it, was a relative stranger, into this painful situation? They'd only known him briefly and hadn't seen him for months. What did she think she was doing?

But as he walked towards her down the platform, with a large rucksack on his back, his bright white hair standing out in the sunshine, she lost all her qualms. There was something about his presence that was calm and reassuring. A memory of the two men smiling and laughing flashed into her mind, as they'd set sail on the Med. They'd formed an instant and strong bond, despite the age difference.

It would be okay.

Nick threw his arms around her and hugged her and as she stood there, breathing in his comforting scent, she herself felt a great wave of compassion from him. Memories of Cyprus flooded her mind; happy memories. As they drew apart, she said, "Oh Nick, it's so wonderful that you're here. It really is."

"How are you doing?" he asked, looking directly into her eyes. She realised few people had asked *her* how she was; everyone had been so concerned about Alex that her grief had been forgotten. David had mourned with her at the beginning, but Beth was *her* friend, and he soon moved on. David had a capacity to disassociate himself from things; his career was all-consuming and a scapegoat.

Tears instantly filled her eyes, and she couldn't speak. Nick took her hand and squeezed it, saying, "Losing your friend like that must have been so difficult for you. Have you had any help ... or therapy?"

"No, I'm just about okay, I think. It's Alex I'm so worried about. He just seems to have disappeared ... to have closed down."

"But you must look after yourself, Charlie. You won't be any help to Alex if you don't."

She knew what he was saying was true; maybe she *would* talk to someone. She couldn't speak to David about her feelings.

But Alex was the reason Nick was here, not *her*, and as they walked towards the car, arms linked, both of them were thinking of *him*.

She had arranged with Alex to take Nick there at six o'clock that evening, so, as it was only three, she took him back to hers first, to freshen up from the journey. He'd never been to this part of the world before, so to fill in time, she showed him around their village first, pointing out local landmarks.

"What would you like to drink? Tea, coffee ... beer?" she said, after they got to the house.

"Tea would be fine, thanks," he said, relaxing into her sofa. The children weren't home yet, so they could speak easily without interruptions. "So ... how is Alex coping now? How long is it since ..."

"Four months ... I can't believe it. He's coping ... just. But to be honest, he seems completely lost without her. It's going to take a long time ... but maybe you'll be able to get through to him? I think if you went down to his boat at the weekend and sailed for a while, it could help. It's something that he's always done, something he's done without Beth. Maybe he'll be able to find himself again."

"Maybe ... but I won't put any pressure on him. If he wants to go, we'll go. If he wants to do nothing, we'll do nothing. I'll let him dictate terms."

Charlie dropped him off at the set time. She'd decided not to go in, so she waited to make sure Alex opened the door. When he eventually did, they shook hands ... no emotional hugging. She had a momentary feeling that this was a bad idea, but then Nick was ushered through the door and disappeared. All she could do was hope.

Alex rang the next day and asked if Darcy could come over, which was a good sign. Charlie, of course, said 'yes' but purposefully didn't ask why; she was determined not to interfere.

She offered to collect her, but Alex said they would drop her on the way to the boat, so she got her answer. She felt a little lift of her spirits.

Maybe this would be a turning point.

# Part 3
## 2018

Sarah Catherine Knights

# CHAPTER 9

David retired from the Air Force a few years later. Charlie was taken by surprise; he'd talked about it, but she didn't think he'd actually do it before he *had* to. His whole life was flying, planes and the camaraderie of his colleagues, but he began to realise that he wasn't going to make Wing Commander. He wasn't a 'yes' man and was too argumentative. He didn't enjoy having to kowtow to the 'powers that be'.

So, he decided there were other things he wanted to do with his life. For example, he'd never really taken golf seriously, and he wanted to learn how to play well. He was going to treat himself to having lessons. Playing much more tennis too was a priority; he knew he could be a lot better, if he had more time. Improving his squash was another contender for his attention.

The other thing he'd absolutely set his sights on was buying a house in Cyprus. Since that holiday and after several sorties to Cyprus since then, his feelings had strengthened. David spent much of his down-time glued to his phone, looking at Cypriot houses for sale.

He didn't discuss with Charlie the fact that they'd have to sell their UK house to achieve this dream. He glossed over that.

Charlie decided to have a retirement party for him. He'd already had a send-off on the camp, which consisted of drinking copious amounts of booze at the bar and a few drunken speeches, but she wanted to have a more sedate party at home with family and friends. It was a momentous moment in David's life; his career had been everything.

The weather was beautiful, fortunately, as the party was in their garden at home. Charlie put on a cold buffet and there was champagne, music, and laughter. David was on his best behaviour and seemed to relish his future. Charlie worried that this euphoria would evaporate when he faced the reality of life without purpose.

It was here, in front of everyone, that he announced his plans during his speech.

"As soon as is possible, Charlotte and I will be off to Cyprus to live, where we'll spend our days loafing around, getting as brown as berries and doing as little as possible!"

This was met by a certain amount of surprise, and eventually, loud whoops from his audience. "There's a lot to do before we get there, of course; the main thing being selling this house. So this might be the last time we ever have a gathering here. Could you, therefore, all raise your glasses, and say, *'To Cyprus!'*"

He raised his glass and everyone shouted, '*To Cyprus!*'

"And I'd like to say, you're all welcome to come and visit ... but not too often! The sun always shines, the booze always flows and the sea's always warm!"

Everyone cheered again and looked at each other, wondering if this was just 'all talk'.

Charlie was standing at the back, smiling, but deep down she felt sick. She liked Cyprus, what she'd seen of it all those years ago, but she was still struggling with the thought of going there for good. It had been a great holiday and she could see it was a beautiful island, but did she *really* want to live there? In her mind, Cyprus was forever tinged with sadness now. She often thought of that swim with Beth when the two of them were alone. They'd said they'd be friends forever, didn't they?

David was so persuasive and she could see she was going to get swept up in his desire to go. Charlie would miss their children so much. Lou would be all right, though; her life was sorted. She'd followed in her mother's footsteps and had got married and had children early. Harry, her husband, was right for her in every way and the children were adorable. But what about poor Will? He was soon off to uni and it felt as if they would be abandoning him.

She'd miss this house too ... and the culture of the UK. She'd even miss the weather, the seasons, the unpredictability. There's only so much sun that could take the place of an English life. She knew she was being indecisive; when she was there, she'd loved it ... but now the reality of David's dream was just too close.

Alex and Darcy were at the party, of course, and Alex came up to her after the speech. By now, he'd come out of his grief and anger at the world. He lived a quiet life, tending to his animals, loving Darcy ... missing Beth. They were, of course, still friends, but that closeness had gone and they didn't see each other much.

"I didn't realise your plans were so definite," he said, looking concerned.

"Neither did I, Alex."

"I know he's talked about it, but the way he was talking then, it sounded like he's made up his mind. Do you want to go? How do you feel about going to live abroad?"

"I don't know, I really don't. There's no reason from my career point of view; I want to leave, anyway. I've had enough. But I was looking forward to doing ..." She stopped and wondered what she was going to say. "I was looking forward to just living here: seeing more of the kids, being a grandma, maybe even getting a dog at last, taking up sailing ... I don't know."

"Maybe you've got to say something, Charlie. You can't let him bamboozle you into going to live there if you don't want to. Apart from anything, we'd miss you. I'd miss you." He looked directly at her; she knew she represented a connection to Beth, which Alex didn't want to lose.

"But you know what he's like, Alex. When he gets an idea in his head, it's impossible to change his mind. He's been going on and on about it, to be fair. It sounded half-hearted when we were on holiday, but ... it's not just a whim."

"No, I know, but the reality is here ... now. He's retired, and he's just announced to the entire party that you're going. I think it's time to say something. You've got to stand up for yourself, Charlie. It's your life he's disrupting."

"Yeah, you're right. I know you are." She could feel her stomach churn at the prospect of confronting him and trying to make herself heard by him. Alex could see her anxiety and put his arm round her shoulders. She loved the feeling of having an ally. How crazy that she should think like that about her own husband.

"You must ... and anyway, you can't go, I forbid it," he smiled.

"If we go, you can always come and visit. As he said, the sun's always out. You would come, wouldn't you?"

"Yes, we will, of course, but it won't be the same here without you."

That night, after everyone had gone, Charlie tried to bring the subject up. It was completely the wrong time: they were both tired and David had got the red wine out and had carried on drinking. Slumped on the sofa, they were watching something neither of them cared much for, and when a commercial break started, Charlie thought ... now or never.

"So ... did you mean what you said?"

"Huh?" he said, without taking his eyes off the screen and taking another swig.

"About Cyprus."

"Yes, of course I did. This is the moment I've been waiting for. We can finally bugger off and get away from this weather."

"But what if I don't want to?" she said. Charlie tried to make her voice neutral, not confrontational. She really couldn't face an argument.

"Of course you want to, Charlotte. What's keeping us here? You're stopping teaching ... so what's the attraction of staying?"

"Well, the kids, for a start."

"They're grown-ups now. You've got to let them get on with life, without interfering all the time. Cut the apron strings."

"Well, Lou's okay, I know that ... but Will still needs our support."

"What that boy needs is a kick up the arse. You've always been too soft on him and look how he's turned out."

"He'll be fine, David. Don't be so harsh on him. Even though he'll be off to uni, where will he go in the holidays?"

"He could come out to paradise. That's not too much to ask. Or stay with friends. Get a holiday job? Anyway, whatever ... I'm going. Take it or leave it."

Charlie didn't know how to respond. Was he threatening to leave her if she didn't comply? Perhaps it was the booze talking.

"So, I don't get a say, then?"

"You've had years to say something. Why are you complaining now I've retired?"

"I've never said I *definitely* want to go. You've always assumed. I agree Cyprus is a gorgeous island but there's a big difference between going on holiday to a place and living there. What would we do with ourselves?"

"All the things we were going to do here ... but in the sun. How can you object to that?"

"I'm not sure, David, I'm really not. Can't we think about it for a while? Why did you have to announce it like that? We haven't ever really discussed it properly."

"Oh, for Christ's sake, Charlotte. We've talked about it endlessly over the years. We've even looked at houses on the internet and you've never said *anything*."

"Well, maybe I didn't think it would actually happen. Maybe I was hoping we could make a joint decision; maybe I found it difficult to talk to you about. Honestly, David, sometimes you just don't listen to me at all."

David stood up, grabbed the remote control, turned off the TV, and flung it on the sofa.

"I'm going to bed. Thanks for ruining what was meant to be an enjoyable end to my career." He stomped out of the room and slammed the door, leaving Charlie shellshocked and shaky.

She turned the TV back on again and stared at the screen, thoughts churning in her head. She was going to have to go along with him. It was clear to her now. As she'd said to Alex earlier, once he'd decided on something, he was like a bolting horse, galloping out of control towards the end of the race. Too bad if she fell at Bechers Brook behind him.

She attempted to 'see' herself there. There she was ... lying on a sun lounger, walking along a beach, sipping wine by the sea with Cypriot music playing. Why didn't she want this for herself? Many people would kill to have this offered on a plate as a future scenario. But she'd never liked change; perhaps that's what frightened her? Would they make friends out there? She didn't want to be a typical ex-pat if she went. She'd want to socialise with Cypriots and not stick to the enclave of Brits, but would David be prepared to break out of his very British self and mingle with the locals?

Charlie was going to have to convince David that if they went, they would do things *her* way: socialise, get out and about and explore the island; come back to the UK as often as possible to see the kids. If he agreed to these things, then perhaps she'd do it. She could persuade herself it would be an adventure and if it didn't work out, they could always come back, couldn't they?

"Hey, Charlotte, look at this one. It's perfect: three bedrooms, two bathrooms, a good sized garden and an amazing sea view. We could afford it too," he grinned.

"There are probably thousands of houses for sale in Cyprus we could afford, David," looking at the pictures halfheartedly over his shoulder. He'd shown her several houses in the past few days. They all looked similar, and she couldn't get excited about a house she'd never seen in reality. Maybe there was a noisy road right next to it? Maybe there were terrible neighbours next door? Barking dogs? All the things that estate agents don't tell you about.

"But this is in a perfect spot ..."

"Yes, I'm sure it is, but there are a lot of hurdles to jump before we can even contemplate it and by then, this one will have gone."

"Don't be so negative. I know the timing's not right as we haven't sold yet, but our house is going on the market next week and you never know, it might sell quickly."

Her heart was beating fast. The thought of not living in this house was so scary. She'd never wanted it in the first place; it had been David's choice to buy it all those years ago, but it was her home now, and she couldn't imagine living anywhere else.

"I'm going to email the estate agent anyway and see what the situation is with that house."

"Okay, but don't get your hopes up. There'll be plenty of others, I'm sure."

They'd approved the photos of their house and the agent said the brochure and online listing would be ready in a couple of days. Charlie looked at the pictures and couldn't believe it was happening, so she was taken aback when the agent rang and said there was a couple who wanted to look round.

"But it's not even officially on the market yet, is it?" she asked, trying to mask the panic in her voice.

"No, not quite, but Mr and Mrs Simpson were in the agency today and are specifically looking for a house in your exact area. They've sold theirs, so they're ready to go. I explained about yours not coming onto the market until Monday, but I showed them the details and they're really keen. I told them you're moving abroad and want to get on with it so ... good news all round. When can they come?"

Charlie looked at her mobile as if it was too hot to hold. This was so typical; anything David set his mind to always fell into place. This couple was going to buy it. She felt it in her bones. How crazy it would be if the first people who looked round it bought it?

She said, "They can come any time ... just let me know." Her voice was trembling.

"Great! I'll get back to you with a time. We'd prefer to show prospective buyers round ourselves, so if you could pop out for an hour, that would be super. Okay, speak later," and he was gone.

David was, of course, thrilled with the news. Charlie had to keep telling herself that, of course, the first people wouldn't buy it. That would be ridiculous.

The agent rang back that day and they arranged for the viewing to be on Monday at two o'clock.

David took her out for a late lunch when the agent and the Simpsons were there, and they talked about their future. Charlie tried to sound enthusiastic and even convinced herself that it was a good move. The house in Cyprus that David had found did sound lovely; it had everything they needed and was in pristine condition, according to the agent that replied to David's enquiry.

Charlie found it hard to imagine that strangers had been poking round her house. She felt unsettled and didn't sleep well that night. The agent had rung them later and said they'd liked it, but had said little more. Maybe her prediction about them buying it was wrong? Or maybe, the couple were like David would be, keeping their thoughts close to their chest, in order to negotiate the price down.

Only time would tell.

As it turned out, the first couple didn't buy it, but the third couple did. Their own house had sold and completion was due any time and they offered what David wanted, so it was a done deal. Charlie couldn't help feeling pleased for David. He really wanted this. She could see that now ... but her own life was feeling out of control.

"Right, let's book some flights out there for next week. We may as well get on with it, otherwise, we'll find ourselves with nowhere to live."

"It's all happening rather quickly," said Charlie. She was running down a hill without being able to stop.

"That's good, isn't it?"

"Yes, I suppose so." If David had been the type of man who could read other people's feelings, he would have heard the anxiety in her voice, but he just wasn't like that. It wasn't his fault, that's who he was.

She spoke to Lou on the phone, who sounded excited for her; Will, less so. He said, "Are you sure it's what you want, Mum? Don't let Dad push you into it."

"No, I'm fine about it, Will. We can always come home, if it doesn't work out, can't we?" she said, sounding bright and cheerful, despite her worry.

Charlie had only been to Cyprus once in her entire life; David, of course, had been so many times with the RAF that, to him, it was just another flight. When they boarded the EasyJet plane at Bristol, she was full of trepidation. How would she feel as they landed? Would she get her mojo back after weeks of feeling lethargic?

It was a gorgeous day when they stepped out into the sunshine. The ochre-coloured land greeted them with that special smell that Cyprus air seems to emit: a mixture of heat, dust and herbs.

David waited for her at the bottom of the steps as she stumbled down, holding her small case. "Isn't it wonderful to be back?" he said, before marching across the tarmac towards the arrivals building. She had to admit, it was lovely to feel the warmth of the sun on her skin; when they'd left England, it had been lashing down with rain. What a difference. The sky here was piercing blue, with no clouds; the air, so clear that it was as if she was seeing the scene with laser-corrected eyesight.

They took a taxi to their hotel along the seafront at Paphos; it wasn't the same one they'd stayed in before, but nearby. As she looked out of their room with a sea view, the sea had its normal mesmerising effect on her; it stretched to the horizon, as flat as a mirror; gleams of light were dancing on the surface. Immediately below, in the gardens of the hotel, she could see a large rectangular pool, with umbrellas and sunbeds ranged around it in perfect symmetry.

"This is wonderful, David, isn't it? It's bringing back all those happy memories of our holiday. I know it's been a long time since the accident, but I can't get used to the fact that Beth once was with us here and now she's gone. We had such fun together here."

"Life's cruel," said David. "But you can't dwell on the past, love. We've got to get on with our future. Life's too short and all that."

"I know ... but Beth was my best friend ... and I feel I haven't got one anymore."

They were both standing, facing the sea. David took her hand and said, laughing, "Aren't I your best friend?"

"Yes, of course. I didn't mean ..." She didn't know what she meant, but she knew she missed Beth every day.

"Come on, stop being maudlin. Let's unpack and pick up those rays before they go. It's already three. Darkness comes quickly here."

They made their way down to the pool; Charlie got straight into the warm water that had been heated by the sun all summer. She swam a few lazy lengths, feeling her body stretch and relax; she was the only person in the pool. David lay on a sunbed, eyes closed, his EarPods in, determined to disassociate from the world. After her swim, Charlie lay next to him and read her novel. She felt content, happy even, as she lay there.

To an onlooker, they looked like a married couple enjoying a late summer holiday, but it was, in fact, the start of a new life.

---

The very next day, David was on a mission to visit as many houses as possible. He'd contacted several agents and arranged two viewings that day, and three the next. The house sale back home was continuing without hitches, the couple wanting completion as soon as possible.

She and David had plenty of discussions about where in Cyprus they wanted to end up. Neither of them knew the island very well; David had only ever stayed near Akrotiri, Limassol and Paphos, and Charlie's knowledge was based entirely on their holiday. So, at breakfast that first morning, when David said, "Shall we draw a circle on the map around the camp?" she agreed. There was no point going to the mountains, Larnaca, Nicosia or Latchi. They wouldn't know where to start. As for northern Cyprus, that didn't even enter their heads.

Maybe in the future they'd visit, but neither of them wanted to live there.

"So, where are the two houses today?" said Charlie.

"Well, we're meeting an agent this morning, here in Paphos. It's along the coast on the other side of town, towards Coral Bay. The second one, at 3 pm, is with a different agent in Pissouri; I've been there a few times on nights out with the crew, so I know it. It's a big village. That's the one I showed you a week ago. This morning's one looks good, but not sure about the location."

Charlie wasn't sure what she felt about any of it; it all seemed unreal to her. It might have been different if they weren't having to sell their UK house, but as it stood, it was such a big decision. She told herself just to look at the houses and forget the implications of them.

David was right with his instinct; the first one was a pleasant house, but it was stuck on a small estate, not near any village or shops. It was a stone's throw from a beach, but had no pool and only two bedrooms. She knew immediately she didn't like it; she had some sort of visceral feeling the moment she saw it; *not for me*. Was she going to persuade David to her view?

The moment they were back in the car on their own, she told David how she felt and he agreed with her. "Yes, I don't think two bedrooms are enough, even though we could have a sofa bed in the sitting room, as the guy pointed out. We definitely want at least three. I liked the fact that it was so near the beach, though, did you?"

"Yes ... but it wasn't a very nice beach, was it? And the shops are miles away."

"Yeah, let's forget that one."

As they climbed the steep hill into Pissouri village later, Charlie had a moment of clarity; this was more like it. She'd like to be part of a proper community and this village, spread over a wide area with its central square, appeared to offer just that. The agent was driving in front of them and finally came to a stop outside a modern house at the end of a no-through road. The sea was all around them, but it would be at least a ten-minute drive down to it, as the house was high up.

The agent opened the front gate and showed them inside.

"So, as you can see, it's open-plan and bright and airy. The people who own it have never lived here; it was an investment and they've been letting it out."

Charlie liked the feel of it the moment she stepped inside; she could see the kitchen was perfect and everything had been painted neutral colours.

"Follow me upstairs," said John, the English agent, "and you'll get the idea of how spectacular the position is, from the balcony." And he was right. As they went onto the balcony from the main bedroom, the full vista spread out before them. The blueness of the sky, meeting the turquoise of the horizon, stretching as far as the eye could see.

"Wow, this is stunning. Sold!" said David. He leant on the railings and sighed. "What do you think, Charlie? And look at our pool; just the right size and a manageable garden around the house."

Charlie was surprised. She'd always thought David would be more guarded and cautious. But here he was, saying 'sold' and 'our pool'. The agent must be rubbing his hands, she thought.

"Yes, what a view," she said. "Can I see the other bedrooms?"

"Of course, follow me," said John.

There were plenty of cupboards in all the bedrooms and both the bathrooms were pristine. Both had showers and one had a bath.

"I'll leave you two to wander on your own. I'll be downstairs on the patio. Take your time."

When he'd gone, David grinned at Charlie. "I love it," he said, quietly, as if he'd suddenly remembered to be a canny buyer. "It's perfect."

"Yes, I like it. It's a good size for us; we could easily have Lou and the family here, and Will, but it's not too big for us when we're on our own. A good size garden ... and I could swim properly in the pool; it looks like a reasonable length."

"Yea, I agree with all that. Let's have a wander outside. I have a good feeling about this."

Over the next few days, Charlie persuaded David to look at other houses, but his heart was set on that second one. They saw one in Limassol, but it was too built up there. One in the foothills of the mountains, but that was too remote and another one in Pissouri, but that didn't have a view. There was one near Kolossi Castle, but it didn't have a pool; they travelled out of their comfort zone to Lefkara, but that was too far. They even had a day trip to Larnaca, but they were both drawn back to the Pissouri one and asked to go back for another visit.

They both decided that the second one was 'The One'. Their future home in the sun.

# CHAPTER 10

The day they flew to Cyprus together to start their new life seemed unreal to Charlie. As they touched down, she gazed through her window at the speeding, brown earth that was rushing past. She felt no sense of joy or excitement, just resignation.

It was November, 2019; Will had left for Birmingham uni to study English the previous month, and she was worried about him. He felt so far away from her. Would he survive? She wished she was still there for him, so he could come back home whenever he wanted. But ... maybe it was a good thing that she wasn't at home for him to run away to? He would have to 'get on with it' as David said, and maybe being self-reliant would be good for him. He'd been fine on his gap-year travelling round Europe with two school mates; it was this degree that was worrying him. It wasn't really what he wanted to do.

As they waited for their luggage to arrive on the carousel, Charlie's mind was occupied with thoughts of both of their children. She already missed them and the grandchildren so much. But soon they were piling the cases onto two trolleys and trundling outside to find a taxi big enough to take it all. The rest of their belongings were being shipped out and would take a few weeks to arrive.

They eventually settled into the taxi, David talking to the driver animatedly about his new house. Charlie, however, pressed her forehead to the window, watching as her new homeland drifted past. She felt alienated, alone, and sad. Why had she agreed to this? Why did she think this was ever going to be a good idea?

When they pulled up outside their new house and the taxi driver had driven away, they walked around the gardens, leaving their luggage on the front patio.

"Isn't this amazing, Charlie? It's all ours ... we can forget the grey skies of the UK forever." Charlie looked around and felt totally disorientated.

He walked over to the pool, squatted down, and dipped his fingers in, and as an afterthought, picked out a floating leaf. "It feels okay, actually. I suppose it's still retaining the heat, but it'll soon get chilly with winter coming. Maybe you should have a swim while you can?"

She didn't feel like swimming; she didn't feel much like doing anything.

"Where's the key to the door?"

"It's in the key safe. Here's the code," and he sent it on a WhatsApp message to her phone. He continued surveying his garden round the side, pulling out the odd weed.

Charlie opened the front door. The smell of the long-empty property hit her, but it looked clean enough. They'd bought some of the previous owners' furniture. The sofa and armchairs looked lost in the centre of the open plan room. They would have to go shopping as soon as possible to get a table and chairs. They'd also inherited a fridge and other white goods in the kitchen, and a double bed, so they could 'camp out' until then.

She went upstairs, opened windows and doors to the balconies, to let in some fresh air. There was a definite feeling of a closed-up house that wanted to 'breathe' the air again. She stood on one balcony, leant against the railings and said to herself: *You can do this ... you can. So many people would love to be in your position. Get to grips.*

She stared at the serenity of the surroundings and wondered why she couldn't feel excited. Here she was, surrounded by the Mediterranean, palm trees and total silence ... she closed her eyes, breathing slowly and deeply, trying to stay calm. She must see this through, for David's sake, as well as her own. If only she could FaceTime Beth; she'd have given her courage.

"Where are you?" she heard David shout.

"Up here! Admiring the view," she said. "Come and join me." If she made herself *sound* okay, maybe she *would* be?

Soon, he was next to her, their four hands together in a row on the railings. "We're going to have such a great time here, Charlie. I can feel it ... no more work, no more worries. Just sun and enjoyment."

She turned her head towards him and put one of her hands on one of his. "It's beautiful, David. I love the smell of the air. And this view ... we'll never get bored with this." She kissed his cheek, and he turned to her and, placing his hands on either side of her face, he kissed her mouth.

"This is us ... forever. Thank you for doing this with me, Charlie. I know it was *my* dream ... I know you had your doubts. How do you feel ... now you're here?"

"I had doubts, David. I can't deny it. It'll take me a while to adjust, but I'll get there. I'm sure I will."

They kissed again and then she said, "Let's sort the unpacking and then ... shall we go out tonight to a taverna and celebrate? I'll shop tomorrow."

"Yea, definitely. Some of them will be closed now after the season, but there are bound to be a few open."

That night, after a shower and a change of clothes, they walked into the square, Charlie feeling determined to make the best of it.

They were going to hire a car the next day before buying their own. David told the waiter they had just moved to Cyprus, and he welcomed them with kindness. They drank prosecco and red wine, ate Afelia, vegetables and chips, followed by yoghurt, nuts and honey, and talked about what they were going to do with their week. There was talk of visiting Ikea in Nicosia; of discovering local shops in Paphos; of joining the gym at the local hotel and of swimming at a different beach every day. The alcohol gave Charlie a buzz, and she began to think that it did, indeed, sound fun.

They walked back up the hill together, hand in hand, in the coal-black darkness. The street lamps burned amber and helped them find their way at first over potholed pavements and random speed bumps, but then the lamps stopped and the darkness was absolute. Only one car passed them on their entire walk; it felt as if they were utterly alone beneath the Cyprus sky. The milky way was clearly visible, and it felt as if they were in their own personal planetarium. David pointed out various constellations as they walked. Charlie looked up at the stars with wonder; they were never as bright in England. It was truly magical.

Everything would be okay.

Soon, their eyes became accustomed to the dark. They could hear something moving near them and realised there were some goats in the bondu near the road. They all suddenly raised their heads and stared as Charlie and David passed. Bats fluttered and zoomed overhead and in the far distance, they could hear a solitary owl. They lingered, not wanting to go back inside. The night here was their friend, and they wanted to embrace it. Charlie saw Cyprus's potential mapped out in the sky above.

They had to make up the bed when they got back, but soon they were snuggled up together and fell instantly asleep. It had been a long buildup and a very tiring day, and they were finally here.

The next few weeks were filled with lots of shopping trips. They began to realise that shopping in Cyprus wasn't as straightforward as shopping back home. Often they would get to a shop that someone had recommended to them, and it was shut at that particular time of day, or on that particular day of the week. It became a joke between them: they would say things like: *As it's a Tuesday at one o'clock, do you think they'll be open?* or *It's a Friday at 4; maybe they've gone home already?*

But eventually they got what they needed and their containers arrived from England, so the house started to feel more like home. They'd bought a truck from a garage in Limassol after a lot of wheeling and dealing, and David loved his new toy.

They began to meet people. David wasn't that bothered and was content with just the two of them hanging out at home, but Charlie joined a yoga class and they both joined the gym at the hotel. It had an indoor pool and spa too, which proved useful as their own pool was getting cold. They met mainly ex-pats and socialised, going to tavernas and even playing some tennis matches. Charlie was always rather wary when they went out, in case David drank too much, but often he would be on his best behaviour when out with new people, but would then polish off a bottle of wine when he got home.

He was very partial to watching sport on the TV and found what they could get on their own TV was rather limited, so he started frequenting local sports bars, which showed all the main football and rugby matches. Charlie didn't mind him going alone; she had no desire to watch sport, but she worried about the alcohol consumption. On the odd occasion she went with him, she noticed there was a hard-core group of regulars and David had become 'one of the lads'. She was pleased he'd met some fellow sports fanatics, but not so happy about the constant pints, glasses of wine, and shots.

They had a strange Christmas together, just the two of them. Charlie had always loved having a houseful, so this was not her idea of fun, but there was no alternative. They booked into a taverna, which was offering a traditional turkey dinner for a reasonable price. There were a few other people they knew there, Christmas music, decorations and silly hats, but it wasn't the same. When they got home, they FaceTime'd with Lou and the children and Charlie felt an overwhelming sadness when they finally clicked the red button. Will had been there too, but spoke little and appeared subdued. She felt sick to her stomach at the realisation that she was losing contact with him.

Of course, *nobody* knew at that moment in time that humanity was hurtling towards the pandemic. Christmas and New Year came and went in Cyprus. The weather got colder; snow fell on the Troodos. Everyone was innocent of what was to come.

Charlie and David went off for adventures in their truck, braving the snow up Mount Olympus for the first time. The beauty of the mountains bowled them over. It was another world up there. Charlie couldn't ski, but was happy for David to go off and ski for a couple of hours. She sat in the warmth of a café, drank cocoa, and read her book until he returned.

They drove to Latchi and walked to the Baths of Aphrodite, explored the Akamas peninsular and drove to San Raphael, and walked along the beach. They wandered the backstreets of Paphos and Limassol. Every week, they went somewhere new, in between shopping, socialising, playing tennis and making their home and garden as welcoming as they could.

Charlie had to admit to herself that she was enjoying it. It felt as if she was on an extended holiday; it didn't have the feel of real life, but she was slowly adapting. She hardly heard from Will, but Lou was in constant touch with pictures of the children or the latest news from work. She tried to put Will out of her mind. He'd call her if he needed her, she was sure, and Lou gave her titbits of news about him. He was just getting on with his degree and hopefully making friends.

The first news of an unknown virus started filtering through at the end of January. Charlie read the news, but it didn't register; two people had it in the UK, but that was miles away from them.

But when two more people brought it to Cyprus in March, she felt a sense of unease.

"What do you think about this virus, then?" she asked David. They'd been listening to Radio 4 while they ate breakfast outside, as usual.

"Not a lot really," he said. "We're out here in the middle of paradise; I hardly think it will affect us. Don't worry about it."

She had agreed with his optimism at that point, but she had become obsessed with the news. Schools in both the UK and Cyprus closed and on 23rd March she couldn't believe that the UK totally locked down. How was that going to even work?

She phoned Lou immediately and realised how disastrous it was: no school, Lou and Harry working from home.

"God, Mum, this is so awful. It's scary. I hate living in London. We're stuck here now ... but at least we've got a garden, I suppose. Think of those poor people stuck at the top of high rises? And I've somehow got to help the kids with their reading and writing and do my own work? How can I do both?"

"You'll have to share it with Harry ... you'll find a way. What about Will? Have you heard from him?"

"He says he's totally stuck in his hall of residence. It's a bloody nightmare."

"I'll text him. Poor Will. This is the last thing he needs."

But soon, Charlie and David were in exactly the same position. David was so angry about it. Cyprus had gone for one of the strictest lockdowns in Europe.

They called it a 'stay-at-home order' and it was exactly that. They couldn't go anywhere without permission: they had to send a text to a government system to get approval before leaving the house to do only a few essential things, like buying food, going to a doctor, or even going for a walk.

"Fucking ridiculous," said David. "Totally over-the-top reaction. We're effectively prisoners in our own home, for gods' sake. So much for coming out here to explore and enjoy ourselves."

Charlie texted Will but got little in return. She was so worried about him. All lectures had stopped, all seminars cancelled. He was meant to study online, but he was so demotivated.

Charlie and David tried to put on brave faces to start with. They went for their hour's walk religiously. Charlie felt that just simply getting out of their house and garden gave them at least a little time to forget, but it wasn't long before David refused to go. "What's the point?" he'd say.

Instead, he started getting up late, spending his afternoons lying in the sun and hardly getting off his sunbed. He would occasionally flop into the pool for five minutes and swim half-heartedly, but he'd then get out and lie down again. He started having a couple of beers at lunch, and then the 'evening' drink started getting earlier and earlier. Charlie would join him for a glass of wine, but he would continue until he went to bed. He wasn't interested in Charlie's advice about keeping fit, his alcohol intake or his weight gain.

TV became very important to both of them; they watched endless box sets, series, dramas, documentaries and comedies, just like everyone else. Charlie, however, was determined to keep active. She made herself swim fifty lengths every morning; followed fitness videos; practised yoga; tried to learn Greek online and went through all her photo albums. David slipped further and further away from her and into himself. Without the Air Force or sport or his adventures in his truck, he had nothing he wanted to do. Charlie tried to encourage him to write about his time in the Air Force. He started this and was, at first, enthusiastic, but he'd never done anything like it before and he soon got disheartened and stopped. He'd do crosswords and suduko but this could only occupy him for an hour or so. The days were endless.

She'd try to get him to go food shopping with her, but he hated wearing a mask. He'd give her a long list of all the alcohol he wanted and she'd buy it, thinking she was actually enabling his behaviour.

With all the different phases of the pandemic: the easing; the second lockdowns; the vaccination rollouts; the SafePass introduction; the Omicron variant and gradual lifting, they remained locked together in silent antagonism.

Charlie couldn't seem to reach David anymore. The 'old' fun David all but disappeared during those two years. He was angry at the world and impossible to talk to. Charlie was forever trying to be the appeaser, the helper and the facilitator, but they didn't see eye to eye on anything and they eventually drifted so far apart, they hardly talked to each other.

# CHAPTER 11

It was September 2023. The pandemic had finally gone and life was almost normal again. Except that David had not gone back to his former self and Charlie and he were simply existing together in their paradise. He did make an effort to go out again and occasionally they would meet up with old acquaintances for meals, but his sparkle had gone. He began to spend a lot of time in sports bars again; Charlie understood his desire to be with male company, but she often wished they had something they did together.

On this particular day, the sun was setting as Charlie drove up the hill towards their house. She never grew tired of the scenery and was tempted to take her eyes off the hair-pin bends. Off to her right, the sky was burning pink and orange, any wisps of clouds becoming purple shadows. Houses on the hillside were turning apricot, bird silhouettes rising and diving above the valley. She had the window open and the warm air fanned her face, blowing her hair and cooling her neck. During the day, she had to have the air con on in the car and the windows closed. It was just too hot not to, but the evening temperature was just becoming bearable now. She glanced at the gauge on the dashboard; it was still twenty-nine degrees. Funny how she now thought that was a possible heat; a few years ago she would have passed out, at the thought.

At the top of the last bend, she passed some sparse greenery. There, standing with its head drooping, was the bay gelding she passed most days, tied up by a long rope. It had no shade, flies were buzzing around its eyes and for the life of her, she couldn't see what the poor thing ate or drank. There was no visible bucket and nothing that could be mistaken for sustenance. Every time she drove this way, her heart would sink at the sight of him; he was skinny and if ever an animal could look depressed, this was it. As always, she drove on, wishing there was something she could do, but David wouldn't have it; he said it was their culture, and she had no right to interfere. She physically shook her head, trying to rid her mind of the image.

She carried on along the road with the speed bumps that took her by surprise every day. She knew they were there, but they weren't highlighted and unless her mind was focussed, she would hit them at too fast a speed and the old truck would shudder and jolt her back to reality. The truck had very little suspension and every minor bump in the road felt like a deep pothole. It was just about okay in the front, but if she ever had to sit in the back, it would make her feel sick with its violent reaction.

Going round the tight lefthand corner, she met another truck coming the other way. The driver didn't slow down or acknowledge the fact that she had had to steer towards the wall; he just ploughed on, oblivious to everything. *Thanks for nothing,* she muttered to herself. She got to the end of the road, swung right and onto the last road that led down the hill to their house. The sky was now getting redder still and she couldn't help it. She would have to stop and take yet more pictures of the sunset over the cliffs and sea. Charlie did this so often, she wondered what she was hoping for this time. She always thought that *this* sunset, *this* sky, would be the best shot. *After three years of living on this island, you'd think I'd have stopped this relentless pursuit of the perfect sunset picture by now*, she thought.

Pulling into a lay-by, she slid out of the car. She only had her iPhone with her, but she took several shots, some standing, some crouching down, some zoomed in, some wide angle. She glanced in the photos app; they looked like many others she'd taken but until they were on her laptop, she couldn't be sure. This new iPhone really was amazing. She'd always loved taking photos; in the past, she'd used a proper camera, which she still had hidden away in a drawer in their bedroom, but these days, the mobile phone was enough for her.

She realised she was putting off getting home. David exuded unhappiness these days, and the house felt as if it reflected his mood. She felt peaceful and content, standing alone, gazing at the sublime sunset.

Nothing could touch her here; she felt invigorated and, somehow, the peach light filled her senses with hope.

Reluctantly, she climbed back into the truck and drove the short distance to the house. Sitting for a moment, enjoying her own company, she gathered her phone and shopping from the front seat and got out. She heard the familiar sound of the laughing dove and found comfort in it. It was all she could hear; no traffic, no voices, no music. The unutterable silence sometimes depressed her, sometimes filled her with joy. Today, it made her apprehensive. Should she broach the subject? Should she suggest they went back to the UK as he was now so unhappy here?

She opened the gate and walked to the front door. He must have heard the truck, but there was no sign of David coming to help her with the shopping. Before she even opened the door, she knew what would be waiting for her.

---

Charlie dumped the shopping on the table and began unpacking it, putting everything into the fridge in the right place. She liked everything neat, and she shopped every day here; gone were the days when she did huge online weekly shops back in the UK. Here in Cyprus, she preferred choosing fruit and vegetables herself and getting them as fresh as possible. It also gave her something to do.

Having put it all away, she automatically put the kettle on and looked out of the window. David was in his usual position on the patio: sprawled on a sun lounger, a table by his side on which was the inevitable bottle of red wine. He was wearing a pair of old trunks, his naked chest a mahogany brown. His long, hairy legs stretched out before him. She glanced at her watch, thinking to herself it was getting earlier and earlier. But these days, he needed no excuse to open a bottle.

She opened the back door and walked out.

"Hey, I'm back," she said, stating the obvious.

"Yes, I can see," he said, turning his head towards her. "Good shop?"

"Yes, actually, it was. I got us some fresh sea bream for supper and a watermelon. It's huge."

"Great, but you know I don't like watermelon. Why do you insist on buying them? They're just sweet, watery slush."

"Oh ... you ate it last time I bought one. Anyway, it's not compulsory to eat it. Are you happy with sea bream?" she said, trying to keep the weariness out of her voice.

"Yes," he said. "I'll light the barbecue soon."

David reached for the bottle and sat up, swinging himself into a sitting position. He topped up his glass, took a large gulp of wine and then lay back down, as if it had been a tremendous effort. He picked up the cigarette that was burning in the ashtray on the table, took a deep drag and blew the smoke upwards towards the darkening sky.

"Okay, can you light it? I'm starving," she said, knowing that he'd do it only when he decided.

Dusk was so short here, it went from day to night in a flash; no time to prepare herself for the long night ahead. It was only during the day when she could tell herself that she was happy.

She went back into the house and set about tidying up some unwashed plates and cutlery in the sink. She felt resentful as she scrubbed the dried-on food. Why couldn't he at least do that?

As she picked up one plate to dry it, it slipped through her fingers and smashed loudly on the tiled floor. The noise was deafening and little shards went everywhere, skidding along the floor surface, spreading far and wide.

"Fuck," she shouted, before she could stop herself. She had bare feet, having taken off her flip-flops as she'd come in, to relieve her feet from the sticky heat. She reached for the broom and began sweeping the broken china away from her, reaching for her flip-flops, which she'd dumped on the bookshelf. He must have heard the noise, she thought; *don't come and help, will you?*

If she was honest, she was glad he didn't come in. He'd have only berated her for being clumsy and would have made a real meal of helping. With her sandals now on, she gathered it all into a pile and then brushed it into a dustpan. Searching for any stray pieces, she walked around the room, glancing under chairs and then, finding none, she poured it all into the bin.

She put on some new potatoes to boil, washed some lettuce, prepared the fish and grabbed some crisps, which she put in a bowl and went outside.

"What happened then?"

"I dropped a plate," she said. "Are you going to light it, then?"

"Yes, give us a chance. What time is it, anyway?"

"Six."

"Well, there you are. It's hardly late."

"I know, but as I said, I'm hungry and I'll just end up eating crisps. I'll light it ..." she said. She'd done it loads of times before.

"Charlotte, I said I'd do it. God, you're so impatient."

She hadn't got the energy to argue, so she went back to check on the potatoes and sat down inside. She didn't like being in the house when it was so warm outside. It felt stuffy; at least outside there was a faint breeze, but when he was like this, she'd rather not be near him. These days, the evenings were always the same.

Eventually, he lit the barbecue at about seven, by which time she'd consumed a small packet of peanuts and half a big bag of crisps and didn't feel hungry anymore. She laid the table out on the patio and they sat together in silence. He scrolled through his iPad and she read her book. This happened most nights; they seemed to have run out of things to say to each other. He, by this time, had consumed nearly one and a half bottles of red and she could predict that they'd go inside, turn on the TV and he'd be asleep within seconds. At least he didn't smoke in the house.

It's strange how you can be with someone and still feel lonely, she thought. When did all that love that she'd felt for him years ago start leaking away? Did she love him at all anymore? She loved the David of the past, but she couldn't say she loved the man he'd become. If only he'd snap out of it. What would it take to get him back on track? She decided she'd definitely talk to him in the morning about what would make him happy again.

When they'd finished and they were sitting together on the sofa, her feet in his lap, the TV chattering away, she felt maybe it wasn't as bad as she thought. She and David rubbed along together; they breathed the same air. They'd produced two gorgeous children; was there any more to life? Here they were, living in an idyllic spot on their beloved island of Cyprus; they had enough money to live; they had no real worries. Maybe that was all life had to offer?

At ten, she woke him up and forced him to stumble his way to bed.

"I'll be up in a minute," she said, as he went upstairs.

"Okay, see you up there," he mumbled.

She tidied up, went outside and switched off the pool lights and the lights on the patio, leaving her in absolute darkness. The stars were incredible, and, for a moment, she leant against the railings edging the patio, and looked up at the night sky. She felt utterly alone.

The stars always made her think of Will and Lou, under the same sky, under the same stars. What were they doing at this precise minute? She felt an ache inside; she missed her children so much.

Charlie climbed into bed next to David. He was already snoring peacefully, oblivious of all her worries and thoughts about their future. She must have fallen into a deep sleep about half an hour later.

Later, she would look back and wonder when his heart had stopped ... because in the morning, David was dead beside her.

---

She knew, instinctively.

Despite his heavy drinking, he was an early riser and was nearly always up before her. When she woke, she was lying on her front with her face turned away from him. The strong, early sun was shining through the gap between the bottom of the heavy duty blind and the floor. There were no sounds outside: no traffic; no birdsong; no human conversation. They always left the sliding door open to get some air into the room (with the mosquito netting across the gap) so the silence penetrated the room with its deadening blanket. She lay still, wondering what had woken her. Had David just left the room? The click of the door usually woke her up. But ... she knew he was still in bed.

She slowly turned her head towards him and moved onto her side. He was absolutely still, on his back, as usual. There was no sound of breathing. The sheet was up to his chin; all she could see was his tousled, sleep-messed grey hair and his lifeless face. She knew that if she touched him, he would be stone cold.

Her heart was beating uncontrollably, knocking her chest with its intensity. She was very much alive, she could feel the blood pounding everywhere is her body. Her mind was racing. She had to touch him, to be sure; put her hand on his face.

As she did it, she snatched it back instantly, as its clammy coldness just confirmed what she already knew. Without warning, she vomited on the bed, her stomach cramping and reacting to the reality of the situation. Her mind went completely blank, and she lay back, banging her head on the headboard. She lay motionless for what felt like a long time. It was as if her brain had closed down. She did not know what to do.

She sat up tentatively, rubbed her head and swung her legs down onto the cool, vinyl flooring. She noticed David's clothes piled on the chair; he always put them there neatly, even when he'd drunk a lot. Opening the blind a little, she glanced across at his expressionless face, peering above the white sheet, almost as if he was already in a funeral parlour. The smell of her vomit was overpowering. She went to the cupboard where they kept clean linen.

Starting by rolling up the vomit, she slowly slid the sheet from his body. His legs were straight, his feet pointing upwards. He was wearing his boxers and nothing else; he'd never owned a pair of pyjamas. His body looked both vulnerable and peaceful, his every blemish visible: the scar on his knee that he got years ago when he fell badly on the tennis court; the long wound where he broke his elbow; the scar on his cheekbone where he'd needed six stitches. His long toes were slightly curled; one arm was by his side, the other was lying across his chest.

She bundled up the sheet and placed it outside the door. Opening out a new sheet, she lay it gently over his body, wanting to protect it from the light. She didn't put it over his face; that was too much. His eyes were closed and if she didn't know, she'd have said he was merely sleeping.

It didn't seem right to cover his face. *He can't be dead, surely?*

Charlie rinsed out her mouth and brushed her teeth to get rid of the acid taste in her mouth. She got dressed, the silence of the house ringing in her ears. Shaking, she found the simple task of finding her clothes and putting them on too much.

She didn't know what to do. She should ring someone, shouldn't she? If only she could have rung Beth, her dearest friend.

Charlie went downstairs and slumped on the sofa in the half-light. She knew she had to do something. Having left her mobile charging overnight on the kitchen top, she went over to it, unplugged it and went to Contacts. She looked for the only person she could think of, scrolling down: a young doctor, who lived in the village and who had a surgery. She'd been to her for various trivial health concerns and found her efficient. It was early to call her. Her phone told her it was 6.45, but she clicked on the green telephone symbol, anyway.

After a few rings, the doctor answered. Charlotte had not cried until this point, but when Dr Theloudes asked her how she could help, she could hardly speak.

"My husband ... has died ... in the night. He's lying in our bed. I don't ... know what ... to do."

There ... she had said it out loud. It was real.

There was no denying it.

# CHAPTER 12

"Come on, kids ... neither of you is remotely ready, and we've got to leave in twenty minutes. Bella, go and find a hairbrush and Jack, do your teeth and get your things together."

Lou wished she didn't have to go through the same routine every single day. Harry was never ready, and she was always stressed because he was always in the shower, on a Zoom call, or still asleep. Why was it always *her* responsibility to get them to school? How had they arrived? Immaculate conception?

"Mum, I can't find my brush," Bella shouted from upstairs. "Where is it?"

"How should I know? Look properly."

"I have," she yelled; Lou could hear her stamping around in frustration. She could hear Jack's electric toothbrush coming from the downstairs loo, so at least *that* was happening.

Where *was* Harry, anyway? She'd left him sitting sleepily on the side of his bed, scrolling through his phone. Surely he should be down by now? Didn't he say he had a meeting in the office at 9.15?

"Harry," she shouted up the stairs. "What's happening?"

After a pause, which was just long enough to wind her up, he emerged at the top of the stairs, hair wet, looking the image of the tech bro he was: fashionable specs, long hair that he was, at that moment, tying back; hipster backpack already on; dressed for his cycle ride to his co-working space, called, imaginatively, Co-Place, an uber fashionable, glass and steel monument to the gods of digital working. Having tied his hair, he ran down the stairs and went to the fridge, grabbing a box of healthy salad that he'd prepared the night before. Lou stood there, watching, amazed at his ability to ignore the surrounding chaos.

"What time are you home?" she asked, hoping it might be in time to help with the kids.

"Hopefully, by the kids' bedtime; my last meeting's at 4 pm, but you know how these things go on. I'll text."

He snatched a piece of sourdough bread off the work surface and folded it in two with a large dollop of peanut butter and began eating it as he picked up his helmet.

"Must go ... bye kids, have a great day." He came over to Lou, hugged her and kissed her on the cheek, which she hardly had time to reciprocate before he was through the door, running down more stairs to his bike, which was padlocked to the railings that surrounded their front garden.

If only life was so simple, Lou thought, as she contemplated her day: somehow getting the kids through the door on time, fed, watered and with everything they needed for school; walking them to school, which was a fifteen minute route march; rushing to the tube; running up the escalators to the exit; catching the 42 to her office ... and that was all before 9.30. I wish I had a wife like me, she thought. She loved Harry to bits, but god, he was annoying sometimes.

"Mum, I've done my hair, but do you know where my homework is? You know, the thing you helped me do last night? I need it for Miss Thomas this morning. She said we had to bring it in to show her."

"Yes, it's on the side, there, look!" Lou said, pointing. She still thought Bella was too young, at seven, to be given homework — why didn't teachers realise it meant that the parents ended up having to do most of it? Didn't the lovely Miss Thomas not see that I actually have a few other things to do with my so-called spare time?

"Oh, and I need to take in a picture of us as a family; we're making a collage of everyone in the class."

"Great. Couldn't you have told me this last night?" said Lou, quickly kneeling down and rummaging through the cupboard that had boxes of photos she'd promised herself she would put in an album one day. She tipped out one box, flipping through the contents, desperately trying to find a photo she wouldn't mind giving away. At last, she found one: she and Harry were sitting on a bench down in Cornwall, with the kids on their laps. They were all squinting a bit, as the sun was in their eyes, but she felt it gave a good impression of them; they looked healthy, happy and none of them were pulling weird expressions. There was another similar one, so she didn't mind giving this one to the school. I wonder who took it, she thought? It was only last year, and she had no recollection of what random stranger they had asked to take the picture.

"Here you are. This'll have to do," she said, as she handed it over.

"Oh, that's a good one," said Bella. "Do you remember Uncle Will took it? I *loved* that holiday."

The memory flooded back into her head like a torrent. When Will was okay. She felt suddenly sad.

"Yea, it was a lovely holiday, wasn't it?" she said, as she stood back up again, rubbing her back. She glanced at another picture, framed on the bookshelf, of Mum, Dad, her and Will all together for once, smiling and laughing on a beach. Will looked so young and carefree in the true sense of the word. Care Free. No cares, no worries.

"Right, I'm leaving and you two have got to be at the door in two minutes. Jack, here's your coat and both of you, here are your packed lunches. All your favourites: a banana, crackers with cream cheese; carrot sticks; baby tomatoes and a yoghurt. Oh, and a couple of biscuits."

"No crisps?" said Jack.

"No, Jack, no crisps. Right, we're off."

They set off up the hill towards the main road, turned left and made their way, slowly, up to the traffic lights where they had to cross. Jack was easier than Bella, but he tended to dawdle, drop things, and not focus on where he was going. Today, it was all Lou could do to keep him walking. He kept seeing cats in windows, or, the latest diversion was a ladybird on a wall, which he insisted on trying to pick up to 'show his teacher'. She tried to keep her cool, but sometimes you needed the patience of the proverbial saint. She persuaded him that the ladybird would prefer to stay where it was.

"Come on, guys, we're going to be late ..." and as the green man lit up, she grabbed his hand and pulled him over the pedestrian crossing.

As they arrived at the school gates, she saw all the usual suspects, looking as if for them the school run was just simply part of their serene morning routine. Did no one else have to work she wondered?

"Bye, kids," she shouted, as she bundled them through the gate into the playground, kissing them as they went. "Have a lovely day ... I'll collect you from After-School Club at 5.30." They ran happily past Mr. Hazel, the Headmaster, who greeted them both by name. She always thought that was impressive. How on earth did he remember all their names like that?

Lou walked away, guiltily feeling relieved that for a few hours, they were someone else's responsibility. She wondered if she had time to collect a coffee from the kiosk; she could seriously do with one. Hell, yes, she would.

While she was waiting in line to order her oat milk, flat white, no sugar, her mobile rang. Pulling it from her bag, she was surprised to see a call from 'Mum'. She never rang in the morning; she was too busy swimming and lounging about in the sun. Lucky cow! Anyway, we'd arranged to speak tonight, she thought. Had she got time to speak to her now? Maybe she should ...

She pressed the green phone and said, "Mum, hi ... I'm just in a ..."

"Lou, where are you? Are you with anyone? Something terrible's happened."

---

If anyone was to peak into the darkened, smelly room, you could make out a lump under the bedclothes, a mass of dark hair on the pillow covering the face of the owner, and hear absolutely nothing, except the gentle snore emanating from the body in the bed. The overall impression was of an unkempt room: curtains pulled but gaping and shabby; clothes piled on the floor and heaped on a chair. The kitchen part of the room had dirty plates piled in the sink and a litter bin full to over-flowing with beer cans. There was nothing that showed that the occupier had a family or friends. The loneliness oozed from every wall, every surface.

It was 10 am and the body in the bed stirred, as a light vibration came from his mobile, which was on the beside table. It was fighting for a place along with a book, a pill bottle, an empty wine bottle and some cash. As it vibrated, it moved slightly; it was hanging over the edge in the first place, so it didn't take much for it to fall with a clatter onto the wooden floor.

Will changed position onto his back and slowly opened his eyes. He moved his hair off his face and lay there for a good few more minutes, taking in the disgusting state of his room.

With a "Fuck," he sat up and leaned back against the wall. "Christ, what a shit hole," he murmured out loud to nobody. He rubbed his eyes, as if this would dispel the sight before him, but unfortunately, it was still as bad when he'd finished. Vaguely recollecting the sound of the vibration, he leaned over the side of the bed and retrieved his phone. He pressed the message app symbol:

> Will, please call me urgently. Why the hell aren't you picking up? Lou.

Will stared at the message for a long time, his eyes not blinking. He rarely heard from Lou these days and what did she mean, *why aren't you picking up?* He then noticed three missed calls from her in the last hour. What the hell?

All he knew was that he needed a coffee before he did anything; he couldn't function without one. Swinging his legs over the side of the bed, he walked the few steps needed to get to the kettle and filled it up, looking around for the coffee. He hadn't sunk so low as to drink instant coffee, but sometimes he wished he *could* drink it; he couldn't be bothered with the faff of washing out the grounds from the cafetière and it was constantly bunging up the drain in the sink. Still, he did just that now, swilling it under the running tap, not caring about the consequences.

He sat back on the bed with his mug full of steaming, strong black coffee and began to feel a bit more human as the liquid hit his throat. His day stretched ahead of him and he could see no light; just existing. Working in a bar wasn't how his life was meant to be. How had his dreams been reduced to this? He looked at his watch; there was only an hour before he had to be there and he wasn't sure he could face it.

Looking again at the message app, he thought, *what the hell did she want that was so urgent?* She'd have to wait until he was at least dressed and ready for work; he hadn't got time now. Lou, with her perfect family and her perfect life.

He opened the door and walked down the corridor to the shared bathroom; he hated it. Strangers' hair in the shower; mould on the tiles, and dirty floors. Showering as quickly as possible, he got out, a towel round his waist. He glanced at his reflection in the mirror; he looked thinner than last time he'd bothered to look.

He dressed in jeans and a loose fitting t-shirt and cleaned his teeth in the sink, trying to ignore the mess everywhere. He forced himself to wash up and even dried most of it up. Was he putting off ringing Lou? He couldn't face her right now. She'd just start on the same track. *Pull yourself together, get a better job, stop drinking, don't take drugs.* She did his head in.

He headed out; he'd call her on his walk to the bar. That way, he could make an excuse to cut the call short — *got to go, I've made it to work.*

As he got to the street, he was walking along when his phone vibrated in his pocket. Reluctantly, he took it out and read the message.

> I didn't want to tell you by text but as you haven't rung me back, I've got no option. Mum's just told me — Dad died in the night. I'm sorry, Will. Ring me. xx

Will looked around, as if searching for something in the distance. His whole body felt drained of blood, his lips were dry, his heart pumping. He leaned against a wall, eyes closed, sweating. The noise of the street crowded round him, filling his ears.

"Are you all right, mate?" someone said. "You look as if you need to sit down. There's a seat here," and they took Will's arm and led him to a wooden bench. "Sit here for a while."

Before he could thank him, the stranger had gone, leaving him alone to face his reality. Tears washed into his eyes; he felt like a child again. How could this devastating event feel so ordinary, so detached from him? Was it that he'd only heard about it by text? Or was it because he was a horrible person whose life was devoid of feeling?

Dad was dead. The father who'd been such a big part of his life and brought him up ... but the man who he'd fought with, who'd wound him up, who'd hated his choices, was no longer part of the world.

The last time Will had spoken to his father, his exact words were: *Fuck off. Why don't you let me get on with my life?*

Well, he'd certainly done that.

After Will got back from Thailand, he couldn't work out where to go. His parents had sold the family home in Wiltshire, so that wasn't an option. Even if they'd still been in the UK, it was the last place he'd go.

His friends were all in Birmingham, but he couldn't go back there; they'd all moved on without him. He wasn't a student anymore, he wouldn't fit in. He wasn't sure if he ever wanted to go back to studying ... maybe it wasn't for him? Three years totally wasted, ruined by the pandemic, looking at books, when you could be out there, doing something, *anything* ...

His sister lived in London. They got on okay, as long as they didn't spend too much time together; after a week in each other's company, they would usually revert to being children, with Lou being her annoying, bossy self and Will deliberately winding her up. They'd end up having horrendous rows and even resorting to the old kind of physical fights they'd had in the past. Lou had such strong opinions about everything; he couldn't compete.

He loved Bella and Jack, though; they definitely helped with the dynamic between him and his sister. They appeared to love him being around and they made him feel 'present' and loved. Harry, he liked, but was jealous of him in a weird way; he'd never want to work in tech, like him, and he'd hate to be saddled with a wife and kids, but ... he envied his success, his stability and his loving family. He could see what a great dad he was to Bella and Jack. Unlike his own dad, Harry had endless patience and was never too tired to play with them. The four of them were definitely a great unit, and their home felt like a haven from the outside world.

They lived in Notting Hill and so he'd moved to London, to be near them. He didn't admit this to Lou. She'd have only taken the mick out of him, but at least if one member of his family was near, he wouldn't feel so alone. He'd always wanted to end up in London, anyway ... so he took the plunge.

One day, he told her he didn't know what to do with his life and she was remarkably understanding. She tried to give him advice, but he wasn't in the mood to listen, but he was grateful that she saw it from his point of view. Harry kept telling him to retrain in computer programming, but it didn't appeal. He could see that computers were where the money and jobs were, but ... he wanted to *create* something; he just didn't know what.

He enjoyed forgetting about everything about his life with the kids, mucking about with them after they got home from school. He loved being fed decent food and sleeping in a comfortable bed in his own room, instead of in a Thai dormitory full of strangers ... but the craving to smoke weed was still there and his sister caught him smoking in the garden on his fourth day with them. She gave him an ultimatum of three days to get out and find himself somewhere else to live.

"I'm not having you smoking dope around the kids, Will ... I'm sorry, you might think I'm being a prude, but I feel really strongly about drugs and you have no right to use them in our home."

"It was only a bit of weed ..."

"It may be 'only a bit of weed' to *you*, Will, but to me, it's the start of the slippery slope ..."

"Oh, for God's sake, Lou, don't be such a hypocrite. I seem to remember you getting very drunk when you were a student."

"It's not the same thing ..."

"Alcohol is just as bad, if not worse than weed ... alcohol is a drug, you know."

"Look, shut up, Will. I don't care what you say, I'm telling you, I don't like it. For all I know, you're snorting cocaine in the house, too."

"Of course I'm *not*," said Will, knowing full well that he did just that, only the day before. "But if you want me to go, I'll go." He hated himself for what he'd done and didn't put up a fight. He was probably better off on his own somewhere.

So that's how he'd ended up in his disgusting bedsit, with his shitty pub job, down the road in shitty Willesden.

# CHAPTER 13

*Fuck off. Why don't you let me get on with my own life?*
The last words he'd said to his dad were crashing round his head as he turned away from the pub where he was working. Will couldn't go in, not now; all he wanted to do was to go home, if you could call the shitty bedsit he was living in, 'home'. He wanted to be anywhere but here, on the street. He started walking back in a daze.

As he opened the door to his smelly little room, he felt as if he was going to be sick and went and lay on his bed, the curtains still closed, the light putrid and yellow. He stared up at the ceiling, his eyes unfocussed, his mind in turmoil. He couldn't get his mind around it: his father was dead.

They'd hardly had any contact with each other; when his parents had fucked off to Cyprus, he'd been relieved. He missed his mum, but his father's ever-present criticism of every aspect of his life had seeped into the very pores of his body, making Will not only hate himself, but loathing being anywhere near his father.

That's why he hadn't visited them on the island; he couldn't face it. And the bloody pandemic.

Will had decided long ago that his father hated him. It went back to when he was deciding what subjects to take for 'A' levels; Will was artistic and wanted to take arts subjects. His father had got it into his head that he would follow him into the military and, of course, the subjects he needed were science subjects for that. The military was about the last career he'd *ever* considered; why his dad thought like that, God alone knew. He never hassled Lou to join up, so why was it different for him? But it always had been. He'd expected him to play men's sports, like rugby, but Will had always preferred individual sports, like gymnastics and athletics. David just couldn't understand him and when he forced Will to join the local football team, he'd run up and down the sidelines shouting encouragement … and swearing at Will when he missed a goal.

Will got his way with his 'A' level choices; Charlie intervened on his behalf and at a parent/teacher evening, the staff confirmed Will's ability. His Art teacher even said Will was one of the most talented artists he'd ever taught. David was even unimpressed by this information, but found he was outnumbered. When Will made his final decision: art, English and history, his father took it as a personal affront.

Their relationship during those two years went from bad to worse; they constantly argued and Will became more and more estranged from the whole family. Lou had her own life to lead and avoided the constant tension. She was already married to Harry and had two children quickly, so she didn't get involved, but she hated the confrontations between Will and her dad.

Will got into Birmingham university, to read English, but had regretted his choice almost immediately. He'd really wanted to go to art school to pursue his dream of becoming an artist but had, after much persuasion, compromised. Both his parents had said that he could paint as a hobby in his free time; he didn't need to study it, in order to paint, did he? He'd finally given in.

He found the academic study of English mind-blowingly tedious. The essays that were expected of him were too much; the amount of reading he had to do made him anxious. He started missing tutorials and seminars (he'd never read the thing they were discussing anyway) and then he failed his first year exams; he was given the opportunity to take them again and scraped through. The rest of his time at uni was blighted by the pandemic, being confined to his digs and doing most of his work online. He hated it and when he got a third at the end of three years of misery, he couldn't wait to get away.

A group of friends at Birmingham had decided to go backpacking around Thailand; the pandemic was all but over and travel there was now allowed; Will had got some money in the bank that had been given to him over the years, which was going towards buying a house, but he couldn't see a future for himself anymore. He'd withdraw the money and blow it on travelling. He told his parents where he was going, but they weren't happy about it.

Fuck the future.

He started smoking weed in Thailand, but it soon progressed to other, more potent drugs. All his friends were doing it; every beach party they went to revolved around bonfires, swimming, alcohol and drugs. Soon, he couldn't enjoy himself unless he'd 'taken the edge off' with some illegal substance. The local liquor was evil; the combination of that, weed, cocaine and sun, took its toll.

His three best friends were all returning to uni to MAs, so they went home at the end of September, leaving Will with people he'd met out there who were, in effect, strangers. He drifted from beach to beach, sometimes sleeping rough, the rest of the time dossing in cheap lodgings. Some of his stuff was stolen, he lost his passport, and it was only with the help of the British Embassy that he eventually got home.

His savings were now non-existent, and he depended on drugs to give him some self-esteem. His parents didn't know how bad things were. He wanted to talk to his mum, but wanted nothing to do with his father, so he'd texted her occasionally, but when he didn't come back, she frantically tried to ring him to find out what was happening. He eventually picked up and spoke to her, confessing that he didn't have a clue what to do with his life.

"But where are you, Will? We can talk about it. We can help you decide what you're going to do next."

"Mum, I can't come home; you know why. Anyway, where is home? I can't speak to Dad any more ... he won't understand. I'm going to get a job, do *something*, just to earn some money. I'll try to work out what I'm going to do, but I want to do it ... on my own."

"But Will, tell me where you are."

"No, Mum, it's best this way. I'm going to make my own way."

"Why don't you come out to Cyprus? Get some sun, get some perspective ..."

"Can you imagine the welcome I'd get? I really don't think it's a good idea, Mum."

"Look, your dad's here ... he'd just like a word with you ..." and he could hear his father's voice in the background. He was tempted to end the call. "No, Mum, I don't want to speak ..."

"Hello Will ... what's all this I'm gathering at this end? I told you that English was a stupid subject to take, but you wouldn't listen to me, as always. But now you've got to face the consequences; work out how you're going to use this useless degree of yours. Where the hell are you, anyway? Your mother's going demented here."

Will listened to him with a feeling of dread. If only he had a father he could talk to, relate to; someone who understood how he was feeling. Lost ... that's how he was feeling ... and this tirade was making everything worse. He had no idea how he was going to carry on with life. And that's when he'd said it.

*Fuck off. Why don't you let me get on with my own life?* ... and he'd hit the red end call button and had not spoken to either of his parents since. His mum had tried to ring him endlessly, but he'd not picked up.

His Dad had never even tried.

He felt guilt, shame and sadness but ... he also felt that if he'd been a decent father, he would have wanted to help him.

Surely any proper dad would have?

# CHAPTER 14

The day following David's death went by in a blur of confusion, grief, and guilt.

*If only I'd been awake when it happened ... if only I'd tried to stop him drinking himself to death ... if only I'd loved him more ... if only we hadn't grown so indifferent to each other.*

*If only ... he was still alive.*

The doctor had come round to the house within half an hour of their phone call. When she put the phone down, Charlie had slumped on the sofa, waiting for someone to come and take the body of her husband away. She couldn't bear it. David, his essence, she knew, had gone forever. She'd never see him again; never hear his voice again, never feel his lips on hers again or his arms around her. How can someone simply disappear off the face of the earth?

She stared at a large black-and-white photograph taken at their wedding, on the wall opposite her. It was a huge, framed print that had been with them on various walls since that day, so many years ago.

The photographer had been good at capturing intimate moments, and this had been one of their favourites. It was taken at the reception, under the old oak tree. They'd finished all the official photos and were simply chatting and laughing together, oblivious to everyone around them. He'd grabbed a candid shot, without them even noticing; they were far too involved in each other. They were in profile with the sun behind them, lighting Charlie's veil and the leaves that framed them. She was gazing into David's eyes with such love, a love she'd felt for him that she'd forgotten over the intervening years. He was laughing, looking down at her, his hand resting on her face. The picture captured, in one split second, the feeling she'd had that day of absolute happiness and hope. Tears sprung to her eyes, and she sobbed.

She thought of her university days; she'd met lots of guys, had plenty of fun times, but it wasn't until she met David that evening that everything had fallen into place. Until then, she'd wondered why she hadn't felt that overwhelming love and attraction that all her girlfriends had talked about; it was an alien concept to her, and she'd wondered if something was wrong with her. Why couldn't *she* feel passionately about someone? Maybe she was trying too hard? Maybe she wasn't ready? But then this handsome man had walked into the party: tall, sandy-haired, insanely handsome with his military bearing, his easy laugh and his confidence. She felt instantly attracted to him; so much so that she could, even now, all these years later, remember the thudding of her heart, the sick feeling in her stomach and the pull of his eyes across the room. She got herself near him by making some excuse to be at the bar at the same time as him, and it took only seconds before he was offering to get her a drink. They drifted away from their friends to sit together, away from the chaos and noise ... and before long, they were talking as if they'd known each other for years. It all seemed so natural, so easy, and so ... perfect. They exchanged numbers and that night, when she was in bed alone, she could distinctly remember thinking: *I'm going to marry that man,* which was crazy, as she'd only known him for a few hours.

Things had moved very fast after that. They'd got together whenever they could, and David had driven for hours to visit her. They'd snatched weekends when all they did was make love, laugh and talk into the small hours. The fact that they lived miles apart intensified their feelings and before long, it was understood that they both wanted to be together forever. He'd bought her a ring, and he'd proposed one year to the day after they'd met.

They'd married the summer she left uni; there was no time to lose. Why wait? They wanted to be together. Her parents had tried to persuade her to wait at least a year, but she didn't want to hear their sensible arguments. She hated it when David left her. She felt as if part of her was gone whenever he drove away. Marriage felt like it was the answer to everything.

A knock on the door, which broke the silence of the house, brought her back to the present. She stood up, rubbed her eyes and stared at the front door, not wanting to face what would inevitably follow. Until now, it had just been her ... and David. Now, the outside world would invade and make it real.

She shook her head, trying to clear her thoughts, and opened the door to the kind, young lady doctor.

"Come in," Charlie said and tears flooded her eyes ... and so it all began. The doctor was empathetic and professional with her smart clothes, bag and fixed smile; Charlie recognised she needed help and succumbed to her expertise.

"I'm so sorry for your loss. I know this must be the most awful situation for you ... I'm here to help you through it. I will deal with everything. You don't have to worry. Is there someone you can call? Friends, family ... neighbours?"

"I need to call my children, but they're in the UK ..."

"Of course. Is there someone locally you'd like to call? Someone who could come round and give you support?" She hadn't made that many friends here; only one person sprang to mind but ...

"Yes ... maybe ... but I don't think I can deal with anyone else at the moment. Can we just get on and do what we have to do? He's ... David is upstairs. Can you come up and see him?" she said, leading the way.

There was a part of her that wanted the doctor to say that she was mistaken. Had she got it all wrong? But of course he was dead; the doctor spent a few minutes checking, while Charlie stood helplessly by the bed ... but when the sheet was drawn up over his face, she knew it was over.

All those years together ended in that moment.

She could hear the shock in Lou's voice.

"Oh my God, Mum. What do you mean, Dad's died? I don't believe you ... How? When?" and then there was the sound of a commotion, of people talking and Lou sobbing. If only there had been a better way. How could you tell your only daughter that her father was dead over the phone? Charlie felt sick.

"Lou, Lou ... are you all right?"

After a few seconds, Lou came back onto the phone, her voice quieter, shaky. There were people in the background. "Where are you? Are you with people who can help?"

"Yes, Mum. I'm with people. Tell me again."

"Lou, my love ... your dad died in his sleep," she said slowly. Even saying the words seemed unreal. "He died peacefully. The doctor is with me now, so don't worry. I'm okay." Charlie was trying so hard not to cry. Her throat felt constricted.

"But what do you mean, he died in his sleep? How can that happen? He wasn't ill ... surely you'd know ..."

"Lou, I woke up, and he'd died. I don't know why but ..."

"How can someone go to sleep and never wake up again? It's not possible." Lou's voice sounded strangled and strange. Charlie heard people trying to comfort her; a woman was telling her to sit on a chair.

"Mum, I'll come out ... I'll come to be with you. I'll leave the kids with Harry. Oh my God, Dad's dead," she sobbed.

"Lou, Lou, you'll be okay ... you'll be okay. You don't need to come ..." She knew she wasn't making any sense. How could Lou's life ever be okay again?

"Mum, I'm going to go now. I'll ring you ..." and the phone went dead. Charlie stared at it, willing it to spring to life with her daughter's voice again.

She called Will, but his phone rang and rang. It was early in the UK ... but surely he should be up by now? Charlie worried about him constantly and when he didn't answer his phone, which happened all the time, she always assumed the worst. She didn't want to text him. She'd have to try again in an hour.

Where was he?

An ambulance appeared, like magic, arriving down their road and hovering by their gate, an evil presence.

She hadn't called for one; she wouldn't have known how to call for one here.

Two men came to the door. The doctor showed them in and explained they should go upstairs.

"So, we're going to take your husband's body now, Mrs Greene. You don't have to worry about anything for the moment. I just want to make sure you have someone who can be with you."

"I've called my daughter, but my son hasn't picked up." She was looking at the doctor to tell her what to do.

"But is there someone here, in Cyprus?"

"Yes ... I'll phone ... Jane. She'll come."

"Good. I'd like you to call her now, before I leave, so I know you'll be okay."

At that moment, the two men were at the top of the stairs, with David's body on a stretcher between them. How would she ever be okay?

They manoeuvred David slowly and carefully down the stairs; the doctor opened the front door for them. She stayed inside the house as Charlie followed them to the vehicle. They placed him gently inside, closed the doors, and within a few minutes, they had driven off.

Charlie was left standing in the middle of the small road, staring at the receding ambulance. It finally disappeared from view, leaving her utterly alone in the sunny landscape. The sun, the blue sky, the sea were out of place, in this utterly dark moment.

The silence of the surrounds of the house echoed with utter stillness and quiet. Nothing moved, for it was a windless day: the branches of the carob trees on the bondu didn't move, the sea in the distance was as flat and blue as a painting, the cliffs as white as the sheet over David's face. Distant skyscrapers in Limassol stood incongruously on the skyline. The sky itself was a piercing blue, dotted with fluffy, cotton wool clouds. The loneliness of her situation smashed into her mind; they'd chosen this house for its peace, its view ... but now there was nothing ... but silence.

"Mrs Greene ..." called the doctor from the house. "Please come in and we'll call your friend."

Charlie stumbled back into the house. There weren't even any goats meandering through the rocky, rusty earth; they always closed the gate in case they came into their garden, but she shut the gate anyway, through force of habit. One of the countless feral cats that lived nearby met her; it meowed mournfully at her, ever hopeful that maybe, just maybe, today might be the day that she would feed it. David hated the cats and never allowed her to befriend them; he would shout at them and was even known to kick them. She automatically leant down to stroke its back, and it wound its way through her legs. It tried to follow her into the house, but she quickly closed the door.

Would Jane want to come, she wondered, as she found her mobile and scrolled for her number? Jane was the one person she felt she could talk to. She'd only known her for a few months; they'd met randomly at an exercise class and they'd immediately taken to each other. Jane was a widow; her husband had died two years ago, and she'd decided to stay in Cyprus, despite pleas from her only daughter to go back to the UK. Jane was the one person here that knew the true extent of David's drinking; Charlie had told her everything one night when they'd met for a meal at a taverna. She'd told Jane how lonely she felt, how disappointed she was with her life ... but later she felt disloyal and asked her to keep it to herself. She'd felt relieved, however, to have been able to unburden herself. Jane was a good friend.

"Hi Jane ... could you ... come over?"

"Are you okay? Your voice sounds odd."

"I'll explain ... could you possibly ... come ... right now?"

"Of course. Give me five mins and I'll be there."

Jane was sitting next to Charlie on the sofa, her warm presence helping her more than she'd imagined.

She'd arrived at her door in the obligatory shorts and t-shirt, sunglasses and pink cap; she always looked ready for action and went nowhere without her bright red lipstick on her full lips. When Jane saw the doctor and Charlie's stricken face, she'd known she'd walked into something, but couldn't have guessed how bad. The colour drained from her face when she was told what had happened.

Charlie was sitting down with her head in hands. Jane assured the doctor that she could be with her; she didn't tell the truth, which was that she was meant to be playing a round of golf that morning. She would, of course, cancel.

The doctor left and Jane got up and busied herself, making them both a cup of coffee.

"Here you are. Get this down you. You look as white as a sheet."

"It's been such a shock."

"Of course. It must have been terrible for you. I can't imagine ... Poor David."

"Yes, poor David. I can't believe it."

Silence fell between them. "So ... have you told your children?"

"I've told Lou, but I can't get hold of Will. It's a nightmare. I don't know what I can do. This will be devastating for him."

"How was Lou when you told her?"

"It was the worst thing I've ever had to do, Jane. I felt so helpless," she said, wiping her eyes. "I could hear her crying, people helping ... and I couldn't do a thing. She said she's going to come out but ..."

"She's bound to want to ... maybe they could come out together, Lou and Will?"

"Maybe, but she's got two children."

"I'm sure under the circumstances, her husband could look after them?"

"We'll see ..."

At that moment, her phone vibrated. It was lying on the coffee table and they both stared at it, wondering who was calling. Jane leant forward and handed it to her. "It's Will ..."

"Oh, god ..."

"You must answer it."

"I know." She stood up and pressed the green symbol. "Will ..."

"Mum ... I've had a text from Lou. I'm so sorry, Mum ... I can't believe it. What do you want me to do?"

Just hearing his voice, so quiet, so far away, made Charlie cry. She couldn't think of one word to say that would offer any comfort to him. She remembered the fractured relationship he'd had with his dad; the rows, the shouting, the misunderstandings ... David's death would bring no closure for Will.

"Will ... it's been such a shock ... I'm not thinking straight at the moment. I've got my friend, Jane, with me, so you don't need to worry. Maybe you and Lou ... could come out here ... in a few days' time? It would be lovely to be with you both. I need time to work out what to do."

"Of course, Mum ... we'll come out. I'll ring Lou now. I love you, Mum ... I'm so, so sorry."

"I love you too, Will." She added, "Dad loved you, you know that, don't you?"

There was a long pause before he said, "I'll text when I know when we're coming."

"Okay, my love. Bye, Will."

"Bye, Mum."

# CHAPTER 15

"So, why don't you and I go out to be with Mum tomorrow? I'm sure we could get a flight," said Will. They were sitting in Lou's kitchen, both with cups of coffee in front of them, which they were ignoring.

"I'm not sure if I can get away that easily, Will," said Lou, dragging her hand through her hair, tears wet on her face. "I've got two children, a husband, a job, a house ... I can't just drop everything, like you."

Will could see she was really struggling with the reality of everything, and all his brotherly love for her came to him unexpectedly, mixed with anger for his father. How could he just die in his sleep like that? So typical of him to leave without warning.

"I'm sure you could. It's not every day that your father drops dead."

Lou stared at him, her face a picture of grief. He hadn't meant to be so harsh. "Sorry, Sis ... but I'm sure Harry could hold the fort for a few days, and your work would understand ... Mum *needs* us."

Lou had rung Harry, and he was on his way back. Will had felt the need to be with family. Lou had sounded so distraught when he'd eventually spoken to her on the phone.

"I'm sure we can work something out," he said, dreading the reality of seeing his mother.

When Harry arrived half an hour later, he said, of course, he could look after everything and that they should go over to Cyprus to be with their mum. So, they went on the internet and found a flight leaving at 2.30 the next day from Gatwick.

Lou had to buy him his ticket as he had no money, but she didn't question it. Normally, she would have had to make some derogatory comment, but she wasn't functioning normally.

They'd stay for five days.

---

Charlie set out to collect the kids (as she still thought of them) from the airport. She'd looked up their progress on the app and could see they were only about thirty minutes away from landing.

The motorway, as always, was quiet; it was now pitch black and the few lights that came towards her hurt her eyes. She'd done so much crying that her eyes felt weak, sore and stingy, but she was determined to put on a brave face. She wanted to be strong and show them she was coping. She was grieving for the David she'd married, and the many years they'd had together. However bad it had become, she still missed him. She loved him and wondered if she'd *ever* get over the shock of his death. The future looked bleak ... but she didn't want to burden the children with her thoughts. They had their lives to live.

She parked in the car park and walked across to the building. There was the normal hubbub of taxis coming and going and taxi drivers hovering around the door, looking for potential customers. There were even a few holding up signs with people's names on them. She looked up at the board and saw their plane had landed five minutes ago; they wouldn't have luggage, so it wouldn't be long to wait. She watched people emerging from various flights, with friends and family greeting them with hugs. One couple launched into a long kiss. Such different circumstances to theirs; Charlie had to look away.

Charlie visualised David, waving to Lou as she'd come through the large door and realised that it was the last time her father would ever greet Lou. Almost immediately after travel restrictions had been lifted, she'd come on her own for five days and it had been a magical time. As she grew up and became an adult, David had found her easier to deal with; Lou, the child he'd found difficult, but Lou, the grown-up, had become his friend and confidant. She knew Lou would be devastated.

She was just beginning to wonder where they were when she saw Will's face amongst a group of people, with Lou trailing behind him. Charlie waved, and he raised his hand. He looked back at his sister, waiting for her to catch up, and then they both walked towards her. Will simply came to her and lent against her, not saying anything. Charlie put her arms around him, feeling the warmth of his body, smelling his 'Will' scent and feeling his body tremble a little. She turned to Lou and hugged her. None of them knew what to say; there were no words.

"Good journey?" she said, for want of something else to say.

"Yeah, as good as any four and half hour journey crammed in a plane can be," said Will, putting his arm through hers. "How are you, Mum? Are you okay? It's such a terrible shock, you must ..." He couldn't continue; he just drew her into a hug again, squeezing her hard.

"Not too bad, Will. But let's just get you back to the house. You must be exhausted." She led them towards the outside of the building. "It's a shame you won't be able to get any impression of Cyprus until tomorrow. Lou, is the family okay without you?"

She knew she was talking for the sake of it, saying anything that popped into her head, rather than talking about the reason they were here, but Lou went along with it and told her all about the arrangements she'd made before she left, so that Harry could 'kind of' continue working. All her mum-friends had rallied round and offered to have the kids after school, so that he didn't have to leave work early.

As they walked across to the car, Will said, "Wow, it's warm here, compared to England. I can't believe how lovely it is at 9.30 at night."

"Yes, it's around 25 degrees for the whole time you're here ... like a brief holiday for you both."

This was met by silence. What could you say? They were here because their father had died, not for a holiday, but Will had to admit to himself he was glad to be away from Willesden. Why had he never come out here before? Was it pig-headedness or because his dad made him feel so unwanted? Now, he wasn't sure ... but he felt guilty for never having made the effort.

They climbed into the truck and made their way down the long, straight road leading away from the airport that, even in the dark, they could see was lined by bougainvillea. They were soon on the two-lane highway, passing the white, moon-like hills which loomed each side of the road, with large advertising signs lit up with unknown brands and real estate. Charlie had Greek music playing quietly on the radio, which hid the lack of words in the car. They were all thinking about the one person who wasn't there. His presence, or lack of it, dominated the ride back.

Will gazed through the dusty windows at the passing scenery. It felt alien and imposing and he realised how little he'd thought of his parents living their new life out here. They'd become strangers, living their sun-filled lives away from him.

"We're nearly there now, Will. We've just got to go through the village. It's odd that you've never been here before. It will be nice to show you where we've been living. You liked it, didn't you, Lou?"

"Yes, I loved it, Mum. I wished I'd come more."

They continued down an amber-lit road with large detached houses on the left and right, and then they wound round and down a hill. They pulled up outside the house; Will had, of course, seen pictures of it, but seeing it in real life was odd. His parents had been living here, in this house. Why had he felt the need to get away from them? Even if he and his dad didn't get on, he should have been closer to his mum. *I'm such a selfish bastard,* he thought, hating himself.

They got out and Charlie locked the truck, which flashed its lights officiously to say it was now secure. She opened the front door and led them inside.

"What do you think, then, Will? Do you like it?"

"It looks lovely, Mum," he said, dumping his rucksack on the wooden coffee table. "How long ago was it you came, Lou?"

"Last summer, when travel restrictions lifted; I remember I had to have documents about Covid vaccinations. We had such a lovely time, didn't we, Mum? Dad was very laid back and relaxed here. Less stressed than when he was in the UK."

Lou suddenly burst into tears, sitting down heavily on the sofa. "I can't believe he's not here," she sobbed. "It's so unfair; he was meant to have a long retirement and enjoy his life in Cyprus."

Charlie came and sat next to her, putting her arm around her shoulders and pulling her in. "It's hard, really hard, Lou. I'm still coming to terms with it. This house is so empty. But we've got to be strong for each other. Come and sit next to me, Will. Let me have a proper look at you."

Will came and sat on the sofa too, and Charlie took his hand. "I don't feel as if I've seen you for so long. I've missed you both so much. Thank you for coming out. I really needed to see your gorgeous faces."

Will held her hand and squeezed it; he couldn't think of anything to say. Charlie sniffed, wiped away a tear, and stood up. "So, what can I get you to eat? I'm sure you're starving ..."

"Do you know what? I'd just love boiled eggs and toast," said Lou, blowing her nose. "You know how it is at airports and on planes? We've eaten a load of crap in the last few hours: rather disgusting sandwiches, foul coffee and those sickly muffins. What do you think, Will?"

"Yeah, sounds great. Just what I need. Have you got Marmite?"

"Yes, I have. Can't live without it," said Charlie, suddenly remembering David tucking into eggs and Marmite toast soldiers. "Why don't you two unpack? Show Will the bedrooms, Lou and I'll get on and do it."

They all woke up late the next day, even though the sun was piercing bright. Charlie was up first; she was sleeping okay after the initial shock. It was as if her body was trying to re.

She made herself a cup of coffee and went to sit on the patio. It had been her routine to have an early morning swim, even before coffee, while David was alive, but she'd hadn't been in the pool since that morning; it didn't seem right, somehow. So, she simply sat, nursing the warm mug in her hands, taking little sips, letting her skin absorb the sun's rays and thinking how lovely it was that her children were upstairs. She was going to have to tell them what she'd decided to do; what they would think, she wasn't sure. She glanced at her watch; it was already nine o'clock.

Soon, Lou padded downstairs in what she'd gone to bed in, which was a skimpy vest top and some cotton shorts. Her hair was all over the place; she'd always been like that since she was a child; they used to say that she was the definition of someone who'd 'gone through a hedge backwards' and she hadn't changed one bit. She smiled at the memory of her as a child.

"Hi Mum," she said, and kissed Charlie on the cheek. "Did you sleep okay?"

"Yes, I did, actually. How about you?"

"Like a log. I feel awful ... I feel I should have been awake all night, thinking of Dad."

"You must be exhausted though, with the worry and the flight," said Charlie.

"Yes, I'm so busy at home with everything. But ... I had that awful thing when you wake up and, for a split second, your brain has forgotten ... it's so horrible. I dreamt about him, too.'

"Yes, I dreamt about him, too. I hardly ever dreamt about him when he was here. The brain's so weird; I suppose it's trying to process it. Sit down and I'll bring you a cup of strong coffee."

She made herself a second cup and took them both out to the patio. Lou was sitting, facing the sun, her long legs stretched out, head back, eyes closed. "It's so great to feel the sun; the weather's been so miserable in the UK."

Lou opened her eyes and smiled at Charlie, who handed her the mug and she took a loud slurp.

"Yes, enjoy it while you can. You're not here for long."

She wanted to say what she had to say, but couldn't find the words. She waited, watching her daughter drink her coffee and feeling so grateful she was there.

"So ... Lou ... I've decided, after a lot of thought, that Dad would want to be cremated and they don't do cremation here, so I've arranged for him to be flown home."

Lou looked at her, and Charlie could see tears well up in her eyes. "Did you ever discuss it ... you know, burial and funerals and things?"

"Well, not in great detail. You know how it is. We all think it's not something that will ever happen to us. We all try to forget that one day we'll die ... but I know he didn't like the idea of being buried. I remember he said once it gave him the creeps, the thought of being stuck in a box in the ground."

Lou looked away. She said, "And I think he'd want to go home, to the UK. I know he loved it here but ..."

"Yes, I don't like the thought of him here."

"So, the body will be repatriated and I think the cremation will take place in Swindon."

Neither of them said anything, but at that moment, Will wandered out, wearing some old boxers and a white t-shirt. "So, he's coming home, is he? The old man, I mean?"

"Yes, I think it's for the best," said Charlie. "Coffee?"

"Mmm, yes, please."

He sat down and gazed out over the pool and the sea beyond, while Charlie went inside. "It's great here, isn't it? I wish I'd come out before."

"Well, it was your decision," said Lou aggressively.

"Yes, it was ... Dad was always so angry with me ... I didn't want to be in the same place as him."

"But you could have thought about how Mum felt. You're so selfish, Will."

Charlie came back out; as she handed him the mug she said, "He ... he was difficult with you, Will, I know he was. But he loved you, you know. Your dad didn't know how to express it and he couldn't understand why you were so different from him. He thought you'd follow in his footsteps and when you didn't and you had your own opinions, he didn't know how to cope. Actually, he got pretty angry with me, out here too."

Lou sat up. "What do you mean, Mum? Angry with you? Why? He seemed fine when I came out and had that holiday. He seemed so chilled. Rather overweight but ..."

"Well, I tried to hide it from you, Lou. Your dad became ... complicated ... out here. He was all right at the beginning and he enjoyed his new life, but then the pandemic came and ruined everything. Your dad lost his identity; he wasn't a pilot any more ... he didn't know who he was ... he didn't seem to want to do anything. But even when it was gone, he'd lost his spark. I would have liked to explore the island, look at ancient sites, walk. We'd done a bit of it when we arrived, but he lost all interest and just spent most of the time toasting himself in the sun, eating and drinking. I tried to stop him but he wouldn't listen to me and that's when he'd get angry with me, telling me to mind my own business and if he wanted a drink, he'd have one. In the end, I just had to make my own life here. I didn't go off walking on my own, but I joined exercise classes and went to Greek lessons and other things. To be honest, I felt lonely. There's so much of the island I haven't seen."

They both looked at her. "Why didn't you say something, Mum? Why did you suffer in silence? If I'd known, I would have talked to him when I came out; he might have listened to me, you never know," said Lou.

"I doubt it," said Will. "He never listened to anyone."

"Shut up, Will ... for God's sake, don't be so negative about him. The poor man's dead."

"Don't argue, you two. It's all ... too late now. Maybe if he'd listened to me, he'd be alive now," said Charlie, "but maybe he was always going to die then; maybe that was his time."

They were all silent. The lack of noise echoed around them, but an aircraft appearing from their left broke the quiet, making its way towards Paphos airport. Another plane-load of happy tourists arriving on this paradise island. In the distance, a noisy leaf-blower started up, another horrible sound that shattered the peace.

"Let's make a pact. We so rarely have time together; let's just enjoy each other's company ... and try to remember Dad as he used to be ... when he was in the Air Force. Fun, full of life, always playing sport ... that's how we've got to remember him," said Charlie.

"Yes," said Lou, turning pointedly to Will.

"Sorry, Mum. I'll try to ..."

Charlie stood up and walked into the house, saying, "Who wants some cereal?"

The five days went by so quickly; it was such a strange time for Charlie. On the one hand, there were many arrangements to be made and discussed, and on the other hand, there were mundane meals to be made and time to fill. David hovered over everything; he was constantly on her mind and his absence was everywhere.

She loved having her two children to herself. How often does a mother of two grown-up children, who have fled the nest, get to spend five whole days with them? It felt like years since she'd sat with just the two of them ... and talked. It was special, and she felt so unbelievably close to them both again. Despite everything.

Another person she wanted to talk to was Beth. If only she were still alive. She would have known what to do, how to move forward. Charlie missed her with every ounce of her body.

"I meant to say, Mum, I spoke to Darcy before we came out," said Will. "I don't know whether you'd spoken to either of them?"

"I texted Alex. I couldn't face writing him a long message. I don't want to speak to anyone yet, only you two. I feel guilty but I haven't rung him, no. There are so many people I should call. If the post was reliable, I'd write to people, but it's all phone based here."

"You'll be able to communicate with everyone back home and see them at the funeral. I'm sure you've been busy, Mum, but Alex was very upset for you; he rang me," said Lou. "He didn't want to disturb you, so he rang me instead. I told him we were coming out. I said I'd tell you how sorry he was. Maybe it would be good to talk to him?"

"Yes it would, I suppose. He's been through it. God, I wish Beth was still here." Salty tears plopped out of her eyes and trickled down her cheeks. Lou came over and hugged her.

"Alex might be the next best thing, Mum. Call him."

That night when the kids were watching TV, she rang him. "I'm so sorry not to have called, Alex," she said when he answered.

"Oh god, Charlie ... I'm so sorry. I couldn't believe the news ... I don't know what to say, except ... I know what you're going through."

Charlie was sitting in the dark on the patio; an owl was hooting, and the stars were piercing the black night sky. She didn't know what to say next, but it was good to hear Alex's voice.

"Charlie, are you still there?"

"Yes ... sorry, I was miles away. The night sky here is like nothing you see in the UK; for a moment, I was imagining David, up there somewhere. It's so hard to think that he's nowhere ..."

"Look, Charlie, I know it seems impossible right now ... but life *will* carry on. It's taken me a very long time, but I can see the future now. For so long after Beth's death, it was as if I'd ceased to exist too ... but you come out the other end. You never forget, but you find a way to live. You will, too ..."

"Thank you, Alex ... we'll be back in a few days. I'll be in touch. You will come to the funeral, won't you?"

"Of course we will ... and anything I can do, you let me know."

When she clicked off the call, Charlie continued to sit in the dark. She could hear the TV; it was coming through the open back door. The owl continued to hoot, and bats flew through the air like black ghosts. One of the feral cats appeared at her feet. She bent down and stroked its head; it meowed and then settled itself next to her.

She looked up at the stars and thought of David.

# CHAPTER 16

The funeral was as heartbreaking as these things always are. Charlie was determined to be strong, not to cry, to be dignified. She'd been to the doctors and had taken some pills to help with it all, and the consequence was, she felt spaced out, as if she was playing the role of the grieving widow, looking down from above.

There was a huge turnout; David's friends and colleagues from the Air Force were there, along with his sporting pals, family, friends and neighbours. Lou, Harry and the grandchildren and Will supported her through the day, sitting on either side of her, holding her hands at the crematorium. She couldn't give a eulogy; she knew she wouldn't be able to get through it. Lou had offered and gave a tearful, yet heartwarming speech. One of his Air Force colleagues talked about David's career; the celebrant gave a quick but professional rundown of his life.

And then it was all over.

The curtains didn't come round the coffin; Charlie had asked for that not to happen. So, they all filed past the coffin and the picture she'd chosen to have in a frame of David looking young, handsome and full of life, in his RAF uniform. She and the family left first, stopping in front of the coffin for a while. She briefly touched the wood of the box holding him, saying in her head, 'I love you'.

Some people touched the coffin as they passed, some just walked slowly past it. They gathered outside the boring, functional building with its pristine grounds, everyone talking in hushed tones, wondering what to say and thinking how lucky they were to be alive. In truth, they couldn't wait to get away, to be as far away from death as possible. To be drinking and eating ... to be doing anything, anything, but think of death.

They gathered at their local pub, ate some sandwiches, drank some tea, and then everyone dispersed back to their lives.

For Charlie, she didn't know what life she was going back to.

---

Of course, she had no home to go to, so she went back to London with Lou and the family. She'd seen Alex and Darcy at the funeral and at the tea, but had hardly said a word to them. They'd hugged and Alex had said all the right things, but she felt so empty, she couldn't respond.

After a few weeks in London nestled in the bosom of her family, she felt loved and safe. The children were such a help; they distracted her from her own miserable thoughts. She found that reading to them, helping with bath time and walking them to school, was exactly what she needed. This, of course, had always been her intention in retirement: to be a granny; to help Lou in any way she could.

She was exhausted at the end of each day and fell into a deep, comatose sleep. She would still sometimes wake up and forget David was dead, and it was a never-ending shock when her brain kicked into gear. He visited her dreams; he was always young, handsome and fun; as if he hadn't aged at all.

Will had gone back to his flat and started work at the pub again. It was the last thing he'd wanted to do, but he needed the money. Charlie said she'd come and visit him. Lou went with Charlie. She'd never visited Will's flat and didn't like the idea of her mum travelling alone; she seemed so fragile and vulnerable. They set out at lunchtime, leaving Harry in charge. They caught the tube and rattled along at high speed in the anonymous metal box. The noise, the people and the air took them to a world far, far away from the serenity of Cyprus, and Charlie wished she was back there. How did people survive such chaos and lack of control over their lives in this vast city?

They followed maps on Lou's phone and eventually arrived at Will's address. They stood outside, looking up at the redbrick, down-at-heel building on a very busy street, with heavy hearts. At the front door was a list of flats and names, and they pushed a button next to his number. Nothing happened for what seemed like a long time. Then the front door clicked open.

They made their way up some stairs and found his shabby door, down a dark corridor. The place smelled of food and drains, and loud rap music was coming from inside the door opposite Will's. Charlie knocked and soon Will was there, silhouetted in the doorway.

"Come in ... 'scuse the mess," and he stood back to let them pass. "As you can see, it's a shithole."

Charlie kissed him and then Lou hugged him, Charlie thinking that the two of them had seemed closer since David's death.

"Do you want some coffee? I think I can run to that," said Will, putting the kettle on. "How are you, Mum?"

"I'm okay. How are you?" she said, looking around with a sinking heart.

"Yea ... I've been better. I hate this fucking place." At that moment, the rap music was turned up, and the bass thumped.

Charlie wasn't sure what she could say. Lou wasn't so reticent.

"God, Will, how do you stick it? That music would drive me nuts. Can't you find somewhere better? There must be somewhere ..."

"This is quiet, compared to some days. The guy above likes jazz, and there's obviously no carpet up there; he sounds like an elephant walking around at all hours. I have to have my AirPods in most days when I'm here, but I spend as little time here as possible."

He poured the water into the cafetière and got out three mugs. "Take a pew, if you can find anywhere to sit." He grabbed a newspaper off a chair, cleared away a dirty plate off the sofa, and motioned for them to sit down.

Having poured the coffee, he turned to the fridge and sniffed a bottle of milk and, seeming to take a chance, he chucked it into the mugs. He handed them over, and then perched on the remaining chair.

The conversation was stilted; they all wanted to avoid the funeral and the awful surroundings, so they found it difficult coming up with something to talk about. Charlie was so worried now she'd seen where Will was living. This wasn't how she'd envisaged his life; Will was so much better than this. He had loads to offer, but he was losing hope. She could see that now. He looked like a young child, lost in a wood, surrounded by dark trees and evil monsters. She had to help him.

They talked about the pub he worked in; they talked about Bella and Jack; they talked about a TV programme they'd all watched. Charlie couldn't take it anymore.

"Let's have a walk," she said, jumping up purposefully. "We could all do with some fresh air. And we'll work out what you're going to do with yourself, Will. Come on, you two, let's go."

They all were relieved to leave the environs of the building and the area. They marched along the pavement; Lou looked at a route planner and they hopped on the Jubilee line, changed at Baker Street and were soon in Regent's Park.

Charlie said, as they walked along, "Look Will ... I know you want to be independent but ..."

"Not particularly," he laughed. "It was Dad who was always saying I should be, but I've never felt ..."

"Well, you should be, by now," said Lou.

"I know, I know. But it's hard on your own. I don't have anyone here to lean on or talk to. I don't know what I want ... I've got so little money. My life's a mess. I know it is."

Lou linked arms with him and said, more sympathetically, "It'll work out, Will. But you've got to get away from that flat. That's enough to break anyone."

"You're right, I know you are. Maybe Mum, I should come out to Cyprus, start a new life?"

"Of course you can, Will. I intend to go back there and see where my life takes me. It'll be very odd being in Cyprus without your dad. It'll be as lonely as hell. I know it will be, but ... I need to see if I can be there on my own. Like you, Will, I've got to work out what I want. Life's so hard, isn't it?" She linked arms with him. "It would be lovely if you came out. Think about it ..."

"Do you want to live there now, though, Mum?" said Lou.

"Well, we rather burned our bridges, didn't we? Even if I decide to sell up, I've got to get back there and sort everything out. But if I stay, Lou, please come out for all your holidays, won't you?" she laughed. "Thank God for Facetime. What would we do without it?"

As the flight landed in Paphos, Charlie realized she had to embrace her solitary life in Cyprus because there was no other option for her at the moment. She couldn't bear the thought of selling everything and moving back yet; staying with Lou's family had a time limit. She loved them, but they had their own lives. She would give it a year and then decide if she'd stay or go back. Trying to remember why she came here, she recalled David's mindset and her initial excitement about their future in Cyprus. She'd looked forward to the outdoor lifestyle, making new friends, getting fit, exploring the island, and even visiting Egypt, Turkey, and Greece. Maybe she'd go back to those plans ... but on her own. The pandemic had ruined everything for them. It was as if the world had conspired against their new life together, making it impossible. She convinced herself that if Covid hadn't happened, David would still be alive. The virus didn't kill him, but it might just as well as have.

She tried to put all these thoughts out of her mind as she drove in the taxi back to their home on the hill. The friendly driver chatted all the way, oblivious of course of the turmoil her mind was in. She told him she lived here, and he started talking about local news: about the landslide on the 'old' road past Petra Tou Romiou; about their local supermarket being taken over by a Greek company ... and as they entered the village, the lack of any action over the houses collapsing on the hillside. She listened, nodded and gazed out of the window at the glorious orange sky, as the sun was setting in the west.

It was strange to be back alone. As she got out of the car and paid the driver, she felt a certain peace descend on her for the first time in weeks. The car drove off in a cloud of dust, leaving her to absorb the silence. She stood by her gate, reluctant to go inside. A feral cat appeared, purring loudly. She was friendly, this one, as long as you didn't touch her. Charlie attempted to stroke her back, and she ran off onto the bondu. She would be back for food later.

Charlie noticed that the garden looked unkempt after a few weeks of nobody pulling out weeds and keeping the plants in check. There was a thick layer of dust over the glass table on the front patio; the windows also looked as if they'd been in a sandstorm. She picked up her case and walked through to the front, past their truck parked under cover, again more brown than black.

The pool looked beautiful in the evening light; the automatic underwater lights had come on and the water shimmered in its blueness; she'd asked Bill, an ex-pat who did pools, to clean it while she was away and it was immaculate, with only a couple of stray leaves in it. The silhouettes of the surrounding palm trees looked majestic against the darkening blood-red sky.

She sat on one of their chairs, legs outstretched, and stared at the scene as the sky went dark. The rapid descent of dusk in Cyprus never failed to amaze her: there was a dome of deepening hues of orange and purple above and the gentle chirping of insects in the air all around and a hint of perfume wafting by. There was a rustle of leaves as a cool breeze danced against her skin, bringing a soothing sense of calm.

Maybe, just maybe … she could make Cyprus her home? She would fulfill David's dreams for them, and live a good life in the sun.

---

The following weeks went by slowly for Charlie. She was constantly aware of being alone and had to fill the house with noise to trick herself into believing she had company. David had never been one for music; he just wasn't interested in it, so now the house was humming with loud modern music. She didn't need to worry about annoying the neighbours and she found the deafening level she turned it up to lightened her mood when she felt down. If it wasn't music, it was Radio Four blaring out a constant stream of news and chat, or endless podcasts. She often wore AirPods when gardening, so her mind was occupied with others' chatter.

Jane was incredibly kind to her: always inviting her round for supper, as she knew how lonely the evenings could be. Charlie went back to fitness classes with her and rejoined her Greek class; she admitted to herself that she was hopeless at languages and would never be able to converse properly, but she wanted to learn some basics. She made a few more new acquaintances and made an effort to socialise with them.

As the weather slowly warmed up, she went swimming in the sea every day. The sea temperature was still low, but the salt water invigorated her and made her feel truly alive. It was strange that so few other people were in the sea at this time of year; she rarely ever saw another person swimming. But this didn't deter her; she positively enjoyed her swims. She always had to wear rubber beach shoes as she was incapable of making her way over the pebbles in bare feet, and remembered David objecting to wearing them, thinking he was manly enough to cope with stones, but soon realising it wasn't worth the agony.

Memories of David jumped into her head all the time. Trivial things would spark them: the salt shaker reminded her of him putting salt on his food and her, trying to persuade him not to; a single sock emerging from the washing machine would make her think of him telling her to pair the socks before putting them in. The sound of the laughing dove ... David loved that sound; his love of marmalade and how he'd search for it in Cypriot supermarkets, often to no avail, and every time she brushed her hair, she'd think about how he insisted on using hers.

She wondered if her memories would ever fade and hoped they wouldn't. Already she found it hard to 'hear' his voice and wished she had a recording of it. She'd stare at his photograph, trying to remember the reality of him.

It was at the beginning of May that she got a text from Will:

> Hey Mum. Can I come and see you? I've definitely had enough of this shitty flat and shitty job and shitty life now and I thought maybe you'd like some company? Let me know. Love you, Will x

When she read it, her heart jumped in her chest. Poor Will. He was as lost as she was ... maybe they could comfort each other?

She wanted to see him, of course she did, but she was worried that he was running away from life and from himself. He'd never shown much desire to come to Cyprus before, but after the trip a few months ago when David died, perhaps he'd realised that the island had its benefits.

She longed to have another person in the house, but she didn't want him to come just because she didn't enjoy being alone. Maybe it would do him good, though?

She wrote straight back.

> Hi Will. Of course you can come and stay! I'd love to see you. The sun will do you good and maybe while you're here, you can work out what you want to do with your life. I'm so excited to see you; I'll pay for your flight. Love you, Mum x

She transferred some money to him, which she knew would cover the cost of the flight at this time of year and it wasn't long before he'd texted to say he'd been looking at flights and would a date a fortnight away suit her? Will said he'd already left his pub job after a row that he'd had with the bar manager. He'd accused Will of stealing money; he had no proof and Will swore to Charlie that he had done nothing wrong. Charlie believed him and encouraged him to move on. She knew her son, and he'd always been too honest for his own good.

He had to give a month's notice on the flat and he asked her if she could lend him some money so that he could move out. She, of course, agreed on the condition he did, in the future, repay her when he could. She didn't believe in handing money over with no conditions; it wouldn't be good for him.

On the day of his arrival, Charlie woke up with such a feeling of lightness and happiness that she quickly realised she'd been simply existing until that day. To have her son, her beloved Will, coming to stay lifted her spirits immeasurably, and she jumped out of bed, drew back the heavy blackout curtains and opened the door onto the balcony. She rarely went out onto the balcony; what was the point when the view downstairs was beautiful, anyway? But this morning, she leant against the railings, took three or four deep breaths, closed her eyes and absorbed Cyprus and the silence of her surroundings into her very being. May was a wonderful month: not too hot; cyclamen were bursting into flower all over the bondu and the fields were a carpet of green. This would be so good for Will, she thought: to get away from the dirt and noise of London and to immerse himself in silence and colour.

She spent the day getting his bedroom ready, filling the fridge with his favorite foods and preparing supper for the two of them. How lovely to have company when she ate tonight, she thought, instead of a solitary plate on her knees, in front of the telly.

"Hey Will," she called, and waved her arms excitedly as she saw him emerge through the doors into the arrivals building, looking dishevelled and disorientated. He grinned when he caught sight of her and she ran to the end of the barrier. Flinging her arms around him, she said, "Oh, Will, it's so good to see you."

He hugged her back, other people moving around them. Charlie always loved hugging her children, but this hug was extra special; she breathed in his special scent of unwashed clothes, sweat and his favourite aftershave. He had a rucksack on his back, which he now swung down onto the floor with a grunt.

"That's so heavy; I tried to cram as much as possible in it. I didn't bring any hold luggage as I reckoned I wouldn't need many clothes here. I've left a lot of stuff at Lou's."

"I thought you got through quickly! Well done, you're right, you don't need much, just shorts and t-shirts. We can always buy stuff here if you need anything. Right, let's go," she said, linking her arm through his. He swung his rucksack up onto his other shoulder and they walked together out into the fresh air.

---

Charlie had made them a rich beef casserole which had been slowly cooking on a low heat all afternoon. By the time they'd got round to eating it, it was pitch black outside, but still warm enough to sit on the patio, overlooking the oasis of blue, glittering water below them.

When she looked at Will, Charlie was worried: he was even thinner than he used to be, his cheekbones now more prominent, his long limbs without a spare bit of flesh on them. His skin was sallow, his eyes dull. She was determined to find the 'old' Will, to feed him back to health and help him find his passion.

"Have some seconds, Will. There's loads left," she said, grabbing his plate when he'd finished.

"Okay, Mum, that would be great. Not too much ..."

"You look as though you haven't been eating enough, Will."

"Really?"

"Yes, I'm on a mission to feed you properly," she laughed. "What have you been eating in that flat of yours?"

"Not a lot, to be fair. McDonalds ... KFC ... toast sometimes, and if I was really pushing the boat out, I'd heat up a tin of soup."

"Oh God, Will ..."

"You saw what it was like, Mum. Not exactly conducive to cooking a roast dinner. I wouldn't know where to start, to be honest, anyway."

She disappeared into the house and came back with his plate loaded with casserole, another baked potato, more broccoli, carrots and peas.

"Thanks, Mum. This is delicious," he said, tucking into the food with relish. "Dad would have loved it, wouldn't he?"

His remark fell into the darkness with a thud. David's absence was suddenly everywhere. "Yes, he would," said Charlie. "He loved his beef, didn't he?"

They smiled at each other across the dimly lit table. Charlie wasn't sure whether Will was remembering David for 'her' sake ... or did he truly miss his dad? However poor their relationship had been, he'd still lost his dad. Boys needed their fathers ... he was probably like her: she remembered all the good parts of their life together now. All the arguments and disappointments of their married life had faded with his death. Whether or not it was a conscious choice, she only remembered the good times now.

"Will ... while you're here, let's forget the bad times you had with your dad. Let's just remember the fun times we had together as a family. Can you do that for me?"

"I'll try, Mum. I just feel sad we were never very close and we never will be now." He put down his knife and fork. "It was as if I could never truly live up to how Dad wanted me to be. He didn't understand me and ... I didn't understand him."

"Yes, you were different people, but ... it all came from love for you, Will. He wanted you to be successful in life, but he didn't know how to express it. It came out all wrong, trying to force you down a road he thought would help you. But ... he's gone now, and it's time for *you* to decide what *you* want."

"I'm not sure I have a clue ..."

"You will, in time. But for now, you're here and it's time to just relax and enjoy the island. You and I can go out and about, walking, swimming, exploring."

"I can't wait, Mum. Thank you for letting me come. And paying for the flight. You know I really appreciate it, don't you?" His eyes searched for hers, and despite how different they were in personality, she could see David's face reflected in his.

"I know, I know," she said. "You must be tired ... don't mind me ... you go up to bed now, if you want to."

He stretched back in his chair, his skinny legs out in front of him. "I'm so glad I came, Mum. I feel, in some weird way, as if I've come 'home', not escaped. This place is so peaceful. I feel like my mind can think clearly again. I will go to bed, if you don't mind. I'm knackered." With that, he got up and bent over Charlie, kissing her cheek. She put her arms up around his shoulders.

"Night, Will, sleep well. Swim in the sea when you wake up?"

"Yes, definitely," he said. "Love you."

"Love you, Will. See you in the morning."

How wonderful to have another human being in the house.

# CHAPTER 17

They did swim in the sea the next morning, but not as early as she'd planned. She'd forgotten what a late riser Will was when left to sleep in. She didn't want to wake him; he'd had a horrible few months and deserved to give in to his exhaustion.

She peeked through his door at around 10.30 and he was dead to the world: sprawled across the bed on his front, limbs everywhere, snoring peacefully. She had plenty of things to be getting on with, so went back downstairs and out into the sunshine, deciding to clear the pool.

The pool man still came to help clean it, but she enjoyed lifting debris out. She took the net on the very long pole off its resting place along the wall, and sauntered the length of the pool, pushing the net basket just under the surface, catching insects, both alive and dead. Also, leaves and petals and even a white feather floated in, which made her think of David. Didn't white feathers appear when someone died?

She found the task calming; it took her at least fifteen minutes to do it well, and there was great satisfaction to be gained when the water was free of any stray objects or insects. She was staring at her finished work when she noticed a dragonfly; it was flying above the water and wasn't the normal bright blue colour you saw in England, but almost crimson, its wings shiny and translucent. She was mesmerised as it darted, rising and falling above the pool.

"Hi Mum ... sorry I'm up so late. I don't know what happened."

She turned around and looked up; Will was still wearing his nightclothes, his hair unbrushed, looking as if he could do with at least another ten hours' sleep.

"Don't worry, Will. Just help yourself to whatever you want. I bought some Weetabix, there are eggs, toast ..."

"Great, thanks," he said, and he wandered back into the house.

After his breakfast, they packed a cool box with some sandwiches, salad, fruit and bottles of fizzy water and set off down the hill to the beach, where she always swam. Now it was May, there were a few more tourists about, but she went to the end few visitors found; it was a 'locals' spot, tucked away beyond the big hotel, with nothing but the cliffs, the sea and carob trees; no ice cream vans, no lifesavers or watersports sellers. There were sometimes some intrepid walkers who were setting off or returning from a trek along the cliff path to the end of the bay; Charlie hadn't done this yet, but she was hoping maybe she and Will could do it together.

As they were nearing the sea, they drove down past the hotel where several jacaranda trees were in full bloom, the violet blueness of their flowers acting as a canopy. "Wow, they're stunning," said Will.

"They are, aren't they? So beautiful ..." she said, never tiring of them. She parked up in the rough-and-ready parking area beneath the cliffs and they walked down the ramp to the beach, carrying food, towels, shoes and a couple of sunbeds. They dumped everything beneath a tree, in the shade. There were a few old benches dotted around and they sat, side by side, on one of them, gazing at the sea in front of them. They were the only people there; on the horizon was a huge container ship and nearer them, a couple of sailing boats. It was as if the sea was theirs.

"Come on, let's get straight in," said Charlie, standing up. She lowered her shorts and took off her t-shirt, revealing her pink costume. "Race you!"

She quickly put on her beach shoes while Will stripped off. He walked towards the sea as if he was on hot coals, each step seeming to cause him a certain amount of pain.

"Why didn't you use the shoes I brought down?"

"Oh, you know, male pride and all that," he laughed, hobbling slowly.

"Well, you'll soon learn," she laughed. She'd reached the water's edge and was walking tentatively forward. "There's quite a big drop here," she said, "just to warn you."

They now stood together, water up to their knees. "Oh, Will, this is lovely. I'm *so* glad you're here."

"So am I," he said. "Last one in's a sissy," he shouted, as he thrust his arms in front of him and dived into the crystal clear water. He came up like a seal, twisted his head so that his hair flew from his face in a spray of droplets. "It's a bit parky, Mum ... why didn't you warn me?"

"I thought it would wake you up," she laughed. "I've been swimming every day for the past couple of months and it's much warmer now." She swam towards him and they both floated on their backs.

"You're braver than me. This is cold."

"Let's swim out a bit; you need to keep going. If we just float about, we *will* get cold."

They swam out towards the buoys which designated the Sovereign Base Area. It was a longer swim than it looked, but they were both determined to touch a buoy and swim round it.

"You're right, I'm fine now," said Will. "It's not cold at all." His face was shining with enjoyment, his smile lighting his entire face. "I'm going to do this every day I'm here. I feel amazing," and he set off, doing a steady crawl, back to the shore.

They put up the sunbeds and lay in the sun to dry off, a light breeze dancing on their skin. There were still no other people on the beach; just a few cheeky sparrows who seemed almost tame, hopping near them.

Will sat up and got out his phone; he started taking pictures of the little birds who appeared to pose for him.

Then he stood up and, with his flip-flops on this time, walked down to the water, squatted down and began taking shots of wet pebbles, seaweed and low-level shots across the beach to the cliffs.

"Can I see?" said Charlie, joining him by the sea's edge. He handed her the phone, and she scrolled through. "They're lovely, Will. You've got a real eye."

"My phone's mostly full of daft selfies in nightclubs. You know how it is."

"Let's do a daft selfie of the two of us to send to Lou," said Charlie, grinning. So Will went to stand next to her, extended his arm and they took several shots with different backgrounds. "Look up a bit, Mum, get your head closer to mine. That's it. Now smile!"

They reviewed the pictures together: they both picked out the best one. They were smiling and looking directly at the camera. The sea was shimmering behind them and even the horizon was straight. "That's the one, Will. I love it."

"So do I. Lou will be *so* jealous," he laughed.

It was a week later, a Tuesday afternoon. Charlie was trying to show Will all her favourite spots and so they'd visited Melanda beach, Will marvelling at the unspoilt landscape leading to it. He'd said at the time that it felt like they were travelling back in time, before the development of the coast at Paphos, covered in houses and hotels. He had only a few memories of the holiday they'd all had when he was young, and he felt he was only just beginning to see what the island offered. There were no buildings visible down the track leading to the sea, apart from a small shack on a hillside. They drove past rows of vines and fields of wheat on a rough, dusty track, with the azure blueness of the sea as a stunning backdrop.

The meal they'd eaten, sitting just feet above the beach, was delicious: sea bream, Greek salad, Cypriot bread, hummus and tahini, washed down with Keo beer. Having sunbathed for a while to let the enormous meal go down, they then went swimming, heading out to the ramshackle jetty on the right of the bay.

"I'm starting to see pictures, wherever we go," Will said, when they were treading water looking back at the taverna.

"What do you mean?"

"Well, it's so picturesque, it makes me want to paint or something. Look at that tall tree, placed so perfectly to the right of the restaurant ... and did you notice those cars parked under that fig tree?"

"Yes, I see what you mean. Parts of Cyprus really are the definition of Mediterranean life. Some of it's still stuck in the past, as if the modern world hasn't touched it yet. Dad and I went up the mountains twice; you'd be amazed how timeless it feels up there."

They did a slow breaststroke back to the shore, chatting all the way. As he towel-dried himself, Will said, "Maybe I should start painting. That's what I've always wanted to do, isn't it?"

"Maybe ... but, as an alternative, why don't you use my Canon and start taking 'proper' photos? Mobile phones are fine, but the Canon is superb. Have you ever used a real camera?"

"Not really. Could you teach me, then?"

"Of course, I'll try. I've always been keen; I used to love taking photos of you two when you were little, but I haven't got it out for years now. I brought it here, thinking I would, but it's just sitting there, unused. You're welcome to give it a go."

When they got back to the house, Charlie immediately went up to her bedroom to find the camera. She handed it over to Will. "There you are. It's yours if you want it. If you don't like photography, you can sell it on eBay and make yourself some money; I don't need it anymore."

"Thanks Mum, that's amazing. So ... tell me what to do."

They spent the next forty minutes with Charlie showing Will how to put on the different lenses: one zoom, one portrait, one macro; then she tried to explain the f settings, shutter settings and the digital menu, feeling that she wasn't making it very clear. She did, however, thoroughly enjoy passing on her limited knowledge and Will appeared to be fascinated by it all. It was already dark, so it was a bit late to practise, but they went outside together and Charlie explained how he might capture the pool and the silhouetted palm trees. He made several attempts from different angles and soon he'd got the idea of balancing a slow shutter speed and the f setting, to get the maximum light into the camera. "I think I get it," he said, staring at the back of the camera. "It's blurry because I've had to use a slow shutter speed. Is that right?"

"Yes, and the f setting needs to be small in order for those palm trees to be in focus; it's all a balancing act, and the ISO makes a difference too. You'll pick it up really quickly, I'm sure."

And she was absolutely right; over the next few days, Will had the camera permanently round his neck, and he was away ... taking far better shots than she ever had. He loved the macro lens and spent ages doing closeups of the bird of paradise flowers, the bougainvillea and cyclamen. It totally absorbed him and she saw him googling photography advice and watching YouTube videos. She posed for him and watched him 'seeing' the light; he would adjust her head up or down or sideways, seeing the effect.

He suddenly became a different person; he was the same old Will, but he had a sparkle in his eyes, a spring in his step and enthusiasm for life.

"As much as I love you being here, Will," Charlie said one morning, feeling rather sick as she broached it, "what are your plans?" They were eating breakfast in the shade; an EasyJet plane had just flown over the house, with a distant but loud roar, on its way to land at Paphos.

"Well, I don't want to outstay my welcome ..."

"You would never do that, Will. I don't want you to go ... but you've got to think about it."

"Yeah, I know I've got to earn some money. I can't sponge off you forever. I realise that. But the trouble is, I've got no reason to go back to the UK. I don't want to end up back in some foul little flat and I'm enjoying living with you and being in the sun. I've missed you, Mum. How about if I went into the village today to see if anyone wants any help in a taverna? There must be someone who could offer me a job; I don't really care what I do. What do you think?"

"That's a great idea. I'd love you to stay and you might start meeting people your own age if you get out; you can't stay in with me every night. I know I'm pretty boring," she laughed.

"I've enjoyed it, Mum, but maybe it's time to break out! I feel so much better than I did; I've got some energy now. And I've been thinking ... maybe I need to apply for another uni course? I'd love to do something creative. I know Dad didn't think it would be a good idea but ... it's who I am. Are there courses in photography? I really love it, you know. Could we afford for me to do another course, though?"

"I'm sure we can. Wow, Will, that all makes sense. I'm so pleased I gave you my Canon. Maybe it will lead you down a career path? Wouldn't that be incredible?"

A feeling of happiness surged through her body at the thought that perhaps she'd helped Will find something he could be passionate about; he was getting his mojo back. She'd always felt guilty that she hadn't stuck up for him more when David was deluging him with reasons why the Air Force would be a brilliant career for him. What was he even *thinking*? Will was a soft person, a creative person, someone who would *never* have fitted in with military types. She'd let Will down in the past, and she was determined now to put it right.

It seemed dreadful, though, that it had taken David to die for her to fight her son's corner and hopefully set him off on the right path in life.

# CHAPTER 18

It was only a couple of days after their talk that Will found a job. It was the third taverna in the village that he'd approached; they asked him to serve at tables and help behind the scenes, if it was quiet. The tourist season was heating up, though; the village square was full most nights with noisy, happy people enjoying the food, ambiance and laid-back culture. His shifts were to be both day and evening; the pay wasn't brilliant, but they shared the tips out. He'd never waited at tables before, but how difficult could it be?

The walk from the house to the square took about fifteen minutes going down to the village and longer coming back up, but he enjoyed the scenery on his many walks: the tumbling flowers from high walls, the spiky cacti poking out of gardens covered in large needles; the numerous cats sitting on pavements or asleep in chairs, all enveloped by the sleepy, dusty silence, which was only broken occasionally by a noisy motorbike driving too fast, or a four-by-four driving past with Greek music drifting out of windows. His mother had offered to drive him, but he didn't want her to have to do it all the time. He had to start being independent again.

What an improvement on his walk to the pub in England it was; there was no comparison.

He soon settled into the routine. The owner was grumpy sometimes, but if you worked hard and were nice to the customers, on the whole, he was okay. There were a couple of waitresses, one from Ukraine and one from England. Iryna spoke English, was very good with the customers and was only a couple of years older than him. Alice was in her thirties, married and had worked at the taverna the year before so, was 'in charge'. Will discovered that he, too, was good with customers; he enjoyed chatting to them and always tried to be accommodating. He loved Saturday evenings when Spyros, the owner, had live music playing. One week it could be a solo bazouki player, one week a trio and sometimes a great girl singer, with a backing track and a violin. The tips proved to be lucrative and he could give his mum some money towards his board and keep, and still have some left over for himself.

"On Thursday, some friends and me, we go in Limassol for night out. Do you want go with us?" said Iryna on a Tuesday, when they'd finished their late shift and were walking home together. Iryna lived in a flat in a small complex on the way back to his mum's house. It was still warm, the sky was bright, and the moon full.

"That's kind but ..."

"Oh, come on, Will. You said you never do many things ... it be fun. We go to karaoke bar to start and then to club."

"Can I think about it?"

"No, you cannot," she said, laughing. "Why think?" She looked at him out of the side of her eyes with a look of amusement on her face.

"Okay, okay ... you win. But how will we get there?"

"Don't worry. My friend she have car."

They parted company at the fork in the road, Will confirming that he would come; he wouldn't see her again before then. They would pick him up at the same fork at 8 pm.

As he walked in the star-lit silence along the dusty track, with the moon throwing white rays across the sea, he realised he was glad that he'd said 'yes'. He would never make friends here if he turned down invitations ... and Iryna was nice.

He didn't know Limassol, and the night turned out to be a revelation. Who knew there was so much night life going on in sleepy Cyprus? Iryna and her friends were super friendly; they were all Ukrainian. Sofia was the one with the car and then they met up with Olena and Dmytro, a couple who lived in the city.

"So ... you sing, Will?" asked Sofia, as they entered the karaoke bar. She was petite and blond, with an open face. She was always smiling.

"I can sing in the shower," he laughed, "but I don't think I've ever subjected anyone to my voice in public."

"Iryna and me, we love to sing. You sing with us, yes?"

"Do I have to?" he grinned. "I need some alcohol first."

It was months since he'd been out. His sister's words to him about his drug-taking all that time ago had made an impact on him and he'd stopped. With his father's sudden death and his mother's grief, he'd stayed well clear, only occasionally wishing he could take coke to forget everything. Tonight, he was going to 'let his hair down' and drink; that was the only way he was going to sing and lose his inhibitions. His mother had confessed so much about how his father had been reliant on alcohol to get through the pandemic and how it had affected him; he didn't want to turn out like his dad. He hoped drinking heavily wasn't hereditary.

He started off with a couple of beers, but soon they were all drinking shots. He went up to sing with the girls and they all performed a loud and no doubt out-of-tune version of 'Girls just want to have fun'. His arms were around both of their shoulders and he felt freer than he had for months. There was no stopping him after that, and the others had to drag him off to the nightclub. His head was pretty muzzy by then, and all he could remember the next day was dancing for what felt like hours in a darkened, red-lit room to thumping dance music. He had no recollection of how he got home;

he found out later that Sofia, who'd been drinking zero-alcohol drinks all night, drove him home.

"How was it?" Charlie asked the next day, when he finally stumbled out of his room, looking rough.

"Great, thanks. I hope I didn't wake you last night? I can't remember much."

"No, I didn't wake up. Oh dear ... can't you remember anything?"

"Yes, I can, but it's all hazy. They were so nice, Mum. We had such a laugh. I sang and danced all night."

"Well, I'm so pleased you're making friends, Will. That's great. Don't make a habit of getting drunk, though." Charlie didn't want to lecture him, but David's drinking still played on her mind.

Will slumped down on the white plastic chair on the patio. He was going brown, but his skin looked sallow, his hair unbrushed and stubble was growing on his chin.

"Shall I make you a coffee? You look as if you could do with one," said Charlie, putting her hand on his shoulder.

"Thanks, Mum. Don't worry ... last night was a one-off. I feel so terrible. I don't want to feel like this again. I don't know how Dad kept it up."

After his coffee, he changed into some trunks and dived into the pool. Charlie could see him swimming an entire length underwater. He emerged at the other end, put his arms over the edge and rested, breathing deeply. He pushed his hair back off his face and smiled up at Charlie.

"Do you know, I don't remember ever feeling so relaxed ... and somehow ... contented," he said. "The sun is healing me ... I love that I can swim every day. I love that I have a job. I love that I went out last night and sang my heart out."

Charlie didn't know how to answer him. She simply smiled to herself, so happy that her son finally had found his place in the world. If getting drunk, singing and dancing were what it took, then she was grateful.

And that evening, he started looking online for photography courses.

# PART 4
2024

Sarah Catherine Knights

# CHAPTER 19

As the spring weather turned into summer, the heat intensified. Most days, the temperature rose to around the thirty-five degrees mark. She felt she should have acclimatised by now, but Charlie found the heat drained her of energy, particularly around midday. Each summer, however, she could cope a little better, and she knew she'd eventually be okay in the heat. She enjoyed the health benefits of living her life outside and loved that she had a golden tan; she always slathered her skin in factor fifty, though. Hats were a must, she mostly sat in the shade, but just living here, walking around, tanned the skin.

One day in June, Will announced that Alex and Darcy wanted to come and visit; Charlie was taken aback. She'd, of course, seen them in England for the funeral and a few times after that, but they hadn't been in touch much since. Darcy was busy at uni; she was doing architecture and her course was full on. Will and she often texted each other, and Charlie caught up on the news about her father through Will. She heard he was thinking of retiring in November of this year and was shocked to think of him without his beloved animals in his life. She felt sad for him. How would he fill his days?

After Beth's death, she and Alex had slowly drifted apart. He'd been so grief-stricken for years, he'd become a shadow of himself, and Charlie couldn't seem to help him. They'd eventually got on with their own lives, both missing Beth too much. When they were together, Beth was ever-present, like a ghost. It was easier not to see each other. When she and David sold up and left for Cyprus, she felt as if she was abandoning him to his fate, especially as Darcy left for uni at about the same time. During the pandemic, they'd chatted over FaceTime as everyone did, but it wasn't the same. Charlie didn't confide in him about David's behaviour; she felt it was something she had to deal with on her own and dearest Beth was always hovering around their conversation. She found it all too painful. And then David died. Alex and Darcy once more came back into her life, but now their friendship was truly tinged with overwhelming sadness and loss.

"So ... how would you feel if Darcy and Alex came out here?" said Will.

"How come? I never hear from Alex ... I feel as if I've lost contact with him. Don't get me wrong, I'd love ..." said Charlie.

"Well, I have to admit, I kind of suggested they came out. Darcy has got her long summer holiday coming up. Alex is slowing down and retiring soon ... so I asked them out ... I hope you don't mind?"

"No, I'd love them to come. Don't forget Lou and the family are coming at the end of July. Why don't you suggest August ... or September? Either's fine for me."

"Cool, I'll do that. I'll try to get some time off work, or at least reduce my hours while they're here. I think it'll do them good. Darce is like a sister to me, but ... will it be awkward Alex coming, for you, I mean?"

"No, not at all. It's a great idea, Will."

She took the initiative and texted Alex, who seemed excited at the prospect; they were going to come for a fortnight at the beginning of August.

Meanwhile, Will had applied to Bath Spa Uni for a photography degree. The course was exactly what he wanted, and being in Bath appealed to him. He was offered an online interview and needed to get a portfolio together, so when he wasn't working, he was taking, editing and printing his photos.

Charlie was slightly nervous about the prospect of Alex coming out when she thought about it, but she put it out of her mind; soon, Lou would come and she wanted to make their holiday perfect. They both worked so hard, their lives so busy. The kids would love it here; they could be in the pool all day and Lou and Harry could chill.

When Lou arrived, Charlie thought how pale and tired she looked as she emerged into the arrivals hall. Her eyes had dark rings beneath them, and she looked as if she could sleep for a week. Harry was his normal ebullient self, and the children bounced up to her, beaming from ear to ear. Charlie flung her arms round them all, saving a special hug for her daughter.

"It's so wonderful to see you all," she said. "Come on, follow me," and she led them out into the heat, to the truck parked not too far away. It was a particularly hot day; the temperature gauge on the dashboard read thirty-nine degrees when she turned it on. It felt as if they were going to be boiled alive in the car, but Charlie immediately got the air-con going and soon the air that was belching out, turned from hot to warm. Harry, the biggest of them, had sat in the front and Lou and the kids had squeezed onto the back seat. They'd flung all their luggage in the back. Harry now fiddled with the air-vents at the front, trying to direct some of the cooler air into the back as the kids were complaining bitterly, saying things like, "I'm going to die," and "I can't breathe." He went to open the window, but Charlie said, "No, don't do that! It'll be okay in a few minutes," and soon they were on their way, with the fan on maximum, making a loud noise over the Greek music coming from the radio. At last, the air turned cold, and they all settled down.

"I can't wait to get into that sea," said Harry.

"Nor me!" said Bella. "Can we go straight down to the beach, Nana?"

"Yes, can we?" shouted Jack. "I've bought my goggles."

"Me too ... and my flippers," said Bella.

"We can go down to the beach whenever you want to. It's only five minutes away," said Charlie.

"You're SO lucky, Nana. I wish I lived near the sea," said Bella.

And Charlie thought to herself, *Yes, I am lucky.*

---

As they arrived back at the house, Will came out to greet them all; he'd just got back from his shift.

"Hey, sis! How the devil are you?" said Will, holding her by her elbows, face on. Without giving her time to answer, he continued, "To be honest, you look awful. Sorry, but ..."

"Thanks a bunch, Will. I'm knackered. Work's been chaos recently, and we got up at some ungodly hour this morning. I'm sure I look shit ..."

"Mum, I thought we weren't allowed to use that word?" said Bella, punching her leg gently.

"No, you're not ..."

"Well, why did *you* say it, then?" she grinned.

"Sorry, Bella, Mummy's very tired and sometimes bad words slip out. Anyway, Will, you look amazing. Last time I saw you, you looked like I do. Cyprus suits you."

"Thanks, yes ... it does. Come on, kids, I'll show you your room."

Will went through the front door and ran up the stairs and Bella and Jack followed, excited to see their room for the next two weeks. Charlie showed Harry where their room was, on the ground floor, and he took all the luggage in and dumped it unceremoniously by the bed. Meanwhile, Lou had wandered out onto the patio and she leant against the railings, staring at the view. As Charlie joined her, she said, "God, Mum, I need this holiday. I feel bone tired ... I don't know what's the matter with me at the moment."

"Well, you're not going to raise a finger while you're here. You're going to just sunbathe, swim and eat. I'll deal with the kids and give you a proper rest."

"God, that sounds amazing," and she flopped onto the nearest chair.

"I know I said we could go to the beach," said Charlie, "but I think it would be better to stay here today. The kids can swim in the pool and I've got a barbecue organised for tonight. You can swim or sleep or read your book ... whatever you want."

"Thanks, Mum."

Charlie looked at her daughter and worried about what was really going on. Were Harry and she ok? Was Lou ill? She was determined to find out, but now wasn't the time.

As the sun began to set and the sky turned bright orange, the evening was filled with splashes, shouts, dives and bombs into the pool; Lou didn't go in, but Will enjoyed reverting to childhood and Harry floated on a lilo. The children loved the pool. Later, Harry helped Will and Charlie with the grilling of sea bream, sausages and halloumi on the barbecue and Lou ensconced herself on a sunbed and hardly moved, only shifting to the table when it was all ready. There was an array of salad with olives and Feta cheese, new potatoes, crusty bread, homemade mayonnaise, beetroot and garlic salad, all washed down with fresh orange juice, Keo and white wine. Charlie had bought a bumper pack of Magnums from the local supermarket, which she presented after they'd eaten their fill, to the cries of 'YES!' from the children and laughter from the all the adults. As they all crunched into the divine, smooth chocolate, silence reigned; all they could hear was a distant owl and the 'mm's' from people enjoying their treat. The heat had eased off a little as the evening was plunged into darkness; there was a gentle breeze that fanned their faces lightly. Little t-lights flickered on the table, the fairy lights lit the edge of the pergola with small, bright white bulbs, and the pool shimmered with turquoise.

As they sat round the table, reluctant to leave the magic of their first night to retire to bed, Lou said, "Dad would have loved this, wouldn't he?"

"Yes, he would," said Charlie. "It's such a shame that we never *all* gathered here, like this, when he was alive. The pandemic has a lot to answer for."

It was almost as if David was looking down on them all. Charlie thought he'd be proud of his family ... he'd even be proud of Will, who looked so healthy, happy and content with being himself.

They were living his dream.

The holiday, of course, went far too quickly. As with all two-week holidays, the first week seemed to slow down time, with its long, lazy days, but the second week was like living in 'fast forward', hurtling towards the end. Will carried on working as he'd arranged time off for Alex and Darcy's stay, joining them when he could. Their days were spent near water; it was too hot not to dip in to cool off at every opportunity. It was a shame not to sightsee, but this wasn't the time for looking at the ruins at Paphos or Curium and anyway, the children simply wanted to swim and have fun.

Charlie took them down to the local beach a lot; they'd spend the morning down there and then, in the heat of the day, they'd drift back home for lunch in the shade. This usually comprised gorgeous local pitta bread, slit down the middle to make a kind of sandwich with lounza, (a local smokey ham) or halloumi, sharp, tasty tomatoes and the little Cypriot cucumbers, dripping in tahini and hummus. The children loved trying new things and discovered a love for olives.

Charlie was determined to show them Cyprus, a little further afield than Pissouri. They had a day at the water park in Paphos in the first week and a trip to the marina in Limassol during the second week. It ended with a swim on Ladies' Mile beach in the shallow, crystal clear waters. They were up the far end of the beach, away from Limassol, towards the salt flats, where David had taken them when they were on holiday all those years ago.

"That's where Dad used to fly to," said Charlie, pointing to the RAF base in the distance, behind the barbed wire barrier. They could all hear distant aircraft engines and then two jets took off and disappeared beyond the horizon.

"Did he come here a lot?" said Harry.

"Yes, he was always coming out on detachments, but we were never offered a posting here."

"I sort of remember coming to this beach when we were on holiday with Beth, Alex and Darcy," said Lou. "Now we're back, it looks familiar. I think I would have loved living here when I was a child. It's a shame we didn't."

"You said something similar all those years ago," said Charlie, remembering.

"It seems unbelievable that Beth's dead," said Lou. "I know it's been years, but memories of the holiday make it seem like yesterday. I'm glad Alex and Darce are coming here, Mum."

"Do you remember Nick, the boat guy?" asked Charlie.

"Yes, I do. Is he still around?"

"I think so, although I haven't seen him recently. Do you remember he came over to England soon after Beth's death? Alex is going to see him when they come out. They've kept in touch. I'm hoping he's still got his boat. He must be getting on now, though. Maybe seventy or older. I doubt he's still got his business, but who knows?"

Charlie took them home across the wide open space of the shimmering salt flats, the children amazed at the fact that they were driving 'off-road'. After driving down the long track, they passed the entrance to the camp and then down through the aerial farm and back along the old road, past Curium, through Episkopi camp and eventually up the hill to the village. They stopped halfway up the hill and went to the Panorama restaurant, perched on top of an escarpment with the most spectacular views to the sea.

They all had drinks and ice cream, sitting at tables outside as the sun set. It was one of those sunsets where the sky looked like a painting; how could it be real? Purple clouds, tangerine, apricot, and sienna streaks brushed the sky with a kind of magic. They all stood with their backs to it and Charlie did her best to take a selfie, shouting, "Lou, get in a bit ... Bella, move forward ... Jack, I can't see you!" Will was at work ... he would have done a better job, but as it turned out, it was a gorgeous photo. Everyone, including Lou, looked healthy, happy, brown and relaxed; the backdrop of the sunset completing it.

Later, when they'd gone, Charlie made a photo book of the holiday to send to Lou. This picture had pride of place on the cover. "Cyprus, July 2024" was the title. It was filled with shots of the children in mid-air, above the pool or surrounded by splashes as they bombed into the water. There were photos of happy times in tavernas, with tables laden with food and cans of Keo; of the children on water slides at the park, or stroking cats in the village square. Everywhere there were the bright pinks of bougainvillea tumbling, with the sea views beyond. Such happy times.

Charlie could see Lou recovering as she tracked her through the two weeks in her photos. The sun had tanned her skin, her hair had lightened, her face had lost its exhaustion. She didn't feel she could ask Lou what the problem was, so she'd left it, but regretted it after they'd left. It would have been so much easier to ask her face to face, but Charlie didn't want to spoil her daughter's holiday.

Despite Lou's appearance improving, Charlie was convinced that something was amiss. She'd leave it a week and if she hadn't volunteered some information, she would take the plunge and ask.

# CHAPTER 20

Charlie felt apprehensive and excited about Alex and Darcy's arrival; it wasn't quite the same as having family to stay. With Lou and Harry, she'd felt totally relaxed about them coming ... but this was different. She was so fond of them both, but Beth's and David's absence was a huge barrier between them now.

Charlie had timed her journey to the airport so that she'd get there as they came out. She'd set out at 3 pm and waited anxiously by the arrivals board; they'd landed thirty minutes ago, so they should be out any minute. She paced around, watched other people ... and wished they'd come out. If only Will could have come with her, but he was doing his last shift before taking time off. He'd be back later that evening. So, it was up to her to keep the conversation going, to entertain; she just hoped she was up to the job. She looked at her watch; still no sign of them. Maybe the airline had lost their luggage?

She'd just decided to go and get a coffee when she heard her name being called ... and there they were.

Darcy was waving and shouting, her father walking calmly beside her.

"Hi there, you two," she said, as they walked round the barrier, pulling two large suitcases. "It's so good to see you. I was beginning to think there was a problem with your cases!"

She hugged Darcy and then Alex, noting how beautiful Darcy was. She was looking more and more like her mother; her smile, her eyes, even her hair.

"Sorry, Charlie," said Alex, "the luggage didn't come out for ages; rumour had it that there was some technical problem, you know how it is. But we're here now, thank god. It feels like it's been a very long day."

Charlie appraised him; he did indeed look exhausted, and she secretly hoped Cyprus would do its magic, as it had with Lou. She was struck by the fact that he'd lost weight since she'd last seen him. Not that he was ever fat, but his cheekbones were more chiseled and his trousers were hanging off him. His brown eyes with those thick eyelashes were more obvious; she made a secret vow to herself that she was going to feed him up while he was here, like she had with Will. What was it with her and the men in her life? Trying to slim David down and fatten Will and Alex up? She laughed to herself.

She also felt inexplicably shy in his company; as they walked towards the truck, she hoped she could overcome this awkwardness.

"This is so beautiful, Charlie," said Alex as he stood in front of the house. "You can see photos of places, but you have to experience them. I hadn't realised how isolated you are here, for a start. Does it worry you, or are you used to it now?"

Darcy had gone through the gate and had disappeared. She'd said she wanted to dive straight into the pool and was on a mission to do just that. Charlie was standing by the open driver's door of the truck, looking across the bondu to the sea.

"When David and I first saw this house, it was him who was so taken with it, if I'm honest. Obviously, I loved the views ... who wouldn't? But I couldn't see myself living here. Through the pandemic, it definitely was isolated; we hardly saw a soul, but I suppose that was a good thing, in many ways; we felt safe from the virus, here. But as restrictions lifted, I wanted to get out and about, see the island; but by then, David had lost all desire to explore, to do all the things we'd planned to do. When he died, this place felt like a beautiful prison to me. I couldn't go anywhere, I was alone and had no idea how my life was going to pan out, but gradually ... I've begun to see what a wonderful place it is. It's definitely healed Will. Having visitors here, it's opened my eyes."

She hadn't articulated her thoughts like that before to anyone. It was as if Alex had tapped into her innermost mind. She slammed the door closed and walked round to the passenger side. Alex put his arm around her shoulders. "It must have been so difficult for you, Charlie. Living in a foreign country, dealing with David's death. It was all so sudden, wasn't it? Like Beth's. One minute they're there, the next they're gone." He squeezed her and added, "I'm sorry I haven't been a very good friend to you ... it's only now that I realise how 'absent' I've been. Now, being here, seeing your house, it's made me realise how strong you've had to be." He turned to get his case out of the back of the truck. Darcy had already taken hers.

"Come in and I'll show you round," said Charlie.

There was a loud splash. "Goodness, Darcy's already in," she laughed. They walked round the side of the house; Darcy's case was open, with clothes spread out haphazardly on the patio and she was floating on her back.

"You couldn't wait a minute longer, then?" grinned Alex.

"No ... it was absolutely essential. God, I was so hot and sweaty. This is heaven. Are you coming in, you two?"

"Well ..."

"I will, if you will, Charlie ... why not?"

"Ok ... I'll go and get changed. Come with me, Alex, and I'll show you your room."

They went inside; it was cool and bright inside the open-plan area. "I love this," said Alex. "It has a wonderful feel to it. Does it stay pretty cool in these hot temperatures?"

"It's not bad, but when it's this hot, we have to use the air-con. It's built to keep cool, so in the winter months it can be parky. You probably can't imagine it, but we have to have the central heating on quite a bit."

They went upstairs and Charlie showed Alex into the room that was going to be his for the next two weeks. "I think you've got the best view," she said, pointing. He opened the sliding door onto the balcony and went out, raising his arms above his head, stretching from side to side.

"Stunning," he said, then he called down to Darcy, still floating in the water below. "Any chance of you moving your suitcase, Darce? You've made the place look untidy and you've only been here fifteen minutes," he laughed.

"Ok, Dad, keep your hair on," she shouted up. "I'm too busy floating."

"Don't worry, Alex. Will isn't the tidiest of people, either. I don't mind, honestly. It's just nice to have some life in the house."

She came and stood beside him on the balcony, enjoying the fact that he was here. His proximity was comforting somehow; she'd known him so long that, although they'd lost that closeness over the years, it was like having an old friend back.

He turned his face towards her and said, "Thank you for inviting us, Charlie. I think I really needed this. And Darcy has been working so hard this year, she needs a break. It's going to be wonderful." He smiled, and she felt a warmth inside her. They looked at each other for a second, the familiarity returning.

"Thank you for coming," she said, nudging him. "Now, come on, we're meant to be going swimming."

She left him to change and wandered to her room. By now, she'd accumulated an array of swimming costumes and even a couple of bikinis. She couldn't decide which one to wear. Revealing her body made her feel self-conscious; she couldn't remember the last time Alex would have seen her half-naked; most likely all those years ago on holiday. At least her skin was brown now, which made anyone look better. She decided to wear one of her sporty costumes; it was flattering with its high-cut legs and tummy support. She felt good in it, which was the main thing.

By the time Alex came down, she was in the water, chatting to Darcy. She looked up to see him sauntering across the patio, wearing a pair of dusky pink board shorts and shades. He definitely looked skinny, but his body was athletic and toned. As he walked towards the pool barefoot, he yelled, "Ow, ow, ow! These patio stones are boiling," and he hopped quickly from foot to foot, running towards the shade of an umbrella down by the pool. "Wow, I'll have to remember to wear flip-flops next time."

He dumped his towel and shades on a sunbed and tiptoed quickly over the hot patio stones to the steps into the pool, getting straight in. The shallow end only came up to his thighs, so bending his legs, he fell forward and dived under the surface of the water, coming up beside Charlie.

"Heaven," he moaned appreciatively, pushing back his hair with his hands. "I think I can cope with this," and floated in a star shape.

Darcy swam to the deep end and, with the ease of youth, raised herself up with her arms and hopped out of the pool, going to a box by the edge. She got out a large ball, left over from when Bella and Jack were there, and threw it into the pool towards Alex. "Throw it to me, Dad," she said, as she slipped back into the water.

There followed a crazy game of catch, which wasn't as easy as it sounds, as they all threw the ball as hard as they could to make it difficult for the recipient. There were loud shouts, enormous splashes and cries; it went on for at least twenty minutes. Nobody knew what the rules were, or what they were trying to achieve, but there was a lot of jumping, laughing, falling and diving for the ball. They were so involved they didn't even notice Will appear.

"Hey ... wait for me ... I'll just change," he said.

It was their second day. Charlie was up early, and she was pottering around the pool. She'd had a genteel pre-breakfast swim and was now lifting the odd leaf from the pool with the net. Her mobile was on the patio table and she heard it vibrate loudly against the glass.

Placing the net back in its holder, she walked towards her phone. It was a message from Lou. Opening the message app, she read her text:

> Hi Mum – I know you'll be up early so I thought I'd text you with news. I found out two days ago that I'm three months pregnant! I'm still trying to get my head round it. I'm not sure how I feel yet. Harry's over the moon and I'm sure I will be too once I've got to grips with it. Anyway, I thought you ought to be the first to know. Love you, Lou

Charlie stared at the message and re-read it. So *that's* what it was; she knew there was something going on. Her stomach was fluttering at the thought of another grandchild; she loved the prospect. But then her thoughts turned to the fact that she'd be so far away and ... would she be able to help Lou enough? She tried to tell herself that it was six months away and she could always go back to the UK. David had left her with enough money not to worry about things. Would it be a boy or girl? The gap would be big ... would Lou be able to go back to her job? All these questions were rushing through her head; she needed a coffee.

She sat with her mug of steaming black coffee on the patio. She must reply, she thought.

> Hey Lou – that is SO exciting. What amazing news! I'm sure you're reeling at the moment, but you'll soon get used to the idea. You're a wonderful mother and you'll cope. It might seem daunting now, but what an incredible family you have. Harry's so supportive and, of course, I'll do anything you need me to do. Can I tell people? Love you, Mum

She'd just got an instant message back from Lou, saying 'Yes, go for it'! when Alex came downstairs. "Morning," he said. "You're up bright and early!"

"Yes, I usually am these days. I'm one swim ahead of you already! Grab a coffee and come out to the patio."

They sat together in companionable silence, enjoying the intense warmth of the sun. "Mmmm, this is the life," said Alex, putting his face up to the sun like a flower.

"Actually Alex, I've just had some incredible news," said Charlie, not being able to contain it any longer. "Look at this!" and she handed her phone to him. He read it and then looked up, beaming.

"That's lovely news. Another life ... I can't wait for Darcy to have children. It must be so special, Charlie." He handed the phone back.

"It is ... it's weird, you feel so much love for your grandchildren, even though they're not your own children. The large age difference makes it special ... the interconnectedness ... just everything." She smiled to herself.

"I can't wait."

"Typical me ... I'm worrying about living here, so far away when the time comes."

"That's why there are planes, Charlie!" Alex said, laughing. "You can always stay with me if you want to come back. You know that, so why are you worrying?"

"I know, I know. Thank you, Alex. I'm just seeing problems where there are none. It's going to be so much fun with another baby in the family ... any noise from Darce or Will?"

"Not a peep. I think they were up late watching some film or other."

"Yes, I expect they'll sleep in. By the way, does Nick know you're here?"

"I messaged him and said hopefully I'd see him. Did I tell you he's finally given up the business, but he's kept his boat?"

"No, you didn't. Text him back and say we'll come and see him. How about tomorrow? The kids can stay here and laze around if they want," said Charlie.

"Perfect, I will."

---

Will and Darcy definitely wanted to 'chill', so Alex and Charlie set off the following morning for Paphos without them.

They were going to meet Nick at midday where the boat was moored. The new owners of the business had let him keep it there, on condition they could use it, if necessary. Nick suggested they took the boat out.

They had time to spare, so turned off the motorway at Petra Tou Romiou. "You've really got to visit Aphrodite's Rock, Alex. We didn't, on holiday, did we?"

"No ... I've read about it, though."

They turned off into the car park, parked the car, and set off down the tunnel beneath the road. They emerged from its darkness into the light, passing the wishing tree on the left. The sea was flat and calm; the water sparkling with diamonds in the sunlight. Huge rocks loomed large as they approached them, towering above them with majestic power. There was a strange sensation of calm serenity about the place; it was just a beach, but Charlie always felt as if it was more than that. She remembered persuading David to swim in the sea here; it was soon after they'd arrived on the island, before the pandemic. They'd giggled about Charlie getting pregnant by swimming round the rock; she could still see David, laughing at the thought.

She bent down and picked up a pebble. "David and I came here ... I remember us having fun together that day. We even put our initials inside a pebble heart. It was roughly here," she said, pointing to an area of the beach.

"Aww, that's a lovely memory to have, Charlie." He took off his flip-flops and carried them in his hands towards the ocean's edge. Charlie took off hers and they splashed along the shallow water, kicking up droplets of light with their feet.

"It's beautiful, here. I can see why people think of it as having mystical properties," said Alex.

"It's really gorgeous at sunset," she said, remembering the photo she took of Lou, Harry and the kids against a blood red sky here. "We'll have to come back in the future, when there are three children. I got Lou and the family to line up over there in height order, and they were in silhouette."

They strolled back along the beach, pausing briefly at the tree covered in material. "I have got nothing to tie on, but I'm having a secret wish anyway," said Charlie, smiling.

"What are you wishing for?" asked Alex.

"I can't possibly disclose ..." she grinned, wishing both her children luck with photography and babies, as she walked back through the tunnel.

Nick was waiting for them; they saw him sitting on a bench, arms along the back, head back, sunbathing. Charlie called his name and his head came forward. He stood up, holding out his arms in greeting.

"Oh, it's so good to see you two," he said, and hugged them, one by one. Charlie thought that although he still looked slim, healthy and tanned, there was a weariness about him she hadn't noticed before.

"You look well, Alex ..." said Nick.

"I feel it; I'm so much better than when you last saw me. What a mess I was back then. I still miss Beth every day, but I've learned how to live."

"Good, I'm glad. It's hard ... but you come out the other side, eventually." He turned to Charlie. "And how are you coping?"

"It's obviously more recent for me ... but ..."

"I'm so sorry, Charlie," said Nick, coming and giving her another hug. She felt comfort from his warm embrace. "Life's a bitch, isn't it? Come on ... don't let's dwell on sad things. Let's have a sail."

He led the way across the grass and down to the water's edge. They clambered on board and soon were off; there was a light breeze, and they tacked out, the only sound being the whoosh of the water streaming past the prow. Charlie didn't want to interfere; she sat back and draping her hand in the water, she let the world drift by, as Nick and Alex caught up and discussed the boat. It amazed her how well the two of them got on; two men united through a mutual love of sailing.

After an hour or so, they returned to shore. "So, if you're going to retire, Alex, are you going to sail again?"

"Well, I haven't got my half of the boat anymore. I couldn't face it without Beth ... but maybe."

"Now Charlie is here full time, you must come out here and go out in mine whenever you want."

"Exactly, Nick," said Charlie. "There's no excuse now, Alex ... I expect to see you out here regularly." She linked arms with him as they walked up over the grass again. "I'm starving ... do you guys fancy going for a meal and a pint?"

"Too right," said Alex. "A cold Keo sounds just what the doctor ordered."

"Why don't you guys come to my place, meet the cats and then we'll go to one of my favourite local places, just round the corner. How does that sound?"

Nick's flat was a ten-minute walk; it was light and airy, with its own communal pool, which Nick said he never went in; he preferred the sea. The cats were asleep on the sofa and didn't bother to get up when they came in. Nick quickly changed, and Alex and Charlie perched on some chairs, waiting for him. Charlie spotted some photos, and as always, couldn't resist going to have a look. There were two pictures, each of them of Nick and his wife, who looked like a smiley, attractive woman.

Nick came back in and found Charlie holding one picture. "That was taken down by the boat ..." he said. "We'd had the most incredible day out ... I got a stranger to take it of us both. I love that one ... it reminds me of such happy times." Charlie placed it back on the shelf.

Alex said, "It's odd, isn't it? We've all lost our partners ... we've all lost our past ... but somehow we've kept going. You have to, don't you? Because in the end, it's the only option. To keep going."

They all fell silent, remembering.

They walked round the corner to the taverna. The men drank Keo and Charlie had one brandy sour as she was driving. They ate a myriad of little dishes, as meze was the speciality of the house. The waiter just kept bringing more and more until Charlie thought she'd never be able to eat again. They were sitting outside, under the shade of vines growing over a structure; grapes were hanging down in enormous bunches beneath the canopy. An old man was playing gentle bouzouki music in the corner; cats slept in the shade, waking occasionally to argue over food. It was a magical, sleepy, hot and perfect end to a perfect day.

Charlie looked across at Nick's kind face, so wrinkled after years of the sun. Deep lines framed his blue eyes on each side; his tousled, white hair looked longer than before; his face was older. He'd transmogrified into part of the culture, part of the landscape itself.

As the men chatted on, she was happy to listen and observe. Alex, her one link to Beth, father of Darcy, friend to her, godfather to Will ... was looking relaxed and happy; his face had caught the sun from the sail. His cheeks and forehead had a rosy glow, his brown eyes and dark lashes somehow emphasised by the tan that had already added colour to his skin. He looked so handsome and when he laughed suddenly at something Nick said, she realised she'd really miss him when he left. She tried to shake the thought from her mind. There was plenty of time left. Why was she already leaping forward to when he'd leave?

"So ... we ought to be getting back, Alex; to see what those two reprobates are getting up to back home," she laughed.

They paid the bill and arranged another sail in a few days' time. At the truck, Charlie kissed Nick on the cheek, reluctant to leave him; she wished she'd visited him before. He cut a lonely figure, and she hated the thought of him going back home to his cats. Nick slapped Alex on the back and they hugged a man-hug. They got in the truck, waved and drove away.

"Let's invite him over to the house, Alex."

"Yes ... good idea. I'll find out when he can come. Thanks for taking me there today, Charlie. God, I love that guy."

"My pleasure," she said, glancing at him.

They were on the very un-busy motorway back to Pissouri. "It's really lovely having you here, Alex," she added, deliberately keeping her eyes on the road this time. She gripped the steering wheel tight, wondering if maybe she'd overstepped the mark.

"I love being here," he replied. "It's as if I've re-found you. I feel properly alive again."

Charlie stared through the windscreen. "Beth would be so pleased for you, Alex. You were everything to her."

"And she was everything to me," he said.

# CHAPTER 21

The holiday drifted on through the heat and bath-warmth of the sea. Darcy and Will went out on their own a few times; Will was now insured to drive the truck, so they went into Limassol and met up with Will's Ukrainian friends. Charlie said Will could have the truck as long as he didn't drink, AT ALL. Will agreed to this; Darcy didn't drink either, to keep him company.

On the nights they were left at home alone, Charlie and Alex would barbeque fish, or the biggest port chops you've ever seen. They enjoyed marinading the meat, and stuffing a whole, gutted fish with parsley and lemon, then wrapping them in foil. A large bowl of salad always accompanied each meal: lettuce, rocket, tomatoes, peppers and spring onions, all drenched in virgin olive oil and lemon juice, from lemons picked that day from Charlie's own tree. They rarely drank any wine; they were content to have wonderful fresh orange juice mixed with sparkling water and lashings of ice.

They'd sit companionably on the patio, sometimes just reading after the meal, or maybe going inside and watching TV together.

Their days were full of swimming wherever they could, be it in the pool or the sea; it was so hot that they wanted to be within minutes of water. Alex's favourite beach, like Will's, was Melanda; he loved the cool, crystal clear waters, the taverna perched on the edge of the beach and the blissfully empty surroundings. The four of them went there several times; they'd sit for far longer than they needed to after the meal, in the cool of the shaded restaurant. Will and Darcy would eventually wander off to cook themselves on the sunbeds, but Charlie and Alex would linger, drinking Cypriot coffee or eating an ice cream. It was so peaceful, with a gentle breeze flowing through the taverna, gently lifting Charlie's hair and fanning their faces. They were always somehow reluctant to drag themselves away, to stand up and go back to the beach, which was, of itself, as calm and quiet as could be; just the whisper of a single wave folding itself slowly along the edge. Neither of them wanted to lie in the sun for too long, so they would find beds with umbrellas and lie next to each other, reading. They were so close to the water; it was almost lapping at the legs of the beds. They would slowly lift themselves up after a while, to walk the couple of steps that were needed to reach the sea, bending their legs and flopping backwards in unison, laughing at each other as they kicked their legs and drifted out to sea.

Charlie felt that, at last, she was reveling in her new home. Life was utterly peaceful, and she was content.

Halfway through the holiday, there was a musical event at the amphitheater. Charlie hadn't been before; David wasn't interested, and then everything stopped. But this time, she wanted to go.

They were having breakfast with Will and Darcy, who were now getting up at a reasonable time; Darcy didn't want to miss a minute of her holiday and they'd already done twenty lengths of the pool. They were both very competitive and were always trying to beat each other, either in speed or by how many lengths they'd done that day.

"So, do you all fancy going to this concert, then? It's on tonight. We can get tickets at the entrance. It's an Abba tribute band ..."

"Oh god, Mum," said Will. "I think maybe we'll pass ..."

"Don't be a spoilsport, Will," said Darcy. "I love Abba."

"Really?"

"Yes ... always have."

"But this is a tribute band. It'll be shit."

"Why? They might be fantastic. We won't know unless we go," said Darcy, eating a piece of toast. "Live dangerously, Will. You might enjoy it!"

"Well, I'm happy to give it a go," said Alex. "You know me ... I love music. Can you dance there?"

"I'm not sure, but I don't see why not," said Charlie. "I've heard people talk about dancing at the bottom of the steps, in front of the band."

So, much to Will's consternation, they made a night of it. They got there at seven, bought the tickets and some raffle tickets, in aid of a dog rescue charity, and went in. They stood at the top of the steps, admiring the spectacular view across the land to the sea. It was quickly filling up with all age groups.

"Hey, Charlie, we should have dressed up! Look at them," said Darcy, pointing to a group of girls about her age, completely togged out in Abba gear.

"Wow, I didn't even think about that. Oh well, too late now, but we'll have fun, anyway. Where do you all want to sit?"

"In the middle, at the top here, I think," said Alex. "That way, we'll see them straight on and get the view."

They'd bought a cool box full of snacks and drinks. Charlie had heard that everyone brought cushions as you had to sit on the cold concrete steps, so she'd bought four. She was glad she had, as two hours on stone could have been brutal. They plonked themselves on their cushions in a line, swigged at some bottled beer, and just simply watched as the amphitheatre filled up. By seven thirty, when it was going to start, it was at least two-thirds full. Everyone seemed up for having a good time.

The band trouped in from the left, two girls and two boys, looking very authentic. The main girl had the patter; she sounded Swedish and made quite a few good jokes. When they started playing and singing, Charlie was relieved; they were, in fact, extremely good. The audience, from the get-go, were up for joining in: standing and swaying, singing along, clapping and shouting their appreciation. On about the fourth song, they invited people to dance and loads of people almost ran to the bottom. Charlie glanced at Will, who was at the end of their line. He was still looking sceptical and tried to distance himself from it all, but she could see that Darcy wasn't going to allow him to be so superior. She was singing the words loudly, loving every minute.

"Come on, you lot," Darcy said, "we're all ... and I mean ALL, Will, going down to dance." She pulled Will into a standing position and dragged him down the steps. He looked back at Charlie with a look of incredulity on his face. She laughed, stood up and said to Alex, "Right, come on ... now's your chance to show off."

They went down the steps, carefully looking at their feet, as it was now dark and the steps had all but disappeared from sight. Darcy and Will had gone into the crowd and were right at the front. She could see Darcy singing away to 'Super Trouper'. Will was grinning at her and dancing awkwardly. Alex and she stayed at the edge.

"I honestly can't remember the last time I went to something like this," shouted Alex into her ear. "It's such fun!" and he grabbed her hands and started throwing her around. Her mind went back to the summer ball all those years ago, when she learned she wasn't such a bad dancer after all; he made her feel as if she was flying. This time, it was exactly the same; they boogied one minute, fake-ballroom danced the next, jived the next. He had a unique ability to interpret the music with whatever style came to him. The band sang 'Waterloo' and everyone went crazy; she looked across at Will and even *he* was dancing properly now, flinging his arms around.

The band announced there would be an interval after the next one, and they launched into 'Slipping through my Fingers'. Charlie had always loved that one; all the couples on the dancefloor started coming together, arms around at each. Alex looked at Charlie, opened his arms, and she slipped easily inside his embrace. Their feet moved slowly, expertly to the music, unlike a lot of others who were just circling each other.

Charlie put her hands on his shoulders, almost keeping him at a distance, but then gradually gave into the slow, gentle lyrics and moved her hands onto his back, placing her head on his chest. She could feel the vibrations of his voice as he sang along. She knew the song was about a mother feeling sad at the speed at which her daughter was growing up, but the words felt poignant to her at that very moment.

*'What happened to the wonderful adventures, The places I had planned for us to go, (Slipping through my fingers all the time), Well, some of that we did but most we didn't, And why I just don't know.'*

Such a feeling of sadness swept through her, filling her eyes with unexpected tears. Poor David ... all those wonderful adventures that never happened. It was as if Alex could sense her sudden change of mood. He took one of her hands and squeezed it gently. The song ended with the lyrics:

*'Sometimes I wish that I could freeze the picture, And save it from the funny tricks of time*
*Slipping through my fingers.'*

The holiday, at this moment, was magical, and Alex felt the sentiment of the song. The ability of music to draw people together was there for all to see. Charlie and Alex almost had to drag themselves apart as the song ended, and the band bowed three times to loud whoops and clapping. Suddenly, the real world was all around them once more.

"They're amazing, aren't they?" shouted Darcy as she pushed through the crowd to them. "You've got to admit, Will, they're great, aren't they?"

Will laughed and said, "You win! I enjoyed myself. Let's get another beer."

Alex quietly dropped Charlie's hand, and they walked up the stairs. The raffle was drawn after a quick speech about the work the charity does. Alex turned his head to Charlie and said, "Maybe you ought to get a dog? There seems to be a genuine need here, and it would be brilliant company for you?"

"I agree. I've always wanted one. Maybe ..."

Soon the band came on again and they all danced non-stop for another thirty minutes. The last song,

"Thank you for the Music" became like an anthem; everyone in the whole amphitheatre was singing so loudly.

This time, Alex and Charlie faced each other and held both of each other's hands, shouting the words:

*'So I say ...Thank you for the music, the songs I'm singing, Thanks for all the joy they're bringing, Who can live without it, I ask in all honesty, What would life be, without a song or a dance, what are we, So I say, thank you for the music, for giving it to me.'*

Charlie felt euphoric when she was singing. They were swinging their arms backwards and forwards to the beat. She looked up and saw the piercing, star-lit night sky.

At that moment, it was great to be alive.

---

There were only four days left. The end of the holiday was counting down, each day going quicker than the last. Alex and Charlie had been sailing with Nick twice, and one evening he'd followed them back to the house for supper.

Charlie had bought enough food to feed an army, which was lucky, as Will invited Iryna and Sophia, too. The young ones all frolicked in the pool, while the 'oldies' prepared the food. Nick had brought some huge prawns, which he put on skewers with peppers, courgettes and onions. Alex had insisted on barbecuing some sheftalia, as he'd so enjoyed them one night in a taverna; there was halloumi, grilled to perfection, brown and chewy; spicy, sticky chicken drumsticks and corn on the cob. There was a large, round loaf of Cypriot bread covered in sesame seeds, salad, dips and olives, and an enormous bowl of buttery new potatoes.

The young ones came when they were called, like hungry dogs, and tucked in, as if they hadn't eaten for a week. They sat, dripping wet in their costumes, the warmth of the evening drying their skin in seconds. The sky turned lobster red, then burnt orange and pink, as they sat round the table, a mixture of ages and nationalities. They ate until they could eat no more. There were mandarins on the table, and everyone peeled the skins lethargically, the pockets of sweet juice exploding in their mouths.

"I'd like to make a brief announcement," said Nick, banging the end of his knife on the table, to quieten the chatter. Taken by surprise, everyone stopped talking and turned to Nick to listen to what he had to say.

"First, I'd like to say, 'Cheers' to Charlie, in particular, for inviting me here tonight," and he raised his glass; everyone said 'Cheers' too, smiling at Charlie. "It's been such a lovely evening, and one that I'll cherish. I can't think when I last enjoyed a meal so much. So ... to my announcement," and he looked at Alex. "Alex, I've loved our sailing trips together. It's been an absolute pleasure; you've taught me so much and I hope, maybe, I've been able to teach you a bit too." Alex raised his glass to Nick.

"I've been advised by my doctor ... basically, he says I shouldn't go sailing any more." There were murmurs around the table and Charlie looked at Alex. "I'm getting a bit past it, and my old ticker is under strain. It's not a good idea for me to go out on my own anymore ... so I've taken his advice, which, I know, is unusual for a man." Everyone laughed. "So, what I'm trying to say is ... Alex, as my surrogate son and wonderful friend, I'd like you to have the boat. I don't want to sell it, and perhaps when you're out here next, you would take the old man out for a tootle around the bay ... so ... what I'm saying is ... she's now .... yours."

"Mate ... you can't just give her away ..." said Alex, looking overwhelmed.

"Yes, I can ... and, more to the point, I *want* to. I can't think of a better person to take her on, and I have an ulterior motive ... you've got to come out here regularly to look after her. No excuse." Alex smiled and Nick raised his glass, laughing, and said, "To Alex ... and Charlie ... and the boat! May they have some wonderful days together, just like my wife and I did." He took a drink of his wine.

They all looked at each other. Alex said, "I don't know what to say ..."

"That's so kind of you, Nick," said Charlie. "Unbelievable."

"You haven't got another one to spare, by any chance?" laughed Will.

"Don't say anything, mate," said Nick. "Just enjoy it. You and she will be very happy together." He was being deliberately obtuse with his use of 'she'. Charlie knew he was. Or was she letting her imagination run away with her?

She felt tears prickle her eyes, and she looked down at her hands. What a lovely man Nick was. What a generous thing to do. He could easily sell his boat, but he'd chosen to pass it on to Alex. She couldn't help agreeing with him. Now there was a reason for Alex to come out again. He would *have* to come and maintain his boat ... and she felt inexplicably happy.

The prospect of him leaving the island was filling her with dread. But now ... he'd have to come out again, wouldn't he?

---

Charlie was determined to show Alex a little piece of the mountains before he left. She'd only gone twice when David was alive, each time to the classic tourist places of Omodos and Lefkara. They were beautiful, but she didn't feel they represented the peaceful village life she wanted Alex to experience; in those villages there were lots of people trying to sell lace. It was beautiful, but she didn't particularly like the hard sell. She'd heard from Jane that there was a village only about thirty-five minutes from Pissouri that was more what she was looking for.

"Do you fancy going up the mountains today, Alex?" she said on the Thursday before he was leaving. "It won't take long and it may be just a little cooler up there, you never know!"

"Yes, that sounds great. Shall I ask the kids, or would you rather we go without them?"

"Oh no, let's ask; they might enjoy it." It was only 7.30 am and there was no sign of life from them yet.

They emerged at 8.30 am, both looking worn out. "Wow, why are you two looking so knackered? Heavy night?" said Alex.

"Yea ... we ended up having a late one," said Darcy, looking across at Will with a grin and flopping down on a chair.

They'd walked down into the square and still hadn't got back when Charlie and Alex eventually went to bed.

"We met up with some Brits at a bar, and we ended up having a long snooker tournament, along with lots of sambucas," said Will, groaning and dragging his hand through his hair. "I need to pull myself together. I've got to send off my portfolio today." He sauntered towards the pool and dived in, like a seal, emerging from the depths at the other end. He pushed himself up and hung over the edge, as if he was exhausted from the effort.

"So, going up the mountains today doesn't appeal?" said Charlie. "We're thinking of going ... but it sounds like you're busy?"

"Yea, Mum, thanks but ... hey Darce, you can go, though?"

"Nah ... I'm good. I've got a brilliant book on the go. Quite happy to lie here all day. You two go, though."

"Where are you heading, then?" said Will.

"Somewhere I've never been. It's a village called Arsos."

"Well, I hope it's better than its name implies," laughed Will. Darcy was also grinning.

"Cool name," she said.

"Don't be so juvenile, you two," said Charlie, laughing. "It's famous for its wine."

"Well, as you so often say to me, Mum, don't drink and drive. You know it makes sense," and he turned and swam another length underwater, jumping out at the end, as if on a spring. Charlie looked at him; he was now so tanned and fit. His stay in Cyprus had transformed him from a sad, thin, pale boy to someone on the verge of his future.

"So, Alex; we'll set out around eleven. No need to rush, as it's a gentle drive to the foothills. It'll be fun to go somewhere completely new for both of us."

"It will," he said, looking across the table, his eyes staying with hers just a little longer than was necessary. "A day out in the mountains. How wonderful."

They finished breakfast, cleared up, had a swim in the pool, and lingered for a while, catching up on world news on their phones.

"God, these riots are awful ... at least they seem to be putting them all in jail," said Alex, staring at his phone.

"But where are they all going to go? The prisons are already full to bursting," said Charlie. "When I read this sort of thing, I'm just glad I'm here. It's terrible."

"You wonder where it's all going to end. You really do. I think you made a good decision to stay here, Charlie. I really do. It doesn't exactly fill me with joy, the thought of Darcy having to go back when there's so much tension around."

"She'll be okay, Alex."

"I know ... but you can't help but worry. It all seems a world away, here. Listen to that!" he said. "Absolutely nothing. Total silence. Amazing."

"Let's forget the world, and go on an adventure," she said, snapping her phone closed and standing up. "If we didn't read the news, we wouldn't know, would we?"

"Yes, it must have been better in the old days, before newspapers, before the internet, when all you knew about was what was happening in your own community. So much less stressful." He too closed his phone and stood up. "Okay, you two, see you later."

"See ya," said Darcy, blowing him a kiss and turning back to her book.

They drove, with the air-con on full blast, through Avdimou, Prastio and Pachna. They were following Google maps who kindly showed them the way with no problems. The scenery was spectacular; the lack of people enhanced the feeling of leaving the real world behind ... anything that linked them to those terrible headlines. It was like they were driving back through time, through villages sleeping in the heat.

The roads were winding and steep. Charlie had to have her wits about her, negotiating hair-pin bends; The landscape mesmerised Alex: the traditional stone walls threading their way across rough, bare hillsides; the distant, hazy hilltops, the outlines of faraway villages and towered churches.

They arrived at Arsos exactly when the lady on Google maps said they would and followed the signs to the car park. There were only a few cars there; they got out, stretched, and breathed in the slightly fresher air of the lower mountains. The smell was herby, perhaps rosemary, and fruity ... perhaps lemony ... it was like nothing they'd experienced before. They put on their caps, grabbed a bottle of water each from the cool box, and locked the truck.

They meandered, following their noses, down the utterly quiet, old, cobbled streets. Trees, laden with pomegranates, poked over tile-topped walls. Some buildings looked as if they were falling down, with open wooden-slatted shutters, showing glimpses of abandoned courtyards beyond. Large double-fronted doors were painted bottle green or sky blue; red roses grew from untidy flower beds.

They passed houses that looked more inhabited, with steps leading up to front doors. Charlie couldn't resist taking photos on her phone wherever she looked. It was so picturesque; it was as if someone had said: *Set it out, so that it looks how you imagine an idyllic, mountain village to be.*

She couldn't believe her luck: one house had a picture-perfect set of steps: on each step was a flowerpot on either side, with flowering and red-leafed plants sprouting abundantly. There were even two huge pots on the top step, with pomegranates growing from them, forming a tall arch before the wooden front door. And ... a black and white cat was sitting, perfectly placed on the second-to-top step, as if he knew how beautiful he would look in a photo. She showed Alex, who peered over her shoulder, in the shade of a building, to look at the photo.

"It's crazy how stunning it is," he said. He clasped her arm and gently kissed her neck. "Thank you for bringing me."

Charlie stood still, the feel of his lips burning her skin, leaving a mark. She couldn't believe he'd just done that; such an intimate gesture. He was still behind her; he clasped both her arms. "I'm sorry, Charlie ... don't know what came over me ..." he said. He gently turned her round, so they were facing each other. "Sorry ..." he said again.

Charlie was at a loss for what to say or do. She wanted to say, *Don't be sorry ... I loved the feeling of your lips ...* but no words would come. She leant forward and kissed his cheek instead, linked her arm through his, and said, "Let's get some lunch."

The moment had gone, but somehow lingered between them as they walked along, arms linked towards the centre of this wonderful village. The possibility of something ... the chance that maybe there was a new future ... the hope ... even the fear. It melted into her heart in the heat of the day.

They found the central square; there was a languorous, empty taverna under a canopy of vines, laden with multitudinous bunches of red grapes. They hung down beneath the leaves, dripping with fruitfulness. There was just one other couple sitting at the haphazard tables and ladder-back chairs. They sat down and looked through the menu written on an old piece of laminated card. Halloumi, chips and salad was what they decided on, washed down with sparkling water and fresh orange juice.

"What can I get for you, my friends?" said the friendly old waiter; he had black hair, a large belly and a smile that crinkled his eyes.

They gave him their order, which came fifteen minutes later; he insisted on giving them some free wine, which was 'on the house'. The food, especially the chips, was delicious, and they ate quickly, dipping the chips in tomato ketchup. They had small sips of the wine.

As they were tucking in, the old man sat down at a table by the door to the kitchen, with a bottle of wine in front of him. He started singing. Loudly. Not some Cypriot folk song, but a rather drunken rendition of 'My Way' by Frank Sinatra.

Charlie and Alex got the giggles; they tried to keep it under control, but in the end, they couldn't help but laugh. It seemed so incongruous, so out of place ... and even though he had a wonderful voice, he sounded drunk.

"I think it's his party piece," whispered Charlie. "Do you think it's for our benefit?"

"I'm afraid so," he grinned. Leaning in closer, still laughing, he whispered into her ear, "I hope there won't be an encore."

At which point, the man launched into 'I've Got You Under My Skin'.

"Oh god, shall we get the bill?" laughed Charlie; their plates were empty, and she swigged her glass to finish it.

"Let's just listen to this one, and then go," Alex smiled. "I learned this one once for an audition," and he started quietly to sing along with the lyrics. When he got to the lines,

*'But why should I try to resist when, baby, I know so well I've got you under my skin,'*

he looked directly at her, took her hand and kissed it. It was a theatrical gesture ... but had a meaning attached to it. They were still laughing, but underneath it all, there was something more important going on, and they both knew it.

They paid and walked away, down different streets, with different vistas.

# CHAPTER 22

Alex and Darcy left, leaving both Charlie and Will with an emptiness which filled the house; they tried to hide it, but they missed their friends. Charlie missed Alex more than she thought possible.

At the airport, Alex and Charlie had hugged, a long meaningful embrace that had stayed with her. As they'd walked away, Alex had turned and waved and she thought she'd seen her own longing etched in his face. Was she imagining it? He'd promised to come out in mid-November, after his retirement ... to do some work on the boat. She could only hope that he really meant ... to visit her.

Will heard he'd got into uni and was so excited; they went out to celebrate at one of the posher tavernas in the village, which sat on top of a hill, perched high on an escarpment that had stunning views over the entire village, to the sea. It was appropriately named The Hillview.

They sat at a window table, the windows open to the evening breeze that blew softly across their faces.

It was more like fine dining, with crisp, white linen, immaculate sparkling glasses, starters that looked like works of art and creamy main courses which oozed taste and quality. It felt appropriate, as Will was setting off for his future.

"I'm so proud of you, Will," said Charlie, as she raised her champagne glass. "I'm going to miss you like mad ... but I'm totally happy for you."

"Thanks, Mum. I actually can't wait for the challenge. It's exactly what I want to do." He was leaving the next day, to spend a week with Lou in London, then he was going to Bath to settle into his digs. It would be a new and exciting start and he was champing at the bit to get going. He knew he was ready this time.

"When you're with Lou, help her out as much as you can, Will, won't you? She's struggling a bit with the children, work and being pregnant."

"Yes, Mum, of course I will. I'll send you lots of pictures, too."

When he'd finally left, Charlie came back to the house with trepidation: she was going to be alone again. Will was everywhere. He'd left a pair of shoes, by mistake, by the back door; a book he'd just finished was lying on the coffee table; the towel he'd used to dry himself with after his last swim was hanging on the washing line. She could even smell his favourite after-shave in his room.

But ... she wasn't as lonely as she thought she'd be. Having been so busy with other people for weeks, she now found she enjoyed the peace instead of feeling lost. She went back to her early morning swim in the sea, to her Greek class, and she joined a new Pilates class. She and Jane went out in the evenings, including to another concert in the amphitheatre. This time it was 'The Three Degrees', and she loved remembering all their old hits.

Life ticked on in the same way it had, and the heat retreated a little. She could bear to go out at midday if she had to; the bedroom wasn't so hot at night. She visited Nick whenever she went to Paphos; she'd either call in unannounced or call him beforehand. He was always pleased to see her, and she loved the comfort he gave her, with his link to Alex. They'd sometimes Facetime Alex when they were together.

The difference to her 'old' life was that she had *hope* in her life now. Hope for Will; hope for Lou ... and hope for herself. She experienced that feeling when you wake up, as the dawn is just breaking and shedding pink feathers across the night sky, that the day has endless possibilities; that your future is near ... and that the time between sunrise and sunset would be full of magic.

She and Alex were exchanging regular WhatsApp messages. Before he came, there'd been the odd one, but things had changed. They wrote silly little notes to each other several times a week; she'd send photos of his favourite beach or the view from 'his' balcony; of the moon shining brightly above the sea, or the silhouettes of the palm trees against the red sky. She'd say things like, *Pity you're in rainy old England, ha ha* ... or ... *visited your favourite taverna today.* He'd send pictures of his garden, or a selfie with him pulling a silly face ... or a photo of Darcy when she visited.

By the time November came, they were talking about what they would do when he came out. He officially left the vets on 10th November and, encouraged by Darcy, who virtually booked it for him, he bought a ticket to Cyprus for 15th. They'd exchanged a list of places they wanted to visit and found they had similar ideas, although Charlie had more suggestions, as she knew the island better. There was Latchi and a boat trip to the blue lagoon; the old city ruins of Paphos; the top of Troodos ... the list went on.

Charlie couldn't wait.

***

"So how do you feel about being officially old?" said Charlie, laughing. Despite it being November, it was still possible to sit outside for breakfast, and they had croissants, jam, yoghurt and fresh fruit on the table.

"I don't think it's sunk in yet. I don't feel any different. Anyway, cheeky devil, I'm *not* old! I retired early enough to enjoy it. Darcy was insistent that I should come straight out here, so that I didn't have time to think. I am sad, though; I was so lucky to have a job I loved. I'll miss the animals and I'll miss my colleagues ... but

I won't miss the emergency call-outs in the middle of the night, or the early starts. "

Charlie poured him a large mug of coffee and passed the plate of croissants to him. "I shouldn't, but I will," he laughed. "Anyway, enough of me ... how's Will getting on? Have you heard much from him? Darcy said he'd texted her twice."

"Yes, he's been remarkably communicative; he's a different person these days. Will's loving the course. He says he can't believe he's got three years doing something he loves so much." She spread some strawberry jam on a croissant and took a huge bite.

"It's like me ... it always seemed a miracle that I was getting paid for helping animals."

"Yes, if you can find your passion and make it your job, it's a gift. Unfortunately, it didn't really happen to me. I drifted into teaching. I loved sport and thought it would be a good way of earning money ... but it was never a *passion*. I think my kids were ... *are* my passion."

"Maybe you could find something new?"

Charlie blew over the top of her coffee, had a sip, and said, "Maybe ... or perhaps I'll just enjoy ... life. Being here ... with blue skies, blue sea ... beautiful sunsets ... what more do I need?" (*and you,* she thought).

They were sitting on opposite sides of the table, and they glanced at each other. There was a space above the table where their eyes fizzled and crackled for a second. She looked down and said, without thinking, "I love that you've chosen to come out here, Alex." Her words floated around the patio, looking for a place to land. Had she said too much? Had she ruined their friendship?

"I love that it was possible, Charlie. Our friendship is so important to me; we have all that history ... all those shared moments. I love that I can come out here and just 'be'. No explanations needed, no discussions. We can just enjoy the place, the time and each other's company. We know we are thinking of Beth and David ... but we don't need to say it. It just 'is'. It's wonderful to have such a connection and so many joint memories."

They smiled a smile of knowing and understanding over the tops of their coffee. Eyes snapped together, not looking away.

"Let's go visit Nick," said Alex. "I said I would, as soon as I got here. I still can't believe he's given me his boat."

"Okay," she said, smiling, anticipating the day ahead. "I'll just clear up and then we'll go."

They stood up in unison and collected the plates and cutlery together, taking them inside. She loaded the dishwasher. He went back outside to clean the table. Simple tasks, done together. She closed the dishwasher door. He came back in and rinsed the cloth.

"This is nice," he said.

"It is," she smiled.

The three of them walked down to the boat, still moored in the same place. The men talked about the practicalities of owning a boat, one of which was taking it out of the water and anti-fouling. Nick knew people who could help with the procedure, and he said he'd give Alex their names and numbers. They decided it would be a good idea to do it while the weather was cold and the wind more unpredictable; it would be useful to have it in pristine condition for the start of the new season next year.

"They say a boat is a hole in the water that you chuck money into," Nick laughed. "You're about to find out it's true."

"But think of all the pleasure it'll bring," said Alex. "Charlie and I have a lifetime ahead of sailing it, thanks to you." As he said this, he put his arm around her shoulders and pulled her into him. His body was warm against hers; she liked the feeling.

Nick smiled at them, like an indulgent father-figure, and said, "I don't want to speak out of turn ... but I hope you two see what a great couple you make."

Still wrapped in his arm, Charlie smiled up at Alex, who said, "We do, don't we?" and nothing more was said.

They walked to a taverna, had a couple of Keos and some steak and chips. The weather was closing in for a storm; black clouds were gathering, and rumbles of distant thunder were booming from the mountains.

"I think we'll leave now before the rain starts," said Charlie. "I know what it can be like here when it really rains. You've only seen the sun, Alex, but it can be dangerous driving here sometimes."

They arranged to see Nick again and climbed into the truck. Large raindrops were landing on the roof now and red dusty rivulets were running down the windscreen.

"The truck could do with a wash, anyway," laughed Charlie. They were now heading towards the motorway and the rain was coming down in buckets. The thunder was getting closer and jagged fork lightning was sparking across the night sky, giving a spectacular, if quite daunting, light show.

"Are you okay driving in this?" said Alex, looking at her anxiously.

"Yes, we better press on. No point stopping now."

There were very few vehicles on the road, which was fortunate, as when the odd one passed them, a huge spray cascaded up towards them.

Charlie bent forward, focussing on the road ahead, peering through the wipers, which were working overtime.

She saw something on the edge of the road in front of them and instinctively slowed down; two eyes were caught in her headlights. She almost came to a halt and said, "Oh god, Alex ... it's a dog. What shall I do?" She knew she shouldn't stop on the motorway, especially in these conditions, but she felt she had no option.

"Yes, pull in, pull in," he yelled, looking back.

They got onto the hard shoulder. Charlie put on her hazard warning lights, turned off the engine and they both jumped out into the downpour. Within seconds, they were drenched, and then there was another loud clap of thunder. They walked back to the bedraggled dog, who was cowering. A car sped fast past them, flashed their lights, and sprayed yet more water in their direction.

Not knowing how the dog would react to their approach, they slowed their pace and Alex said reassuring words. They worked like a perfect team, Charlie going behind it to keep it from running away and Alex, the expert with frightened animals, shielded it from going across the road and grabbed its neck. The dog didn't resist and succumbed to them. With soothing noises and a firm grip, Alex picked the skinny body up and they hurried back to the car. Alex slid into the back seat, holding the dog tight, now covering it with his coat. Charlie turned from the driver's seat and said, "Are you okay? Do you think it'll sit still if I drive?"

"Yes, there's no other choice, is there? Just try to drive steadily."

Rain was still pounding down on the roof; the sound was deafening. The windows were steaming up inside the truck and thunder was still booming over the hills. Water was now running along the road in streams, so Charlie drove as carefully as she could.

Soon, they turned off the motorway and made their way up through the village. Small rocks had been washed off the hillside and had landed on the road. Driving carefully round them, Charlie didn't speak.

She could just hear Alex saying things like, "You're ok," "There's a good boy," and other such endearments.

"Let's get you inside," he said, as Charlie turned off the engine. She came round to his door and together they got the dog inside. They were dripping all over the tiled floor; Charlie went to get some towels and when she came downstairs, she could see Alex gently stroking the dog's head. He wrapped the shivering dog in the towel and slowly started rubbing it dry.

"I think it's a hunter's dog. They chuck them out if they're no good," said Charlie. "He looks a bit like a pointer. God, he's so thin. Shall I get something for him to eat?"

She went to the fridge and remembered there was some cooked chicken left over from the night before. She cut it up and put it in a bowl. He was obviously hungry, but didn't wolf it straight down. He picked at it. She got another bowl and filled it with water. In the meantime, Alex was examining him with his professional eye, looking for wounds, feeling his stomach, looking in his eyes. The dog was sweet-natured and never once complained, despite being frightened.

Charlie hunted around for an old blanket; she also found an ancient duvet that could be used as a bed. She put it in the corner of the sitting room, doubled over for comfort, and placed the blanket on top. He was short-haired so his body was drying quickly and with a few more rubs with a towel, Alex showed him the bed.

The dog sat on it, his sad eyes staring. "Lie down, old chap, snuggle in," he said.

"Poor thing," said Charlie. "He looks so lost. Have you ever seen such sad eyes? I wonder what's happened to him, to be in this state?"

"Neglect, abuse, abandonment ... it's so pathetic, isn't it? Let's let him sleep and then we'll see what he's like in the morning."

The dog stood and curled itself round and round, finally lying down in a tight ball. Charlie and Alex looked at him and then at each other. Charlie went to Alex, and he wrapped his arms around her. She knew they'd done the right thing, but wondered what the future would hold. Would he have some disease? Had he just escaped from someone who would want him back? Questions were flooding through her head. All she knew was that they'd had no option but to stop. They both had understood that, without a doubt.

"I think I'm going to get out of these clothes; I'm drenched," she said, pulling away from Alex. "It sounds as if the rain has stopped, thank goodness."

", me too." They stood together, both looking down at the dog. "Maybe tomorrow we should take him to a vet and have some tests done. It may have Leishmaniasis. It's common in the Med."

"What would it mean if he had it?"

"It's treatable but not curable. He's so thin, and he wasn't that interested in the chicken. It could well be Leish."

"I want to keep him," said Charlie.

"I know you do. I knew it the moment we saw him. Let's wait till the morning."

They went their separate ways to change and when they came back downstairs, the dog was fast asleep.

---

The vet, the following day, said that Rufus, as Charlie had already called him, was approximately eighteen months old and tests soon revealed he was free of Leish. The vet reiterated Charlie's thoughts that he was simply an abandoned hunting dog who'd been beaten and neglected. There was no sign of a chip, so no owner would come out of the woodwork.

He had the most adorable nature: quiet, loving, and he seemed to have an inbuilt gratitude for being rescued. Over the next few days, Alex and Charlie catered to his every need, and he loyally followed them everywhere. They took him for gentle walks across the bondu on the lead, and gradually he began to recover; his appetite increased, and he had more energy. It would be a long road, but everyone was up for the challenge. His tan and white coat turned shinier, with a lot of gentle brushing from Charlie, and his long, floppy ears became like silk.

They didn't like to leave him alone for too long, but on the fifth evening, they went out to a local taverna.

They made sure everything was in place for him and they left, promising they wouldn't be too long; he seemed to understand.

"So ... Charlie, I have something I want to say, or ... I've wanted to say it since I got here."

They were sitting opposite each other at a candle-lit table. It was a traditional place with checked tablecloths, nothing fancy, but a wood-burning stove was throwing out heat, giving the place a warm and cosy atmosphere. There were a few other people, mostly Cypriots, sitting at nearby tables; gentle bouzouki was playing. They'd been given some local bread, hummus and tahini and olives, which they were tucking into and had ordered sea bream, salad and chips.

Charlie looked up from the piece of bread she was slathering in tahini. Alex's eyes had the candlelight reflected in them. She thought how handsome he looked; he was wearing a casual shirt of light blue which suited him. He put down his knife and reached forward and took her hand.

"I have loved being here, with you ... just hanging out, finding Rufus together, walking, eating ... it's been amazing. But ..."

Charlie's heart did a little flip; what was he going to say ... why did there have to be a 'but'?

"But," he continued, "I know the time will come to an end next week ... and I know I don't want it to." He squeezed her hand, and they stared at each other. "What are you thinking, Charlie? What do *you* want to happen?"

Her heart jumped in her chest. She knew she had to say something ... now ... or never. Why was she frightened to tell him? The way he looked at her, didn't he feel the same?

She swallowed and said, "The thing is Alex, even though your Beth's husband ... I ... don't want to let you go ... back to England. I think Beth would see how happy you make me feel ... and I think she'd give me her blessing. What I'm trying to say is ... don't go."

Tears sprang to her eyes; she blinked them back, but they flowed down her cheeks, the candlelight lighting their path. The waiter appeared with their food, and she quickly wiped away her tears.

"I love it here," he said, when the waiter had gone. "I love being with you ... but I'd feel like I'm abandoning Darcy ... she's already lost her mum. How could I leave her?"

Charlie knew exactly how he felt. She felt the same when she came out here all those years ago with David, but part of her felt it was their time now. Darcy, Will, Lou ... they'd all got their own lives to lead, and they were only a flight away.

"Alex, I think Darcy would be pleased and relieved that you've found your own way after losing Beth. She'd be happy for you. I really believe that. You could keep the house, flit backwards and forwards to see her ... and just see if you like the life here."

She couldn't believe that they'd gone from being close friends to *this* conversation, with nothing in between. It was as if it was a continuation of a discussion they'd been having all along. But it was as it had always been with them. They didn't need to verbalise things, they just knew what the other was thinking.

They ate in silence for a while, both of them thinking about the implications of what had just been said. How could things return to how they were before?

They couldn't.

Alex insisted on paying the bill, and they decided they were going to leave the truck outside and walk back to the house. It was cool but a clear, star-spangled night with an ice-white moon lighting the air. They walked slowly, chatting as if they had a lifetime to catch up on, holding hands the whole way.

When they reached the top of the hill where they could see the silver sea and the twinkling lights of Limassol in the far distance, Alex stopped and turned to her. Putting his hands on each side of her face, he kissed her with a passion that took her breath away. It was their first proper kiss, but it was as if they'd done it a million times before. It was as natural, sweet and all-consuming as she'd dreamt it would be.

They walked on towards the house; the lights from it, shining like a beacon over the bondu.

Rufus got up to greet them, they let him out into the garden and then they went upstairs together, into the same room.

# CHAPTER 23

It was April, the following year.

"Shall we go to Petra Tou Romiou tonight?" said Alex, as he put the kettle on. He looked so at home in the kitchen, as if he'd always been there. He glanced at his watch; sunset would be in about an hour and a half. "I know it's obvious, but ..."

"Why is it obvious?"

"Well, it's the place *everyone* goes ..."

"Well, that's because it's magical and the sunset is absolutely stunning there. We've been to so many other places in Cyprus in the last few weeks. It's been truly amazing, Alex; it's what I'd always wanted to do, but Aphrodite's Rock is one of my favourite places ... so, if it's cheesy, I don't care."

Alex poured some water into two mugs that already had tea bags in them. He stirred each of them, added a dash of milk, and handed one to Charlie. They went through the back door onto the patio, accompanied by Rufus, who curled up by Alex, his constant companion.

It was cool outside, but the sun was there, in the blue sky ... as always; there was a slight breeze, making the palm leaves rustle, and they sounded like the sea. They were determined to live as much of their lives in the fresh air, despite the chill in the air. The sun lifted their spirits every morning. They had warmer clothes on: still shorts, but a t-shirt with a fleece over the top.

They sat with Charlie's legs on Alex's lap. Without thinking, he was stroking her legs gently as they sat in companionable silence; the steam rising from their mugs on the table. They gazed at the pool, shimmering in the sunlight.

At that moment, birds appeared from nowhere, screeching with the simple joy of flight, or so it seemed to Charlie. They swooped round the house, rising and diving, appearing to chase each other. One dived onto the surface of the pool and immediately rose and disappeared.

"They look so happy," said Charlie. "It's probably us humans putting our own interpretation on their movements, but ... are they swallows or swifts? Do you know?"

Without hesitation, Alex said, "Swifts. They both come to the island but, can you see their dark underbelly? Swallows are much paler and have other colours on them — blue, green or orange."

"Oh, I've always wondered. I love that you know so much about birds and animals, Alex." She squeezed his hand.

"I hate to disappoint you, but they're just flying around catching insects," he laughed.

"I know ... but they sound and look as if it's the best thing in the world to do."

The swifts continued their fun, swooping and calling, silhouetted against the sky. Alex reached for his tea and took a few slurps. "Do you fancy a biscuit?" he said, moving her legs and getting up.

"Yes, there are some chocolate ones in the cupboard."

As he wandered slowly inside, Charlie sipped her tea with her eyes closed, face up to the sun. She felt so contented, so warm, so loved. How could this have possibly happened to her? No one should be this lucky at her time of life; she'd thought this type of happiness would *never* come her way again. Having someone to do nothing with; to look at swifts with; to eat chocolate biscuits with.

*How I love that man.*

"Here you are, my love," he said, putting down a plate on the table, with just four biscuits on. "I didn't bring the packet out, in case we ate too many; I know what we're like! We ought to set off in the next fifteen minutes, if we're going to watch the whole sunset." He broke one biscuit in half and gave half to Rufus, who looked eternally grateful.

They both had their swimming costumes on underneath their clothes, as usual. Sometimes, it was as if they spent the whole day in them. They tidied up the tea things and settled Rufus on his bed, made sure he had some water, and then closed up the house.

"I bought some towels, just in case; they're in the back of the truck," he said. "You never know, we might be inspired to take a dip."

"Definitely," said Charlie, looking at him as he drove. He was still so gorgeous: his hair, longish, bleached by the sun; his arms, golden brown. He was wearing a pair of aviator glasses which suited him; his profile still made her heart jump in her chest. She put her hand on his leg, stroking his warm skin. Had she ever loved David this much?

They went down the hill, round a couple of hairpin bends, past the poor horse that was always there. Charlie couldn't help but stare at it as they passed, wishing she could rescue him, but knowing it wasn't her place.

As they drove through the hills on the old road towards Paphos, the sun was beginning its slow descent in the far distance. They soon pulled into the car park, which was remarkably full for a weekday evening; other people must have had a similar idea to them.

Grabbing their towels, they made their way down the steps and through the tunnel under the road, Alex leading the way. They came out into the dark blue, pink and apricot skies of the beach, the huge rocks looming in front of them.

They walked, hand in hand, towards the sea, picking their way between several stone monuments to love, some in the shape of hearts. They looked down at each one, wondering who the initials inside referred to. Were they people who had found love in Cyprus perhaps, or were they tourists visiting for the first time? It felt that love was everywhere on this atmospheric beach.

They walked slowly past the rock, along the sea's edge, away from the other couples and families. They wanted to be alone, together, to watch the fire burn the sky.

As they approached the water, they sifted through the multi-coloured pebbles that lay randomly on the sand. Charlie was always looking for the 'perfect' one, although she was never sure what a 'perfect' one looked like. They looked so full of sheen and shimmer when they were wet, and often disappointed her when they were back home, and she was putting them on a shelf, or piling them in a glass jar.

"Look at this one," said Alex, handing Charlie a coal-black one with white specks. She held it in her open palm. "It somehow makes me think of Beth. Is it the blackness of her hair? Or the white specks, so bright and cheerful?" He took it back, holding it in the palm of his outstretched hand. "Let's find one that reminds you of David," he said.

"What would that be like?" said Charlie, smiling, squatting down, so that she could see the pebbles more clearly.

"Oh, I don't know ... large ... solid, with ginger streaks?" he laughed.

"What about this one? It's white and has brown lines and flecks shining through," she said, turning it round in her hands. "David wasn't straightforward, was he? But ... he was a good man ... he didn't know who he was without the Air Force to define him. He lost his way here. I wonder if things would have been different if we'd never come here to live? I know it's pointless to say 'what if' but ..."

"You'll never know, Charlie. All you know is that he desperately wanted to come here and he fulfilled his wish. You made it happen for him, even though it wasn't *your* dream; you went along with it. Charlie, you did your best, and that's all any of us can do." He put his arms around her and hugged her tight.

He continued, "We've got to learn to live without them now. We *can't* hang onto them ... they left us on earth ... and we need, somehow, to move on. I think of Beth every day. I'll never forget her ... never. But ... I need to think of *you* now ... and myself. She was the love of my youth; you're the love of my older years."

"That's such a lovely thing to say, Alex. I like to think they'd both approve of us being together. I know if the roles were reversed, I'd want David to be happy. Despite our problems, I loved him. I really did. I still remember the first time I saw him. I love *that* David; that young, handsome Air Force David. I miss him."

They sat down at the water's edge, still holding their stones. Their shoulders were touching, their heads inclined towards each other. The sun was sinking fast, spreading its rays across the sky. They put both their stones down together on the sand, where the water was gently lapping, in front of their feet. All their memories of times past were consuming their minds; Charlie found tears slipping down her cheeks for a life gone. Alex could hear Beth's laughter in his head and could hear her saying, *Embrace the time you have left. Live, live ... life is gone in a second.*

"Do you know what?" said Alex. "We're going to throw these pebbles into the sea, together. When the sun finally drops behind that horizon in a few minutes, we're going to throw them as hard as we can. We're not throwing our past away ... we're laying it to rest, forever in the sea. We're going to live *our* lives now, just the two of us, without our past holding us back. Just think of all the sunsets we haven't seen yet."

Charlie looked down at her stone, round and heavy in the sand. Alex was right. She had *somehow* to make that leap into the future. It was *her* time now; *her* time to live.

The sun sank into the sea, its drop so sudden. They sat mesmerised by the light show.

"Right," said Alex, picking up the stones, handing hers to Charlie. "Come on, we're doing it," he said, standing up and pulling Charlie up by the hand.

She stood up, a little reluctantly at first. She put her arms around his neck and kissed him on the lips. The golden hour of light wrapped them in its embrace. They pulled away from each other and stared into the future, to the horizon.

Alex said, "On the count of three ... one, two ... *three*."

They looked at each other, both drew back their arms and then threw their stones as far as they could.

As they stared at where the stones had entered the water, the red of the sunset glowed around them, like the embers of winter's fire. Alex took off his t-shirt and stepped out of his shorts.

"Come on, what are you waiting for?" He looked at Charlie expectantly, smiling. "Let's go swimming."

She slowly peeled off her t-shirt and shorts, the breeze cooling her skin, before they walked, holding hands, into the sea.

## THE END

# PLEASE LEAVE A REVIEW

## DID YOU ENJOY THE BOOK?

If you enjoyed reading 'Beneath The Cyprus Sky', please consider leaving a review on Amazon. Your feedback helps other readers discover my books and is greatly appreciated.

To visit my Amazon Author Page Click here: https://www.champlinks.com/sl/MTI3ODA=/

# ALSO BY SARAH CATHERINE KNIGHTS

**APHRODITE'S CHILD (Aphrodite Trilogy Book 1)**

When her RAF husband is posted to Cyprus for three years, Emily Blackwell jumps at the opportunity to escape her cosy life in the Cotswolds. Embracing everything the island has to offer, she reinvents herself, only to find that this new life brings its own heartache and tragedy. In a modern take on the myth of Aphrodite, the Goddess of Love, Emily's experiences on Cyprus change her, and she comes to questions everything she thought she knew about herself and her former existence.

But the choices she makes will affect not only her, but everyone she loves ...

**NOW IS ALL THERE IS (Aphrodite Trilogy Book 2)**

In the sequel to the hugely popular, Aphrodite's Child, Emily Blackwell returns to Cyprus to try to mend her broken marriage. She befriends and helps Beth, a young airmen's wife, whose own life is in turmoil.

Their paths lead them back to England, where they meet again in the rugged surfing world of North Cornwall. Just as the Mediterranean influenced her life in Cyprus, so too does the Atlantic cast its spell over Emily's fortunes. Her tangled life eventually implodes and she has to face a drama that Fate has planned for her all along.

But she finds that her Destiny is not written in the stars. It's within herself...

### SHADOWS IN THE ROCK (Aphrodite Trilogy Book 3)

In the third book of the Aphrodite series, Abi Blackwell is a young woman desperate to escape her Devon village and start a new life as a fashion photographer in London. The shadows of her parents' past have haunted her life and she needs to break free.

Her new life turns out to be more difficult than she'd ever imagined. On a shoot in Cyprus, Abi experiences both the worst and the best that life has to offer, forcing her to grow up quickly and to learn to forgive.

But has she left it too late?

### LOVE IS A STATE OF MIND

Anna is in her fifties and is living a contented life. Their children have left home and she and her husband work at the same school. One day, a perfectly ordinary day (or so she thought) they are sitting on a bench during a walk with their beloved Labrador and David drops a devastating bombshell: he's fallen in love with a colleague and is leaving her.

At first, she wants to hide herself away, but, with the help of her friend and her daughter, she realises that there *has* to be life after a long marriage; she must move forward. She makes some huge changes: she leaves her job, moves house and goes to visit her estranged sister in Australia. As she navigates her new life as a single woman again, she discovers she's stronger than she realised.

Can she build a new life, find new love and a 'happy-ever-after' or will she be on her own forever?

If you love humorous and poignant novels about women facing up to the harsh realities of life, then you'll love this emotional and uplifting story.

**LIFE HAPPENS (The Life Series Book 1)**

She was always the beautiful outsider, the one who yearned to have the handsome husband and the perfect family. But she let the love of her life slip through her fingers and from then on, happiness was always just out of reach.

Rachel Holland married an Air Force officer on the rebound and lived a life on military camps that made her feel like a fish out of water. When her husband takes early retirement, she begins to live again. She starts her own business and finds her independence. But when she goes on holiday to Cyprus with her two best friends and their husbands, secrets and lies begin to emerge which will change her life and the lives of everyone she holds dear, forever.

She must now face up to her past and confront her new present. Will her marriage and her friendships survive the revelations? Can she forgive herself, move forward and find the happiness she craves?

The novel is about the powerful bond between three women and one woman's enduring love. If you enjoy women's fiction set on a beautiful Greek island with plenty of drama, you'll love this first book of the 'Life Series'.

### LIFE'S COMPLICATED (The Life Series Book 2)

In the sequel to the bestselling novel 'Life Happens,' Rachel, Jen, and Grace must confront a question that haunts us all: can you ever truly know someone?

The three women have been inseparable since the eighties, but their recent momentous holiday in Cyprus has left them reeling. As they return home and try to pick up the pieces, they realise that their trip has set in motion a series of events that will affect their lives forever.

Rachel is single again, Jen's health is in jeopardy and Grace embarks on a new chapter in her life. As they navigate their way through these challenges, Rachel's sons, George and Harry and Jen's daughter, Amber become entangled in their parents' struggles.

Time marches on inevitably towards the global pandemic and they must all face the two extremes of life: birth and death ... and everything in between.

'Life's Complicated' is a powerful testament to the strength of friendship and how it can define us all.

**'LOVE, HONOUR AND ANNOY'** – a humorous memoir about a (very) long marriage

Have you ever wondered how on earth two people can be together for fifty years? It seems like a miracle to me and I'm living it.

In 'Love Honour and Annoy', I try to figure out how Peter and I have survived such a long partnership. We met, by chance, in 1970 and despite me getting cold feet and postponing the wedding for a year, we got married in 1976 and embarked on this incredible journey together. Spoiler alert: it hasn't all been love and roses. We've annoyed each other intensely a lot of the time, but we've also been best friends, produced three amazing children and found our way through the bad times.

This memoir doesn't reveal the secret of a perfect marriage, but our stories will make you laugh and you'll see why, despite everything, we're better together. It is a humorous and heartfelt reflection on life and marriage, from the perspective of a seventy-one year old woman, who feels she's only just getting started.

**'MARVELLOUS MABEL AND HER AMAZING BALL'** – a children's book about a Labrador with an obsession with her ball.

Can Mabel change her behaviour, with the help of a group of friends? Marvellous Mabel, a lovable Labrador, is obsessed by her amazing ball. It's her favourite thing in the world. But it's becoming a problem, because she can't think about anything else.

When George, a wise old police dog, suggests she joins the VOA group (Various Obsessions Anonymous), Mabel meets a friendly mix of dog friends with crazy obsessions of their own: there's Biggles, the squirrel chaser; Queenie, the food thief; Doris, the hole digger and Boris, the letter snatcher.

Through this heartwarming tale, they must all learn the magic of balancing their addictions to find true contentment.

'Marvellous Mabel and her Amazing Ball' is a story that celebrates how a problem can be much easier to solve with the help of others. You can find happiness together - you just have to ask for help.

**www.sarahcatherineknights.com**

# About the Author

## Sarah Catherine Knights

I'm a British novelist and live in Malmesbury, Wiltshire. I've lived here since 1985, with my husband, Peter and three children and various dogs. The reason we moved here was because Peter was in the Royal Air Force and we were posted to RAF Lyneham. We were then stationed at RAF Akrotiri, Cyprus, at the beginning of the nineties, which was to prove a catalyst for my writing.

I've had various careers during my life: secondary school English teacher, financial advisor, portrait and wedding photographer and teacher of English as a foreign language for business people. It took me sixty years to realise I should have been a writer all along, but having started, I now can't stop.

I did an MA in Creative Writing at Bath Spa University in 2012 and I've now self-published nine books. One of them is a children's book, based on my current

Labrador, Mabel's, obsession with balls, but my main genre is Women's Fiction. I love writing about families and relationships, secrets and tensions; about female friendships and emotions ... and women's resilience. The 'Aphrodite Trilogy' is set in Cyprus, as is 'The Life Series'. My standalone novel, 'Love is a State of Mind', is set closer to home in Bath, but it also nips over to Australia. I have also written a funny memoir about our very long marriage, called 'Love, Honour and Annoy'. My latest novel, Beneath the Cyprus Sky, is set (obviously) in Cyprus and also Wiltshire.

My three children have flown the nest, of course, but often come home for chaotic weekends of dog walks, laughter and noisy meals around the large kitchen table. The whole family has been very supportive and patient with my late career change as a novelist, always willing to help with the plot or reading a new draft.

I'm currently working on a new novel.

Please follow my Page on Facebook: www.facebook.com/sarahcatherineknights/